Praise for
The Patron Saint of Plagues

"A smart, entertaining, eminently readable book."
—Maureen McHugh,
author of *Mothers & Other Monsters*

"Barth Anderson's inventive viral emergency may be
set in a speculative near future, but it has a persuasive
real-world urgency. He nails the gritty essence of disease
detection: frustration, exhaustion, obsession."
—Maryn McKenna, author of *Beating Back the Devil:
On the Front Lines with the Disease Detectives of the
Epidemic Intelligence Service*

"Anderson has some serious writing chops, and he
delivers a page-turner that is at once a medical thriller,
cyberpunk romp and provocative tease...a novel
about race and class, science and faith."
—Salon.com

"A cinematic, futuristic techno-thriller with smarts and
heart...this cleverly managed skein of cliff-hangers
and revelations begs to be filmed."
—*San Diego Union-Tribune*

"Very neat, impossible to put down, and I hope a book
that gets nominated for some awards."
—*Philadelphia Weekly Press*

Also by Barth Anderson

THE PATRON SAINT OF PLAGUES

THE
MAGICIAN
AND THE FOOL

BARTH ANDERSON

BANTAM SPECTRA BOOKS

THE MAGICIAN AND THE FOOL
A Bantam Spectra Book / April 2008

Published by Bantam Dell
A Division of Random House, Inc.
New York, New York

Book design by Lynn Newmark

Bantam Books and the Rooster colophon are registered trademarks
and Spectra and the portrayal of a boxed "s" are trademarks of
Random House, Inc.

Library of Congress Cataloging-in-Publication Data

Anderson, Barth.
The magician and the fool / Barth Anderson.
p. cm.
ISBN 978-0-553-38359-1 (trade pbk. : alk. paper)
1. Tarot—Fiction. 2. Retired teachers—Fiction.
3. Homeless men—Fiction. I. Title.
PS3601.N46M34 2008
813'.6—dc22
2007043433

Printed in the United States of America
Published simultaneously in Canada

www.bantamdell.com

BVG 10 9 8 7 6 5 4 3 2 1

Acknowledgments

Tarot scholar Ron Decker originally posited the connection between Key I (The Magician) and the Egyptian god Khnum.

Thanks to Mark Teppo for allowing me to cross over briefly into his world created in "The Oneiromantic Mosaic of Harry Potemkin" (online at www.farragoswain scot.com).

Thanks to writers in Clarion '98, the Ratbastards, and Karma Weasels for looking at this story over the years.

THE MAGICIAN

AND

THE FOOL

Nicaraguan roosters never need the excuse of a sun to start screaming. A prowler startles one, or maybe it's a pair of headlights or another chicken, but with one loud cluck, that lone rooster sets off a chain reaction of shrieking across Managua. Nicaraguans never seemed to notice; to a local, a crying rooster was like a taxi horn to a New Yorker. You tuned it out or you never slept. Tonight, they started at 3 a.m. This was only his second night in Managua, and Rosemont hadn't learned to ignore them yet. He unwrapped himself from the sleeping priest and slid from bed.

After stepping into sweatpants, he walked around to the main gate leading into the Casa Evangelista courtyard. Enfolded in amniotic darkness, a broad-leafed tree nodding overhead in the night's sultry breeze, he sat by the bookcases in the open-roofed atrium where he could see through the front security gate into the street. Rosemont liked this hostel. He'd been backpacking south from Mexico and this was the fanciest place he'd stayed in since Costa Rica. Meals of *gallo pinto* (beans and rice), a hard-boiled egg, and a little cheese. Fans in the rooms. Showers with no warm water, but no one wanted it. Travelers from all over the world intersected here, some coming with church groups to offer aid, some to see the volcano south of Managua.

From the atrium, Rosemont could hear the Australian couple having noisy sex in the bathroom. Just that afternoon they'd been arguing bitterly, and just as loudly. He could also hear the group of European students drinking, flirting, and lamely trying to be quiet in one of their rooms. After translating for the hostel's cook, who had a crush on one of the French women, Rosemont had left that party a couple of hours ago.

Mentioned in most of the backpack travel guides, Casa Evangelista was an oasis after the trip that Rosemont had taken down from the Segovia region in northwest Nicaragua on Saturday. In exchange for food and board, he'd been picking coffee in that frontier for weeks. The harvest was over now, it was May, so he followed one of the shipments of beans south to market. Hopping aboard a wide wooden flatbed used for transporting one-hundred-pound bags of green coffee, he left the cloud-rinsed farms of the high Isabel mountains. Unfortunately for him, just before reaching the arid, middle regions of the country, Rosemont lost his hat when standing to hand a bottle of rum to a fellow hitchhiker. The man laughed, watching it spin along the dirt road behind the truck, and saluted it.

"Go with God, hat!" Rosemont had laughed too. But when the sun vaulted to midheaven less than an hour later, he was baking like the wet coffee beans drying on wide, concrete patios that they passed along the road—nothing between him and the pounding Nicaraguan sun.

Around noon, as the mountain road stepped down into the deserts outside Matagalpa, his breakfast rum-buzz had worn off and Rosemont realized he was in trouble. He drank all the water in his one water bottle. He traded places to take advantage of what little shade he could get from the flatbed's crossbeam. He draped a T-shirt from his pack over his head, but he was already near heatstroke, dehydrated from rum and sun, and his whole body rumbled in a fevery hallucination of bouncing farm trucks, leafy boughs of coffee growing out of the stuffed burlap bags around him, and his landed-gentry grandparents back in the States scolding him that he'd never secure tenure for himself this way. When the truck stopped in Matagalpa at Cecocafen Coffee cooperative's offices, his fellow traveler had taken pity on him and bought him a couple of bottles of water, offering them with a wry smile, saying, "Vaya con dios, Señor Sin Sombrero." *Go with God, Mr. Hatless.*

While Rosemont sat in the back of the truck, drinking water and waiting for the driver, a little boy had approached him with his palm out. From his sickbed of coffee bags, Rosemont looked down into that hand, and in his delirium, it had seemed the boy was holding a broken shellfish, offering it to Rosemont. He looked into the boy's face for an explanation.

"¿Por favor?" said the boy. Rosemont looked back and realized that the hand had only three fingers.

What we do to kids in this world.

Rosemont nodded at the boy's fingers. "How'd that happen?"

The kid shrugged one shy shoulder. Then he managed, "Angels."

Rosemont hadn't understood, nor was he certain what he'd put into that hand, but it was the last two bills he had in his pocket. "Steer clear of angels, okay?"

The kid took the money, and as Rosemont's truck pulled away from the curb, he baffled Rosemont by saying, "You're the one who should watch out for angels."

The smooth highway to Managua had soon droned the strange warning from Rosemont's mind, and the bottles of water helped drown his thundering headache. By the time he'd reached Managua, well after sundown, the shirt-soaking humidity of the Pacific was almost a relief. With the help of a Finnish cab driver, Rosemont had made his way from the bustling terminal coffee market to the only hostel whose name he knew: Casa Evangelista. He was wary of the religious name—*evangelista* basically meant Protestant—but the Casa's reputation among travelers was sterling. He was greeted in the maroon-tiled atrium by the hostel's proprietor, who introduced himself as Aurelio, though he was obviously American.

"Budget-trail traveler, caught in the desert without a hat," guessed Aurelio. His blue linen shirt was open at the collar, revealing coarse, white chest hair. He took Rosemont's pack and slid it next to the front desk. "German?"

He got that a lot. Rosemont smiled, feeling dilapidated. "Not too many of us down here, but I'm American."

Aurelio laughed and looked him over again. "To quote the Bard," he said, "you do look all horse-piss." Aurelio took Rosemont's hand in both of his and then led him through the Casa's courtyard, where dark palm fronds bobbed, and to the guest rooms. The room that Aurelio assigned to Rosemont had an engraved door, painted with a rough portrait of bespectacled and goateed Carlos Fonseca. He said, "For you, Fonseca, my favorite room." He smiled affectionately. "We have a Sunday service tomorrow morning with Communion. You're invited but not expected to come."

Hector, the bellman and guard, had arrived a moment later with Rosemont's bags, slid them into the room, turned on the electric fan, and set a big dispenser of water on the dresser, flashing a winning smile as he departed.

"I won't attend," said Rosemont over the loudly oscillating fan, again wondering if he'd made a mistake selecting this hostel. "I'm not feeling very well, and—"

"So sleep in," said Aurelio, smiling and stepping back from Rosemont.

An Australian couple came to stand behind Aurelio, just outside Rosemont's room. They were quarreling over money.

Their dissonance wore on him. The welcome firmness of Aurelio's hand had reminded Rosemont how long it had been—weeks—since he'd even touched another human being. He wished that the couple would find a gentler way to speak, that the man wouldn't go.

"Perhaps I'll check back on you later tonight?" Aurelio said. "See how you're feeling?"

It begins, thought Rosemont. He should have said that wasn't necessary, but he was not himself. "Yes, do that."

As it happened, Aurelio did not come back to check on him, and Managua's roosters had woken Rosemont early that first night. The headache he suffered in the Matagalpa

desert was gone, though he'd drifted in and out of a sun-
burnt sleep, drinking from his water bottle, dreaming of
plump red coffee berries and relieved to have the fan aimed
at him.

Hours later, hand bells woke him, announcing the
church service. Rosemont figured *what the hell,* and put on
his last clean shirt, a blue and brown plaid shirt with yellow stripes.

The Casa was set up like a big oval, with the atrium
and gate at the front and the "church" at the back. Really,
the church was just twenty chairs set before a makeshift altar. Guests walking from the rooms on the right side of the
oval to the dining tables and kitchen on the left kept passing behind the congregation of Nicaraguans and international guests who'd risen early to hear the old Anglican
priest.

Much of Aurelio's sermon was lost on Rosemont, who
slouched into a folding chair and leaned back against the
wall. He didn't understand the passages from Ezekiel, the
obscure quotations from modern church fathers. But when
Aurelio began talking about Rome, Rosemont leaned forward. "Saints Peter and Paul were executed," Aurelio said,
preaching in English for the international crowd, "each according to their class. Paul was a citizen of Rome, and
accordingly he was beheaded—a quick and merciful exe-
cution. But Simon Peter, a Jewish nobody, met a nobody's
end, tortured to death by crucifixion—just like his nobody
Jewish rabbi, Jesus, for sedition, conspiracy, and terrorism
on the fringes of the empire."

After the service, Rosemont and Aurelio ate lunch
together and walked through the dismal neighborhood.

Aurelio told him that the Anglican Church was preparing to kick him out for his politics and "other practices."

Rosemont wished the man would take his hand. *Do it. Go on. Do it.*

They stood facing each other, but Aurelio would not look Rosemont in the eye. Then, as if Rosemont were being taken from him, Aurelio admitted, "I would like to hold your hand." He raised dark eyes to Rosemont. "But in this culture, that's a dangerous line to cross."

They bought a couple of Cokes, drank them standing outside the bodega. Strolling back to the Casa, Rosemont put an arm around Aurelio's shoulders. A block later, he took the older man's hand.

Aurelio went rigid under Rosemont's embrace, though he looked with want and fear at the younger, taller man.

"Don't worry. You're safe." Rosemont justified doing this by telling himself that he needed helpers now. He had little money, the coffee season was over, and he was still sick from the heat and sun. He had already erased a line between the French girl and the cook, pressed them together to create a cozy bed of good, compliant feeling in the Casa. The bickering Australian couple had spent the rest of Saturday evening apparently making up, because they were all whispers and coy laughter now, and the sound was soothing to Rosemont, actually relieved his headache. He hadn't interfered like this, not once, since leaving the United States when he'd promised himself never to do so again. *But I need something good. A nest. Something that feels like home*, Rosemont told himself. *Just till I get better.* Before anyone noticed that something was happening, he would move on.

"Trust me," Rosemont had said, smiling down into the priest's eyes. "I'll handle everything."

That night, sitting near the Casa's wrought-iron gate, Rosemont turned the priest over in his mind. The oceanic night air cradled him as he sat, exulting in his body's sated, satiated, and saturated warmth. The peak of gray hair on the old man's chest. The strapping shoulders that seemed to crack at the crucial moment. The salty tang of Aurelio lingered in Rosemont's mouth, and the sermon came like a breeze looking for him through the Casa's barred gate.

On the fringes of empire.

For the first time since leaving America six months ago, Rosemont looked backward at the height from which he'd fallen. Poverty here was not like poverty in the States. No one had money except the impossibly rich, while three-fingered boys begged in the streets. Untethered from a tenure track as an art historian, a respectable neighborhood, and his family, Rosemont had willfully abandoned prosperity and a promising future and had fallen down, down, as if draining from America into Mexico's high plains, Chiapas, Guatemala, Honduras, falling in line behind a trail of migrant coffee workers and hidden jungle farms. Now he had finally landed here, in a destitute neighborhood and a radical priest's bed. Rosemont wondered what was beyond this fringe, if anything could possibly be beyond it. Looking back at the height from which he'd fallen he could see, far above him in the north, America, an immense and ridiculous bird, spreading vast wings pinioned with personal computers, telephones, modems, rear-window defrost, CD players, cable TV, talking cars, and jumbo decaf cappuccinos. Ivy-covered brownstones. University scuffles. Reputation and status; betrayal and sabotage. It all seemed so arbitrary from here; Rosemont wanted nothing to do with that bird. He wanted this road. He wanted it to take him farther into the fringes of the empire, and beyond, if he could find a place where someone like him might belong.

A burst of laughter came from the partyers in the French room. Rosemont closed his eyes. Listening to the mood of the hostel was deeply soothing.

"That's it! Forget it! I'm canceling my trip. I want to stay here forever," someone shouted in English.

"Me too," the French girl shouted. "I'm here for good."

"Good!" the Nicaraguan cook was yelling back. "We'll start a new city, here, inside the Casa. Our city won't join wars like Bush's. We'll populate our new city with Nicas and Euros. Where's Rosemont? If I could—"

A crash of metal on metal and another hysterical burst of group laughter.

Rosemont turned in his chair as he heard several pairs of footsteps rapping down the unlit road outside the Casa. A man appeared, pressing himself against the bars of the gate, eyes scanning the atrium and focusing down the hall to the light of the kitchen. "¡Ayudame!" he shouted. "¡Ayudame!" *Help me.*

House rules said that he couldn't open the gate for a nonguest after midnight—Aurelio's hostel was located in a very rough neighborhood. The man looked frantic as the young guard, Hector, appeared from his office, where he had been listening to his shortwave radio. Glancing back the way he had come, the man fell quiet and looked suddenly dead-eyed with fear. Just then, two running men appeared, and each shoved him hard against the gate as they passed again out of sight, down the street. It was almost as if they were playing a game of late-night tag, and the man was safe, touching these iron bars.

Hector watched them go and stared at the man, waiting for an explanation or a departure, perhaps.

Still clinging to the gate, the man wore a nice dress shirt beneath a suit jacket, a fashion one didn't usually see in Managua's tropical bake. Both jacket and shirt were filthy. "I'm in trouble," he whispered in Spanish to Hector.

"I'm sorry. I am not allowed to open this gate," said Hector. "Gangs in this neighborhood make it unsafe here."

"It's not your gangs I'm worried about. Say, can you give me some food?"

"No, sir. You have to come back in the morning."

"I'm just going to stay here for a moment," the man said, leaning against the wrought-iron bars.

"You can stay there as long as you like," said Hector. He turned and noticed Rosemont sitting in the shadows. He beamed and tipped his baseball cap. "I didn't see you there, Señor Rosemont. Good evening!"

Rosemont smiled sleepily at Hector, unsure if he was breaking house rules by sitting in the atrium this late. He made to get up, saying, "I'm sorry. I just needed to get out of bed for a bit. This heat—"

Hector shook his head frantically side to side. "Stay out here as long as you like." He smiled again, then gave the man at the gate one last scrutinizing look before walking back to the office and his blaring shortwave radio.

At the gate, the man watched Hector disappear, and from down the hall and the bathrooms came sounds of the Australians orgasming operatically. He sat listening for a moment, as if to music, then his eyes drifted over to Rosemont in the shadows. "I have a message for you."

Rosemont pressed back slightly in his chair, surprised by both the man's words and his use of English. "What did you say?"

"He called you 'Rosemont'?" said the man. "You're Jeremiah Rosemont?"

Sitting perfectly still, his body nonetheless broke a sweat. Rosemont laughed a small syllable of disbelief. "Yes, that's me."

The man reached into his suit coat pocket and removed a business-sized envelope, pristine and white, a stark contrast to the condition of his clothes. He offered it through the bars of the gate. "Here."

No one from his previous life in the shadow of the ridiculous bird knew that Rosemont was in Nicaragua, let alone in this city or staying at this hostel. Rosemont was near enough that he could see the envelope in a strong splash of light from Hector's room. The letter was addressed to *Jeremiah Rosemont, Casa Evangelista, Room Fonseca, Managua, Nicaragua.* "That's impossible," said Rosemont, gripping the arms of his chair hard to keep from shaking. "I didn't know I was coming here myself until Saturday night. Who sent you?"

"Don't act like a child." The man held out the envelope with an impatient shake of his wrist. "I've made sure it arrived to you clean, just as the rules prescribe. Now take it."

"What the fuck are you talking about?" said Rosemont, standing like a marionette jerked to its wobbling feet. He stepped forward and took the envelope. "Who sent it? Who are you?"

The man released his grip on the gate and stepped back. "I did my part," said the man. "I don't know anything more."

Rosemont pushed the envelope back through the gate. "Tell me what this is about. Please?"

"Read the message," said the man, backing away from the envelope and Rosemont. "I imagine that your questions will be—" He looked down the street in fright. "Jesus Christ!" Then he turned and ran back the way he'd come, without looking at Rosemont again.

A moment later, a dappled white and tan horse appeared from the opposite direction, barreling up the street after the man. Two figures were crouched and spooned on the galloping horse, and the one behind held what appeared to be a spear. Rosemont threw himself forward against the gate but only managed, before they disappeared out of his view, to glimpse the messenger looking frantically over his shoulder and the horse's tossing tail illuminated by a streetlight.

Shaken, Rosemont stepped away from the gate. He had to remind himself not to crush the envelope in his sweaty hands. When he felt he could walk without his knees giving way, he turned and went down the hall to his room, holding the letter level as if it were a tray of nitroglycerin.

"Rosie!" shouted one of the French girls in English as he passed their room, making him jump. "You have one last drink?"

"One last drink," parroted the cook's assistant in English, though he didn't speak it. His eyes were glazed. "One last drink!"

Rosemont looked in at the ring of drinkers—French, Nicaraguan, a German kid, and an older Swedish woman—and even though he'd been sitting in that ring earlier, the doorway into the room now seemed a portal into a parallel dimension. He couldn't imagine passing into it. "Thanks.

No," he muttered, walking to his room and shutting the door.

After flipping on the nightstand lamp, Rosemont sat on the bed and opened the envelope, half expecting an explosion. Inside, however, was a plane ticket for a flight from Managua to Rome and a note that simply said, *Come, Rosemont. Your opinion is needed.*

Rosemont let the letter, ticket, and envelope slip to the floor, and lay back flat on the hard bed with his hand on his brow. He remained like that through the night, unable to close his eyes or sleep, listening to Nicaragua's roosters scream.

On a hunt for a nice suit, the Boy King leaned forward over his steering wheel as if Lyndale Avenue were pulling him forward. Between Thirty-second and Thirty-fourth, there was an alley that ran parallel to the named streets. On the east side of the alley stood a nice apartment building where mostly young people working downtown lived, and on the west side was a Jewish nursing home. The Dumpsters here were cornucopias, and it had been a whole week since his last harvest.

As he steered his van into the alley, the bumper scraped the high sidewalk. The Boy King needed to sell off some of his junk; it was loading him down. He toed the accelerator, the van lurched toward the Dumpsters, and the Boy King felt an almost adolescent surge of glee as he saw them overflowing with bags and boxes.

Pristine Dumpster diving. "My suit is here," the Boy King said.

There were many ways to Dumpster dive, and the Boy King employed them all at different times according to his needs and wants. Zen trolling: drive and dive. Strategize: gear up, find targets, dig, deal with authority, escape with the loot. The freegan method: think globally and eat very locally (grocery stores *always* threw out perfectly good produce). Fix-and-resell turned Dumpster diving into a profitable venture—Boy King had a vintage 1923 sewing machine in the back of his van that someone threw out thinking it was useless, but the bobbin was merely knotted with thread. He figured it was worth hundreds of dollars, based on his many years of repairing such discarded antiques.

And then there was Boy King Style, which the Boy King himself used only in rare moments. It worked like this: picture the need, go and find it. It was a scary door to open, since often other unbidden events, characters, and conflicts might pass through the aperture of an opened Dumpster lid. Successful Boy King Style depended on how great the need truly was and a vivid imagination to picture it fulfilled.

Today, the need was truly great. He'd landed a job, but the Boy King had been wearing threadbare khakis for nearly two years straight. He dearly needed a new suit.

Eight boxes sat neatly beside the row of garbage cans, more like boxes ready to be loaded into a moving truck than discarded trash, but the Boy King didn't hesitate to park the van and investigate.

Fumbling with his left hand, he opened the top box. Books. He hated books. They were heavy, they took up space, smelled like mold, and rarely earned him more than a quarter apiece. He folded the top box neatly and shoved it aside.

The next box was more promising: CDs. Boy King was lucky to get here before LuLu and the Pipehead Unit. They rarely scored anything *but* CDs. There were some good ones here too, mostly grunge from the early nineties, with some other alternative titles thrown in. Nirvana, of course. Soundgarden. REM. Lemonheads. Blue Mountain. Jayhawks. Down at Cheapo they'd give a buck each for white-boy music like this, the Boy King calculated, loading the box into his van. Slacker music. Someone—roommate, landlord?—apparently had gotten fed up with an aging slacker, chucked his books and CDs into the alley. Breakup, decided the Boy King. An infidelity. With a close friend. The woman's sister. Oops. Boy King laughed as he slid the box of CDs under the end table he'd found an hour before. Yes, the sister, that was right, though he hadn't intended to picture it all so vividly. This stuff had been thrown more in anger toward the sister's betrayal than the hapless slacker whom the woman was ready to leave. The Boy King stood facing the bay of his van and the odd collection of items there—the furniture, vintage sewing machine, bike with training wheels—his hands on either side of the box of CDs, picturing this breakup, transfixed. The guy didn't know that his belongings were out here, trashed. He would come looking for his things. Damn. He'd miss the Lemonheads especially, which would remind him of the heady, better days of this love affair, back when the two of them took road trips to Duluth to hang out with the woman's sister. The Boy King shoved the box as far into his van as it would go, making room for more. He was a sentimentalist, this slacker man, who lingered on old relationships like an alcoholic nursing warm beer. He would be doing this guy a favor, taking these mementos. It wasn't a rationalization. He could hear the rumor of this future like a song through apartment walls. If the guy came home and found these CDs outside in the alley, the Boy King figured, he'd plunge himself into a music-induced depression, savoring the pain of how he'd hurt this girl for many years. That was the music from one future. From the other, the Boy King could hear this guy running downstairs in his Nike Airs to recover the items that the girl had discarded in anger. But the boxes would be gone. The guy would of course be furious. He'd storm out of this relationship, slamming the door on it in indignation. The girl, satisfied by her revenge, would move on, and so would the guy, anger cauterizing both wounds.

A happy ending. All thanks to the Boy King.

The third box was marked "study" but contained old *Playboys,* and the fourth box contained a scattering of junk: a tangled mobile of silver seagulls, broken *Star Wars* action figures, glob-tipped Bic pens, cracked and half-burned candles.

The Boy King neatly restacked the boxes—always leave the trash better than you found it—made a cursory inspection of the apartment's garbage cans, then looked across the alley at the line of nursing home Dumpsters.

He had mixed feelings about diving these. On one hand, they never failed to yield a bountiful crop. That's because (on the other hand) they were the final resting place for items left behind by residents who died in the nursing home. Most ground-scores were expensive canes, telephones for the blind, hearing aids, glasses with dense lenses.

Such items were often in excellent shape and could be resold for a lot of money, relative to the prices that other Dumpster-dived items earned him.

But even more lucrative and disturbing were the personal effects. The music box that played three different Cole Porter songs. The Art Deco mirror. Ancient, black-and-white photographs of grandparents or European relatives—nicely framed. A gold-plated menorah. Diaries, letters, and even jewelry. With no family in the next generation to catch these items, they fell into the Dumpster, not even boxed up like the slacker guy's books were. The Boy King always wondered why the nursing staff didn't take these things. Maybe it was too much for them to scavenge from men and women for whom they had offered so much care and companionship. Or maybe they took only the best treasures, and then only from the clients they didn't know well, leaving the rest for divers like the Boy King to claim.

He lifted the first Dumpster lid and found nothing but cafeteria scraps. The next three Dumpsters held old files. He picked up one piece of paper. An admission form from 1974. Someone apparently had finally converted the old archives onto disc.

The last Dumpster was it. The Boy King's need would be answered there. He could tell the suit was waiting for him like a punch line to a practical joke, and suddenly he wasn't sure he wanted to get a pie in the face. The universe could be a cruel jester when one indulged in Boy King Style. He approached the Dumpster and opened the lid, almost wincing as he saw the suit laid out in its plastic cover, just for him.

It wasn't any old suit. It was a fine double-breasted black silk jacket with flashy pinstripes and matching pants.

Forty-two regular, the Boy King noted, inspecting the jacket's tag through the plastic. Perfect. Thirty-six-inch waist on the pants. Even the shoes, in a shopping bag, were the correct size, eleven D. Way too perfect.

Unsure if he should accept such a fine harvest, the Boy King laid his left hand flat on the suit cover and realized that this was the suit that the nursing staff had *not* selected for burial. The suit they'd chosen for the funeral was less flashy. The man who'd died was quiet and polite. None of the staff had expected to find such a gangster-looking suit in the old fellow's closet. Instead, they'd selected the sober, charcoal-gray suit and a plain white shirt. It was how they remembered him dressed for Sabbath on Fridays for the last three years.

It would have been a crime, though, to bury this beautiful suit in a landfill, let alone to refuse it after specifically asking for it, so Boy King removed the suit from the Dumpster. He unzipped the cover and, holding the hanger, checked the suit's pockets with his right gloved hand, not wanting to take more personal effects from the dead man than necessary. He found two theater ticket stubs placed neatly in the breast pocket like a kerchief: Chanhassen Dinner Theatre, *Guys and Dolls*, 1988. The Boy King smiled. This fellow had dressed the part to see the show. When he checked the back pocket of the pants, however, his smile faded. His mouth dropped open, and the Boy King almost let the hanger slip from his fingers.

On a folded 8½-x-11-inch piece of paper was a symbol drawn in pencil. It was neatly done, the letter of a curious alphabet or a character in a childish code.

Just as the Boy King had seen it for the first time twelve years ago.

Frightened, he looked at the suit. Who could that man possibly have been? How could an old Jewish fellow in Minnesota know to draw such a heinous thing? And if he didn't draw it, then where in the world had he gone in this suit that he would casually place that ancient symbol in his back pocket with less ceremony than a pair of ticket stubs?

Ready to march into the nursing home to start asking the staff questions, the Boy King took three steps in that direction and stopped. No. The explanation was not so literal and probably had little to do with this man or his suit.

It was the Boy King's own doing, he realized. He had asked for the suit, and, as he well knew, when he asked for doorways to open, even Dumpster lids, frightening things came through in the wake of such requests.

But this. Had he known. Letting *this* wrecking ball swing back into his life? He shook his head. He did not need a job nor suit this badly, but too late. Here it was.

Club music pulsed in a passing car, the creamy April sun emerged from behind a cloud, and Boy King put the suit in the back of his Econoline.

T he cab driver pulled up to the curb and shouted something in Italian. Rosemont figured it was either *here it is* or *get out*. It turned out, after a clutch-screaming car ride from Rome International, that the address he wanted (written on the back of the airline ticket) was in the dark-windowed street-maze of Rome's famous Jewish ghetto.

Looking at the row of cramped and unmarked buildings sardined together before him, Rosemont called back to the driver, "This is 24 Vicolo il Bambinello?"

But the driver, having been paid, merely waved at the nearest door and stomped on the accelerator, cutting off three guys on motorinos. Cursing and horn honking trailed off down the street.

Though a small business district thrummed just a few blocks away, here, crumbling houses were piled one on top of another. These tall narrow stone houses were pock-marked with square holes for beams that once supported wooden neighbors, long gone now. Climbing up a tall stoop of stairs to the nearest door, Rosemont figured any one of these houses was centuries older than America.

He knocked, but the door was ajar, so Rosemont slipped inside and found himself in an unlit atrium. Down a long hall before him, he could see a dim rectangle of light shining around a door. The hall smelled of dust and mold, but of sautéed onions, too.

Fearing that he was stepping into someone's apartment, he gingerly walked to the door at the end of the hall, a ready apology on his lips.

"What is this place?" he said into the dark.

Rosemont knocked on the door. He could hear people on the other side talking quietly, the sizzle of frying. When the door jerked open, Rosemont started back in fright. A middle-aged Italian woman with frizzed hair and a greasy apron stood there staring at him.

"¡Lo siento!" Rosemont said, apologizing in Spanish out of reflex. "Estoy buscando—"

The woman said something rapid and demanding to him in a low whisper. Behind her in a cramped kitchen, an older, grandmotherly woman was caramelizing onions on an ancient gas stove. "What are you saying?" the younger woman said in Italian.

He handed her the envelope given to him by the strange messenger yesterday in Managua and shifted to Italian. He was better with Renaissance-era Italian, but he managed to ask, "Miss, do you know this address?"

She scanned it and then showed him a face of resignation, maybe pity. Over her shoulder she said something derisive to the older lady, who snorted her agreement with a contemptuous toss of her head and said what sounded like *Whore*.

Rosemont tried again. "I'm looking for a hotel. I think I am, anyway. Do you know this address?"

The woman handed him the envelope and then wiped her hands on the dirty apron, as if she'd ridded herself of something. "Come. Come." She stepped away from the door and waved him in. He entered and felt his stomach shy from the claustrophobic reek of onions, gas, and garbage. "Through there," she hissed at him in a loud whisper, and pointed to a blanket covering a doorway.

"What's through there?" he asked in English.

"Go, go," said the aproned woman, turning back to a cutting board of chopped green peppers.

Rosemont squeezed against the old woman to reach the blanket, wondering where he was being sent, and lifted the hem.

On the other side was a room with three beds and sleeping bodies in each one, snores sighing in the darkness. Rosemont shook his head angrily and turned back, but both women were already waving him forward.

"We don't want you here. Go. Through there!"

"But they're sleeping. I don't—"

"Shh shh." The old woman hushed him and turned his shoulder with a rough push of her hand. "Don't you wake them. Go."

Rosemont passed beneath the blanket, feeling stupid, confused, but hopeful this might take him to the street on the other side of the block, so that he could shake off the smell of the onions and gas. He tiptoed past the sleepers to the doorway beyond, stopping only to discern the sound of a foreign news service chittering about Iraq from a discarded Walkman on the floor. The room smelled sour, like unclean clothes and sweating bodies, and Rosemont negotiated between the beds, stepping over piles of books and magazines in the smothering dark. He opened the door beyond and quickly shut it behind him, so as not to wake the smelly sleepers, and passed into an open-air courtyard. The fresh air, warm as it was, felt good on Rosemont's face. He looked up and saw white linen and undershirts bobbing overhead on laundry lines sagging between high windows.

Four doors opened onto this sunlit courtyard, and one of them stood ajar with warm light spilling outside. Rosemont could hear American voices through the door. It was marked Hostelry of the Tyros in English and Italian, but there was no address.

"A hostel," Rosemont said to himself as he walked to the door. "This has to be the place."

Inside, the hostelry was a typical check-in room with a pretty woman in a thick purple sweater behind a pressboard desk, a computer buzzing blue light at her face, and a wall full of Roman street maps behind her. The young couple standing in line ahead of Rosemont at the check-in looked ragged and sunburned. Rosemont watched them closely, listening, and wondering if they would give him a clue as to why he had been called to this place.

They seemed tired yet eager, these two, but managed a forced jaded attitude of kids mimicking European travelers with far more miles behind them. "We need a room for the next three nights," the boy said, leaning on the desk, trying to talk sense to the desk clerk.

The woman behind the desk didn't look away from her

computer screen, where she was losing a game of hearts, and she sounded angry. "No."

Rosemont straightened and looked over the boy's shoulder at the desk clerk. By her tone, it didn't sound like occupancy was the issue.

The American girl looked at her partner like he had the necessary key in his pocket and gave him a nod of encouragement.

"Look," said the guy, still leaning. "We ran into someone named Etienne in Prague who told—"

The clerk looked away from her computer for the first time and withered the boy's voice to silence with a toxic stare.

The young woman took up the cause. "This Etienne told us that we could get a room here. We really need a place to stay."

"No. You don't." The desk clerk looked back at her game as if the couple had already headed out the door.

"We—"

"You might know the right things to say for whatever random reason," interrupted the clerk. Her voice was haughty, but her eyes remained cool, kind. "There's absolutely nothing desperate about you, however. No. You're tourists. You have everything you need in your ridiculous Lands' End backpacks, and you have a thousand phone numbers in your *Fodor's Rome* current edition. If you know to say that you spoke with Etienne, then you also know that this hostel is not for vacationers. Or budget travelers. Or backpackers of any kind. Yes?"

The two were clearly disappointed to the point of anger, and the girl in particular didn't want to give up. "We know something's going on here. We know this is—"

"Yes, I'm about to shoot the moon and you're messing me up," said the desk clerk, rolling up her sweater's sleeves. She leaned to her left and suddenly made eye contact with Rosemont around the boy's hip. "Come. Come. You need a room?"

The Americans looked over their shoulders at him. Then with a reluctant sidestep, the boy made room for Rosemont at the desk, giving him a baffled head to toe.

Rosemont readjusted his backpack but couldn't hide the Lands' End label from anyone in the room. "Um. Good evening. Hello," he said in English. His eyes darted left and right as he stepped between the Americans, unsure what was expected of him now. The letter merely said to come to this address and to get a room. It didn't say anything about Etienne or the proper thing to say. "I'm here to—"

"We've got singles and dorms." She unrolled the sleeves of her sweater again, reduced her game of hearts, and pulled up a spreadsheet. "Two singles left."

"Um," said Rosemont with a nervous laugh and glance at the boy. "I'll take a single."

"Why does he get a room and we don't?" the girl demanded, and Rosemont could picture her at three making the same face during a tantrum. "*We'd* take a single."

The desk clerk flipped her bobbed, black hair away from her face as if she were accustomed to having longer hair. "He needs us. You don't. Take it up with President Bush. Okay?"

"Actually, I was *told* to come here," Rosemont said. This seemed important to point out for some reason and hoped it might elicit an explanation.

"By Etienne? Do you know Etienne?" asked the girl. "Who *is* Etienne?"

The clerk blinked her eyes as if to say *ignore them.* "Name?"

The American couple backed away from the desk and huddled with loud stage-sighs as Rosemont unshouldered his pack, reddened from Nicaragua's ubiquitous volcanic dust. "Rosemont. Jeremiah Rosemont."

He went through the typical check-in ritual, but when it came time to present his passport, she waved it away. "We're not registered with the government," she said. "All we need is your signature."

Rosemont jerked his head back in surprise. "No money up front?"

"You don't *have* any money, eh?" the desk clerk said.

He shook his head. "Not really. Just Nicaraguan currency."

She presented him with a clothbound ledger to sign. "Keep it," she whispered. "We're here for you, Signore Rosemont." In her Italian accent, his name sounded like *rosa-moan-ta.* "Here's your key. Your room is on this floor, down that hallway."

The American couple was standing in the courtyard now, and Rosemont could hear them arguing. He turned back to the desk clerk and said, "Can you tell me one thing?"

She'd gone back to her game of hearts but looked at Rosemont as if he'd snapped her concentration from an involved phone call. "What do you want?"

"Do you know what I'm doing here?"

The woman frowned at him, almost in disgust. Then she leaned forward, with a sideways glance at the door where the American couple could still be heard. "No, but I'll give you some advice."

Rosemont nodded and leaned toward her.

"Don't admit your ignorance like that anymore."

"My ignorance?" A surge of anger knotted his fists, and he glowered at her, snapping, "How could I be anything *but* ignorant in a situation like—?"

"Shh! You're here for a reason, and I guarantee you know what it is," she said in a rushed whisper. Rosemont had the distinct feeling she was trying to tell him something before someone arrived to silence her. "I don't care about you one bit. I'm just a volunteer. I don't care why you're here. It probably has something to do with academics, I'd bet. But listen, it's not my job to care. Or give advice." She looked at his hands. "Research, maybe? Are you a historian?"

Her voice lost its irritated edge. She suddenly sounded intrigued by him.

Rosemont said, "Yes. I was an art historian for years. How did you know?"

"It doesn't matter. I don't care what you were." The woman closed her eyes and shrugged one shoulder. Her severe bob made her look controlling and precise, but her haughty demeanor had dissolved. "Besides, they all are academics. Or used to be. Or wish they had an academic track." She looked at him helplessly. "You have to stop beating this information out of me. You have information or expertise that someone wants. There. I said it."

"I do? Maybe," said Rosemont. He wasn't beating information out of her, of course, but understood that sometimes people felt this way when he wanted something from them.

Rosemont's academic track had evaporated two years ago—seemed like decades now, for all it mattered to him.

That Rosemont—the wunderkind who'd papered, at the tender age of twenty, newfound sketches of noted tarot artist Beneficio Bembo, and who, as a result of the attention, came to value reputation and prestige so dearly—that Rosemont was gone from the world. Everything had been stripped from him, beaten out of him, literally, by two men who didn't appreciate the compelling effect he had on the unsuspecting, like this desk clerk. That Rosemont had laid his precious burdens down in Austin, Texas, on an emergency-room gurney, with a fractured skull, a broken collarbone, and a scary, scary loss of blood. This Rosemont had been happy to leave that one behind but old habits were hard to break. "I don't know what anyone might want of me," Rosemont said, coaxing the desk clerk. "That's all. Someone wrote me and I came."

"Yes, you came. You came," she said, as if he were tearing the words from her. She glanced at the Americans out in the courtyard and whispered, "You flew to Rome willingly, is that it?"

"That's right."

"For no good reason." She gave him a little frown with her eyebrows, encouraging him to speak. "Why would you do that?"

Rosemont laughed. "It wasn't even a question," he said. In Managua, he hadn't even debated with himself whether or not to take the tickets and fly to Rome. He looked at the desk clerk hard. She seemed careful and trustworthy, so he said, "It's the opposite for me. Standing still is the dilemma—that's when troubles always find me."

"I see. Fan clubs form around you, eh?" she said. "Little cults of personality?"

He nodded, staring at her, wondering if she'd sensed

that he had deliberately compelled her to speak. "Sometimes."

People always noticed eventually that there was something strange about Jeremiah Rosemont, that things were not as they should be. They always identified him as the catalyst, the hot coal under the bed of leaves causing flames to leap suddenly. The disappearances and reappearances of children. Visitations from the dead. Strange personalities overtaking people. In those moments of crisis and anguish, some people, especially students, used to turn to him—while some turned *on* him. That's what happened with those two rednecks in Austin. Rosemont's magnetism simply repelled instead of attracting, soothing them, and it had been about to happen again in the Casa Evangelista in Managua, a repeat of shocking events in Estelí, Kansas City, Des Moines, Austin.

"So this is a safe haven for people like me?" Rosemont said.

Her face was serene and kind as she looked at Rosemont. "It's more like a gate you're passing through. I don't think you'll be back." She lifted her hand for him to leave or be quiet, and said in her imperious voice, "It's just my advice. I don't know you from a hole in the street, I don't care, and that's the way I like it. Now go. I have to get rid of the queen."

Rosemont decided he shouldn't press, though she'd clearly been compelled to speak and answer his questions and could have answered more. "Thank you. Thank you."

He turned his back on the desk clerk and looked down the hall she'd indicated. From a high, circular window at the far end, washed-out sunlight reflected on linoleum in the dark hallway, and he wondered who else was staying in this bizarre little hostel. He was safe here, she said, but he wondered what her definition of safe was.

Rosemont was about to head down the hall to his room (he was still wearing the same clothes he'd worn on Sunday in Managua) when something feathery and magenta flashed by the window of a nearby door. He looked back at the clerk but she was absorbed in her game and hadn't seen it. He opened the door and stepped out into a little winding street. The door, on a spring, slapped shut behind him. He glanced up the street, which was narrow and curved up a low hill. Running up the middle of it was a man or woman in high-heel boots and fishnet stockings, a blazing magenta feather boa trailing behind. Uphill, the little street bent out of sight behind high buildings. Here, where Rosemont stood, the buildings were cramped together so that the sky was just a long crack of dark blue overhead. He hadn't seen the hill when the taxi let him off, and the buildings here looked newer, yet somehow old—from another era. Rosemont couldn't tell where he was. Hadn't he just come around to the other side of the building?

He looked back at the door but could only see a wall.

"Hey."

Rosemont put his hand on the wall and ran it over the dusty surface but couldn't find hinge, seam, or latch. Stepping back from where the door should have been, he scanned the wall up to the eaves. No windows. No balconies. Just a broad, flat, red-brick wall.

"Hey!"

Walking toward him, an old couple, the man holding a chaise longue, glared at him.

"Is this . . . ?" He was about to ask if the Hostelry of the Tyros was nearby, but recalled the desk clerk's conversation with the American couple. It was a safe house of some kind. Even if this couple knew about it, they wouldn't talk. "Good evening," he said in English.

As she passed, the brittle old woman made an inscrutable gesture at Rosemont. It didn't look friendly.

You're safe here, the desk clerk had said. *It may be the only place you're safe.*

Rosemont hung his head and leaned back against the blank brick wall. He looked down into his hand and realized he was still holding his room key. It had the number five scratched into it.

"Rome," he said, slipping the key into his pocket. "I'm in Rome."

4

The Boy King's van cut through the shadows of palatial mansions on Franklin and came to a stop at the intersection with Hennepin Avenue. While he waited for green, the ancient sigil that he'd just found in the pinstriped suit filled his mind's eye. His van idled in anticipation, and he took comfort knowing that the whole continent was at his whim from this red light.

He could turn left and get onto Highway 94, head east through St. Paul, into the wildernesses of Wisconsin. A beautiful hiding place, Wisconsin, but someone like the Boy King would be all too trackable out there. Wild and remote, but not remote enough. Or, from 94, he could veer south on Highway 35, which bifurcated the country and connected to the Intercontinental Highway in Mexico, and hide out in a bigger and better urban tangle like Mexico

City. *Or, I could go north,* he thought, looking up Hennepin where the wide boulevard bled into Highway 94 flowing west. *Make for the wastes beyond Fargo, and continue west to Seattle or even press northward to Winnipeg, and away.*

But any of those escapes would mean starting over, and, while it had taken him years to do it, he'd finally created something here. Corrections. Connections. Then rhythm. He dared not call it home or even think the word, but this city protected him now, and it didn't make sense to sacrifice it quite yet.

So instead, the Boy King's van rumbled east on Franklin, then down Lyndale, past the bustling Wedge Co-op and its conflation of urban tribes and landed gentry, through a bouquet of boutiques, past Lake Street. When he first came to this city, Lyndale and Lake was a heroin hot spot. Grunge bands wailed into the frozen Minnesota nights from grimy flats. Now it was all Merlot and money—far more want than need.

The Boy King checked his watch for the date. Thursday. Lara would be drinking bourbon at the Dream Machine today, and she once asked him to come see her before making any decisions about leaving town.

Older than the Khemet mud, he thought, hypnotized by the flow of traffic as he drove. *Why here? Why now?*

Dream Machine Laundromat was a scummy slot of washers and dryers located north of his warehouse on the West Bank, and it was here that Boy King had first met his best friend, Lara, several weeks ago. He didn't know Lara's last name, didn't particularly think they had much in common, but he'd grown to rely on seeing her once a week at the Laundromat, and he liked that. After sliding his van into a parking stall, Boy King peered through the plate-glass window. There was Lara, sitting cross-legged on a washing machine, and her two roommates, Gitana and Jackie, perched across from her on dryers in graffitied leather jackets. A bottle of Beam sat between them.

"Hello, you washwomen."

They looked up at the Boy King and his craggy face as he let the Dream Machine door swing shut behind him.

"Shut *up*!" Lara laughed and hit him on the arm with a flap of her hand. "I was just talking about you." She leaned backward, seemingly to swing her light brown hair away from her face, but she was giving him an appraising look under drunk eyelids. "Gitana, get a Dixie cup."

He liked these kids. They never turned their noses up at him, even though he knew he smelled perennially of stale beer and cigarette ashes from diving. "I found my suit."

"Cheers." Gitana handed him a Dixie cup of bourbon. "Now you're ready for your gig, right?"

Gig. Ready. The words scared Boy King, but he tried to smile at Gitana as he took the drink.

"I got him that job at the restaurant!" Lara said. "And I think it's fuckin' *right on* that you're gonna stay in town this winter, Boy King!"

Gitana caught Boy King's glance and winked at him. "We've been here since ten this morning."

The Boy King leaned against the washing machine next to Lara and self-consciously folded his right, gloved hand into his pocket. It was nice to join them, to have some friends. This circle had developed very recently, Lara and her pals from the art school, none of whom seemed to mind how low to the ground he lived or the fact that he squatted in a warehouse. Sometimes he even met them and their barfly buddy Garbus for drinks at the Wiggle Room Saloon. If he wanted, he could choose to hear a note of condescension in Lara's comment about him wintering in Minneapolis, his migrant life—the twang of smug magnanimousness that sounded in the voices of people with means—even small, modest means. But Lara couldn't help it. She was drunk, and her effusion genuine, he knew, so Boy King chose not to be bothered. It had been a long time since he spent enough time in one place, where people recognized him, smiled at him, put a drink in his hand. The fact that he looked and smelled like some sort of mad street pirate didn't seem to matter to Lara, Gitana, or Jackie.

The bourbon tasted sweet and sharp and he paused, looking down in the cup, then past it, at his gloved and broken right hand. The smell of bourbon always took him to crazier times. He forced a smile. "Here's to some fucked-up shit."

Gitana and Jackie raised their cups, mouths wide with a tandem laugh. "Fucked-up shit!"

"So you found your suit," said Lara, emptying her cup and holding it out to Jackie to refill. "You start the gig at Dona Mia soon. Everything's good." Lara gave him a vampy look, about as smoky as anyone could look while sitting on a washing machine. "And yet . . . you came to see me." She lowered her voice even more. "On Dream Machine Thursday."

The Boy King spread his hand as if he'd been caught in the act. "So true. I'm here for the magic."

"Something's *not* good?"

The memory of the symbol made Boy King wince. He took another little sip of whiskey and put the cup in his left hand. "I need some answers."

Lara took off her leather jacket, covered with her handwriting in white paint, and sat in just her tank top and jeans. Lara wore tank tops even in winter, deliberately exposing the tiger tattoos on her shoulders. With one pale hand, she reached into her pants' thigh pocket and removed her tarot deck. She patted the washing machine behind him. "Up here."

Biting the cup of bourbon, Boy King joined her atop the washing machines. Across from him was a wall-length mirror. He blocked it out, afraid of the maddening reflection he knew lurked there.

"Jackie, be a thang and fold my whites?" said Lara, unknotting the silk tie that bound her cards.

Jackie clearly didn't like the idea. She had sharp, pixie features that made her look demonic when angry. In a snotty singsong, she said, " 'Jackie, drive me to the war protest. Jackie, do my laundry.' Diva."

Lara shuffled the cards and plunked them down in front of the Boy King, then immediately picked them up with a hasty apology. "Oops! I forgot! You don't like touching them."

The Boy King wrapped his hands around the paper cup, as if warming himself, but really he was just finding something to do with them. For safety reasons, he handled his own tarot deck only, but he'd been about to pick up her cards. In the mirror on the other side of the Laundromat, Boy King could feel his reflection looking at him.

"Don't worry," she said. "I'll absorb the evil for you." Lara dealt ten cards facedown, placing six in a cross and four alongside in a column—the arrangement she always used whenever the Boy King asked her for a reading.

There was a lot of drama in the way Lara read, which

was fine with Boy King. After dealing the cards, she stopped and closed her eyes, summoning strength or peace of *something,* he figured, and she held her splayed fingers over the cards for a long, quiet moment. The Boy King didn't believe this mumbo jumbo was necessary, but Lara was a very accurate reader, so if she needed to cut open a chicken beforehand, he'd sit patiently and wait for the squawking to end.

Finally Lara flipped over the first two cards, which were crossed at the center of the spread. She looked at them the way she might look at a couple on whose conversation she was eavesdropping. "Yours is a story of hiding and discovery. Here's what I mean. First? You were a bullied disciple. Then? You were a warrior surrounded by all his favorite weapons. This is a transformation of chopped wood to billows of dark smoke. But we're not concerned with that— for now. This is merely the swinging bat and sailing ball, not the final score. Does this make sense to you?"

It made no sense whatsoever. "Yes, of course."

Gitana opened a dryer and started hauling out black skirts and black pants. "You two are insane."

Boy King nodded and smiled to encourage Lara. He was waiting for that tenth card—the final score. "Go on."

Lara flipped over the next four so that a larger cross of cards was now revealed. "You can't go far from your past, ever, though you constantly strain at its leash like a frightened, beaten dog." It went on like this, card after card, with Lara scattering her surreal pearls, most of which rolled past him ungrasped, but some of which struck him with startling resonance: "The sleuth who almost caught you many years ago never had a chance, did he?" and, "The danger with camouflage is forgetting your own, true skin." Lara's readings were a bit like randomly spinning the tuner on a radio, which is how he'd recognized what she was, sitting in this Laundromat a few weeks back, listening to her dole out mad readings to her eager and easily mystified friends. But she always accessed a channel, heard something that others couldn't—it just meant patiently waiting through opaque oracles like, "Dead animals lying unburied are vexing you," or, "We daily taste the most acrid hope," and, "You dangle from the sky like noon."

"These last four cards," Lara said, "speak to the intangibles in your situation—what you must know but cannot now see, nor face—what you dread and long for. Understand?"

She said this part every time. "Oh yes. Yes, I do."

"There's a telescope aimed at a distant star. You know it's aimed correctly, but you cannot see the star, no matter how long you stare through that telescope."

That much might have been true—in an obscure, metaphorical way. He had the strange Egyptian image in his own pocket but didn't understand what it portended, and he couldn't get it out of his thoughts. "What do you advise?"

Gitana was folding a black knit top. "She doesn't do advice, Boy."

"Not my department. Sorry," said Lara, decanting some more bourbon. "Now shut the fuck up. I got the final score."

Boy King clenched his teeth, bracing himself.

"You will never see what is right in front of you," Lara said, slurring her words a bit, "until you realize something salient about that sleuth's case."

The Boy King shrugged. "And that is?"

"That you aren't the sleuth."

"I'm not the sleuth," repeated the Boy King, oblivious to what she meant. He waited for clarification, but Lara answered by finishing her little drink. He prompted her, saying, "I'm not the sleuth?"

"No, you're not. You will never find the Holy Grail."

"I'm not in the *grail* business."

"That's good, because the sleuth is still on the case."

"I thought you said I *wasn't* on the case."

"No, I said you weren't the sleuth."

The Boy King gritted his teeth. Maybe he'd gotten here too late in the day for a coherent reading. "What are you talking about, Lara?"

"I never said there *wasn't* a sleuth."

Boy King reworked the sentence in his head, as if translating. "Okay," he said vaguely. "So who *is* the sleuth if I'm not the sleuth?"

"See? I told you! You don't see what's right in front of you!" She signaled touchdown. "Vindicated!"

Boy King shouted. "How am I supposed to see what's in front of me?"

"You *can't* see what's in front of you."

"Not with a reading from you! If I'm not the sleuth, then who *am* I?"

"God, you two," said Gitana, shaking her head.

"You," said Lara, scooping up the cards, "are *the Grail*."

The Boy King was about to argue with her and send this Abbott and Costello card-reading into yet another pass, but he suddenly stopped. He wondered if this was more random Dada poetry, or her eerie channel of truth. The Boy King put his hands flat on either side of him, as if to keep the washing machine that he was sitting on from flying into the air. *"What* did you just say?"

Lara righted the cards and then tied the silk tie around them again, making a little Windsor knot with her fumbling fingers. "Did I fucking stutter? You're the goddamn Grail, okay?"

The Boy King felt the distinct urge to grab Lara and wring something cogent out of her. He figured he wasn't going to get the answers he wanted so he said, "Are you saying that this sleuth is after *me*?"

"You tell me."

"No, you tell me."

"No, you tell me!"

He looked at her warily. She might have even planted the Egyptian symbol in that suit, laid it out for him to find. She looked up at him, caught him staring, and seemed to start. Something could have overpowered her, manipulated her into leaving that symbol where he could find it. But no. Lara didn't have any lies in her, he could tell. What she was saying had merit, whether she understood the implication of her words or not, and that was usually the way with readings from the uninitiated. "There's something who wants something from me," he said in a low, rushing whisper to Lara, "and it will kill me to get it. So if you know something concrete that will help me."

Lara turned her face to him, and he could see she finally realized that he was scared, that her words had frightened him. He could also see that the oracular moment was over. Her eyes were too glassy with booze and they held a little spark of fear for her friend. "Do you need a place to stay?" she asked. "Are you in danger?"

A place to stay. He almost spat at her. No lies in her,

maybe, but the yawning gulf that surrounded Lara was so wide she couldn't see people clearly, couldn't see Boy King as anything but homeless, helpless, tragic. *Do you need a place to stay? Can I give you a crust of bread, so I won't feel so guilty for knowing you?* If it weren't for that receiver inside her that plugged Lara into signals beyond her gulf, her do-gooder reflexes would dominate, and she and Boy King would have no friendship at all.

"Yes, I'm in danger," said Boy King, all but snarling. "That's why I wanted this reading, to see if I'm safe or not."

"Who's after you, Boy?"

He decided it was time to find out if Lara was truly friend or foe. Boy King removed the piece of paper that he'd found in the suit just an hour before and laid it on the washing machine. Across the way, his reflection was waving in the mirror, trying to get his attention. Boy King closed his eyes and said to Lara, "Have you seen this before?"

"What is it?" Lara picked it up and examined it. "Looks like an animal, maybe."

He'd hoped that seeing it would bring in something more coherent through whatever spooky channel she accessed, but no. Her expression was sincere, ignorant, and she had no access to the people who revered this sigil. Boy King took the paper back and slipped it into his pocket. All the hiding had gotten him nothing. Walling off that past, burying the names and stories from that time, and freeing himself had simply delayed the inevitable. As soon as he decided it might be safe to accept a job, to find a suit to wear for his first day, the Boy King announced his presence, stuck up his head—and, voilà, a warning from Our Lord the Spinning Wheel.

"Boy, what *is* this thing?"

"It's a symbol," Boy King told Lara, "of a very old cult. Egyptian, but not really. Older than that civilization. Older than the Khemet mud, as we used to say."

Lara frowned and gave him a slow, besotted blink. "But what does all that mean?"

His lips twitched into a little smirk. *Now look who's asking for clarity?* The Boy King lifted his eyes to her. "It's a calling card from the sleuth. I found it in the pocket of the suit that I just Dumpster dived. Someone is letting me know that they're after me."

Lara frowned. "That doesn't make sense."

"No. But it's true."

"I believe you that something weird is going on, Boy. But I mean, if someone was after you, why would they alert you?"

"Hmm." Boy King straightened. He hadn't thought of it that way. "They like to toy. To terrorize. But you're right." The symbol filled his vision for a moment, and he saw it as he had first seen it, cast in gold on a chain around the neck of the six-hundred-year-old man. He blinked rapidly. "There's nothing good that comes with this symbol. That's all I know. I think I need to get out of town. I think I should get in the van and—"

"Look," Lara said, grabbing his gloved hand.

He flinched and yanked it away. "Don't!"

She held up her hands, placating him, but she looked frightened. Boy King glared at her furiously and knew she was trying to decide if he was so bonkers that she should cancel his Dona Mia's gig for him. The moment passed, and her shoulders went from squared to whiskey languid. "If someone wanted to kill you they'd just *do* it, Boy. They wouldn't put a note in a suit and leave it in a Dumpster that you might or might not find," she said, her voice still hot, "right?"

Boy King didn't understand much of why things happened the way they did, but maybe Lara was right. Maybe the symbol of the ancient cult portended something other than a visit from the old man. Maybe things had changed. Boy King certainly had. "Could be."

"Dona Mia's is expecting you to come."

"I know."

"So you can't run off now."

"I don't know. Might be the best time, Lara."

"After all I've done for you?" She was teasing, but she wasn't kidding. "How long has it been since you had an address, a phone?"

"I don't need those things."

"A van that runs good? A visit to a doctor? Being able to pee somewhere other than an abandoned lot?"

The pat answer was that he didn't care about those things, either. But he stared at her and wondered if he did.

"Just hang tight, Boy," Lara said. "I think you're wigging out because you're afraid of this job and the change. That's what I think is going on."

He grimaced. More of her slumming art student crap. She could leave this world of homeless people, war protests, and shitty Laundromats anytime she pleased. He wondered what she would say if he told her what he was really afraid of—the casual, bizarre cruelty, the laughing torturers, the warning he'd been issued twelve years ago while his lover sprawled on a machine shop floor. *They're coming for you. You have to escape!*

But she'd said the right word. *Afraid.* He allowed himself a rare look at his reflection, the image of himself there. At least it looked like him now. It didn't used to, and maybe that meant things were changing for the better, becoming less dire. That's how the game operated, after all. Those who thrived on power lusted for acquiescence, surrender, and fear. Their lives were streamlined into the hunt for ever greater pools of it, drinking deep from them; the mere fact that he'd been in a state of panic in the hour since he'd found the symbol might have done more to announce Boy King's location than a flare shot straight overhead and exploding over the city.

For the longest time, Boy King had adhered to the motto that if he had nothing to lose he had nothing to fear. During those early days of homelessness, his reflection was a horror, a reminder of the horrors from which he was running. But that was different, now, and maybe *nothing to lose equals nothing to fear* was the wrong strategy. Maybe if he bolstered his life with a little muscle and stopped living it so close to the bone . . . Maybe Lara's world was safer because of its smug fearlessness and confounded belief in itself. Did hope trump fear? It could. It might.

"Okay. Me and my suit will be at Dona Mia's tomorrow. Like I said."

Lara grinned. "Cool." She held the bottle of Beam over his cup without pouring. "Promise?"

Boy King smirked at himself. Was he going to live in abandoned buildings his whole life? It was time. He'd been on the fringes of firelight for too long. Time to rejoin the human tribe. "Hit me."

She poured. "Gitana, he's actually going to read tomorrow. Wait till you get a Boy King reading. It's five-alarm yikes."

Gitana was buttoning down the collar on a dress. "I'll draw up a press release."

This was so brazen, so needlessly forward after all these years of careful solitude. But it was done, he'd promised, so he drained the bourbon. "In for a penny, in for a pounding," he said, and edged the empty cup across the washing machine for one more.

If urban planners had been paying attention, they might have noticed that the tail end of River Boulevard, the half-block that jutted toward Highway 35 like an accusing finger, began disappearing from records about a decade ago. Street maps of Minneapolis started shaving off that little finger, that 650-foot stretch of road, where an abandoned blond-stone warehouse from the last century and two Edwardian duplexes sagged against each other. Just as well that no one noticed. Most families didn't want houses so close to the highway, and enterprising businesses couldn't use the tiny Bryce & Waterston livery that didn't have a parking lot or modern loading docks; development would cost them more than it was worth. Or, at least, that was the thought that made their eyes drift away from this amputated section of River Boulevard.

Five families of Hmong and Eritrean immigrants lived in one of the Edwardian mansions-turned-duplexes. The other was occupied by a squatting theatrical collective in the bottom flat and a prostitute named Farah in the top. Neither the immigrant families nor the theatrical collective, nor the Boy King, paid rent. In fact, only Farah was connected to civic commerce in any palpable way.

The Bryce & Waterston livery made the other households nervous, so the Boy King had the building to himself. Pulling in from *Thirtyfivedub*, he parked his van up River Boulevard, well away from the warehouse but still within view, and walked a circuitous path through an abandoned lot of thistle and quack grass. Entering through a side window where he'd leaned a plywood board, he was home.

It was April, so the chilly warehouse was invigorating when he left the warm sun outside. Boy King stayed here in spring and fall but in the cruel Minnesota winter, and the very hottest pit of summer, he lived either in the Econoline or in the shelter on Twenty-eighth if he could get in. Now, Boy King stood in the center of the ancient loading bay and took in the cool, moist air of the warehouse. He loved it here, but for the first time he was considering staying in Minneapolis year-round, and that meant a change. With the prospect of a job like the one that Lara got him, he found himself thinking about things like an apartment. Could he earn that much money? A telephone? Maybe a desk and a room where he could put books that he would buy with his earnings. Bryce & Waterston was too cold and wet past September for such plans.

Boy King had just placed his hand on the wall, ready to ascend the railless stairs, when something on the loading-bay floor caught his eye. A rock, he thought at first, or a brick. The building was crumbling, and the occasional scattered brick on the floor wasn't unusual.

But this brick had eyes. Like a turtle? Didn't it? It was hard to see, nestled in an unnaturally dark nook of shadows below the stairs.

Boy King stood with his back to the rough, blond brick of the warehouse wall, and the cool dampness of it chilled the backs of his bare arms. He dared not move, trapped in a silence shattered by geese barking overhead and traffic rivering along the highway. Slowly, a square of sunlight elongated, drifted across the floor, and swallowed the figure in light.

Now he could see it clearly. Not a turtle, but a tiny car. A van.

His van.

Boy King turned his head ever so slightly, cranking his gaze sidelong so that he could look through the open doorway at his van. Still there, on River Boulevard. Doors shut. Windows rolled up, snug as an Econoline bug.

Now that natural light had been thrown on the model, Boy King could see that it was more than just a clever rendering—it was an exact replica, complete with slightly hanging forward bumper and a dented cargo door. It was a marker. Someone was watching him. Someone was here and had found him despite Boy King erasing the paths that such searchers used. He couldn't fight the force that was coming. No, it wasn't coming—it was *here*. Had it been the decision he'd just made? Did these things happen that quickly? Had the promise to Lara alerted a spy? Or was this some older trap finally springing? In the old days, he'd discounted Khnum as a complete joke, but he never would again.

You're the goddamn Grail, okay?

Lara's words scared him deeply. It wasn't revenge, recovery, justice, or hate that compelled the "sleuth," as Lara put it. It was him. *Doesn't matter what I have or what I give it,* he thought, looking up at the top of the stairs that led to his secret home.

Stepping toward it, Boy King traced *BK* on the roof of the miniature van with his finger. It was made from mud. Nile mud, he knew. He told the van as he picked it up, "I renounced my power over an evil world a long time ago." He paused. "But I'm back in it now."

He walked to one of Bryce & Waterston's shattered windows and released the replica into the air like a trapped bird. It broke away from Boy King's hands and sailed east, as though it were just another goose or duck making for the Mississippi, where river mud would meet river mud.

"I'm not a grail. I'm just my own self."

5

Around him, the winding Roman street was filling with what seemed to be festival-goers. Smiling people with lawn chairs and blankets strolled up and down the street with an air of anticipation. A few wore wild and garish makeup, above their staid collared shirts and casual skirts. Nearby, someone was lighting off bottle rockets.

Rosemont scrutinized the wall again. He'd been waiting for some time to see if a traveler would arrive and open the secret door. But maybe it only opened out and the indifferent desk clerk had simply let him walk out without warning him. He hoped he could walk around to the front and pass through the kitchen of angry ladies and the dormitory to find the hostel again. He figured he should do that soon, but now he could smell meat grilling somewhere down the block and his stomach led him away from the wall. He hadn't eaten anything since the little Salisbury steak on the flight into Rome.

Rosemont set off down the narrow street in the direction of the enticing smells. As he walked, though, he remembered that he didn't have any money. He had Nicaraguan currency, but the corona was so devalued he couldn't even exchange it at Rome International. How was he going to eat in one of the wealthiest cities in Europe? The thought made him anxious—and hungrier.

"Oh, God. What the *fuck* are you doing here?" a voice said in English.

Rosemont turned his head this way and that, trying to find the speaker's voice, which resonated as if from inside a garbage can.

"Jeremiah? This is... Oh, this is just fucking rich. Ow. God, that hurts my... Wipe that idiot look off your face and come here!"

Rosemont glanced at a parked Volvo and saw that the trunk was open, cracked just a bit, but held in place with bungee cord. Someone was in there, stuck in the trunk. Rosemont reached for the cord to unhook it, but the voice hissed at him.

"Stop that! There's no time. You have to help me. You have to trust me, okay? I know it doesn't make sense, but it will."

"Who are you?"

"You don't know who I am?"

Rosemont said, "No."

"No?"

"No, I don't know who you are!"

"Then, um." The man in the trunk stifled laughter, coughed, and then collected himself. "Let's save *that* moment of joy, shall we? You see that building there? That one with the steps and the blue door?"

Rosemont saw it. It was less than thirty feet away, atop a short stoop. There was a group of young discotheque boys smoking on the steps wearing glistening fairy wings on their backs, a funny contrast with their muscle shirts. "Yes, I see it . . ."

"You have to walk up there. Go in, and on the desk by the marble staircase is a red three-ring binder. You have to grab it and walk out here and then you have to let me out of this trunk, and then we're going to run like hell. Got that? It's got to be quick, clean, and you have to act totally—"

"I'm not walking into a stranger's house," Rosemont snapped.

"Look, shut up."

"I'm not stealing anything. Not for some guy in a trunk."

"They're going to kill me if you don't help me. They're not supposed to, but they will. And you're not exactly sitting pretty, either. You got a message, right? A spooky dude in the middle of the night? A letter addressed to you with a plane ticket in it, probably?"

Rosemont pulled his hand back from grabbing the bungee cord and bent over, saying, "Yeah. Yes, what is this about? Can you—"

"Don't talk into the trunk, you fucking moron! Christ, act like you don't know I'm in here!"

Rosemont stood straight and leaned against the Volvo, looking down the street at the revelers. "How did you know about that? Why am I here? Who was that? Who sent him?" Though he was supposed to be acting cool, at that moment there wasn't a nonchalant bone in his body. The more that his questions spilled out of him, the more he scooped the air with his hands, shouting, "You have to tell me *something*—none of this makes sense! I mean, I came all the way from Nicaragua! Who was that guy? How did he know where to find me?"

"Now, don't go William Shatner on me," the man in the trunk said. "I'll tell you everything I know if you help me out. Deal? Look, it's a cakewalk. They all left after they threw me in here. There's no one in that house. It's unlocked. I know, because I left it unlocked. Walk right the fuck in there and grab the red binder—you'll see it, I swear to God—and come back here."

Rosemont shook his head as he walked away from the Volvo. "I can't believe this. I can't. I can't do this." He started down the street, walking away from the man in the trunk. Then he stopped and pressed his fingertips against his forehead as if keeping his thoughts or his brains from spilling onto the street.

"Rosemont? You have to! Where are you going? Ah, God, I'm in a pool of windshield wiper fluid or something!"

Still shaking his head, Rosemont turned back to the building with the blue door and looked at the young men in fairy wings and wraparound sunglasses sitting and drinking on the stoop. They didn't seem like they lived there—just partyers parked on available stairs. Maybe he *could* walk in. Maybe they wouldn't stop him. Maybe he could get some answers.

"Rosemont? Come on! Cowboy up. Let's go."

The man in the trunk knew about the crazy letter deliverer. He knew about the plane ticket. It didn't make sense, but walking away now, after coming halfway around the planet, didn't make sense, either.

Rosemont shouldered his backpack and marched toward the cluster of men on the steps.

As he approached, they parted for him and he walked up the stairs, reaching into his pocket as if for keys and trying to look like he belonged here—as best as an itinerant traveler with Nicaraguan mud on his work boots could. He blocked the lock with his body, mimed unlocking it, and prayed that the freak in the trunk wasn't lying.

A breath later, he was inside.

Standing in a high-ceilinged foyer with thin diagonals of white daylight illumining a pale marble staircase before him, Rosemont felt a desperate sense of panic. For whatever reason, he'd pictured that this would be a set of offices, that he would be taking something from a receptionist's desk.

But no, this was someone's private residence. Cheap picture frames filled with shots of the same five members of a bespectacled family lined the walls. A pile of folded laundry on the bottom step of the stairs. Stacks of books on the floor, awaiting shelves or cardboard boxes. Two teddy bears in a toy wagon waited for a child to come play with them. A valiant neatness barely staving off clutter. Rosemont hadn't stood in a house like this in many years, a house with so much life and loneliness.

On the floor, at the foot of the stairs, he noticed a perfectly round dot. Rosemont stepped closer and looked down at it. Black and gleaming like paint. He knew what it was a second before he touched it, but he couldn't stop himself from letting the dot turn his fingertip red. The blood was already starting to congeal, making a circle of darker red upon the wood floor.

Rosemont winced and wiped his finger clean on his boot. He was about to back away but he saw another black dot before a shut door beside the stairs.

"Don't do this," he told himself as he reached for the knob.

Rosemont slammed the door shut a quickened heart-beat after he'd opened it, a perfect photograph of what he'd seen in the little bathroom emblazoned in his mind's eye. He leaned against the banister, looked down at his chest, and realized he was starting to hyperventilate. He took a few deep breaths and coaxed himself to think clearly.

"Okay. Lot of blood in there. That's the way it is. Okay."

He nodded, then shut his eyes hard, scrunching them tight, but the last thing he'd seen, the person's hand with a piece of wood nailed to it, was getting the better of him. The nail had driven a piece of paper against the wood, an impossibly clean, white piece of paper against all the red in the room.

Rosemont's eyes rolled heavenward. "Oh, don't do it, man, don't do it, don't do it, don't do it."

But a second later, he was opening the door and shutting it again, almost immediately.

Standing in the foyer on unsteady knees, Rosemont clamped his palms over his eyes. "Aw, shit."

A big woman, rumpled and housewifey in her way. Jeans and cheap tennis shoes. On the piece of wood nailed to her hand were written characters from an alphabet that he didn't recognize, and on the white paper he'd seen the typewritten words "Your presence is requested" and "Rome," before hastily shutting the door.

A copy of the very same letter that he himself had received in Managua.

Rosemont took two steps toward the stairs and leaned his full weight against the banister, breathing deeply through his mouth and exhaling hard through his nose. "Sure." The blood-and-feces smell behind the door had been strong, clinging. "It'll be a lark. Why not take that ticket," he said between breaths, "and just fly to Rome?"

So there were more people who had received the same letter, being called here. But someone wanted the recipients gone in a pretty ritualistic way. Was it really a match to his own letter? Maybe he hadn't read it correctly. A sickly, low laugh rattled from his chest. He couldn't open that door again.

He was about to push himself away from the banister and slip out the door when he saw, under a stack of mail on an oak secretary by the stairs, a red, three-ring binder. In front of it, a bandana was folded neatly on the shelf.

A dizzying nausea made the print on the bandana—the vaguely familiar paisleylike flowers—rise from the cloth and dance upon his retina. He grabbed the red binder and bandana and shoved them into his backpack. He wanted to vomit and rid his body of the vision of that poor woman, but before he zipped his backpack shut, he looked at the cover of the binder and read the computer-generated label there:

Dr. John C. Miles
Ligget & LaSalle University

Rosemont put a hand over his mouth, staring down at the name of the author. He pulled the binder out of his backpack and a shower of the tiny paisley bandana flowers fell to the floor as he opened the binder to the first page and the title there:

THE REFUTATION OF ROSEMONT

Rosemont's head jerked back.

Immediately, he shut the binder and looked at the cover again. *John C. Miles.* Rosemont opened it again and glanced at the beginning of the manuscript but realized it was written as a letter to the editor. The manuscript was addressed at the top to *Antiquities Journal Monthly,* a magazine to which Rosemont had regularly contributed years ago. But the letter had a title, *The Refutation of Rosemont,* as if it were an article.

Dear Sir,

Did you know that Jeremiah Rosemont picks his nose? In his sleep, he picks his nose...

What the hell was this? A slanderous attack on him? Rosemont's eyebrows furrowed in anger as he tried to make sense of the article, wondering if it had actually seen print in *Antiquities Journal Monthly.* He continued reading.

Dear Sir,

Did you know that Jeremiah Rosemont picks his nose? In his sleep, he picks his nose. Did you know that? I have no beef with you. To sell copies of your ludicrous magazine, you frequently publish the excitable dithering of Dr. Jeremiah Rosemont, he of the undercover pick, the somnambulant harvest, and I don't bite my teeth at subscribers of *Antiquities Journal Monthly (AJM),* either. Though, for the duration of this letter, do your best to keep up with the smart kids, ok, Gentleminded Readers?

That was Miles, all right. His irascible, irresponsible attacks—his patented blend of jest and bile. Was it possible? Rosemont's head turned toward the front door. The Volvo. Was the man in the trunk John C. Miles? Rosemont should have recognized that voice of all voices, one that went with Austin, the Circus of Infinite Wow, the highest and lowest moments of Rosemont's life. Miles could never have disguised his voice well enough. Rosemont scanned down the page.

No occult origins for tarot, eh? Rosemont, Rosemont, Rosemont. I'm surprised *AJM* and its high premium on adventure (!) and mystery (!!) bought your tidy little turd of an article.

Rosemont shut the binder just as he'd shut the bathroom door, blocking his eyes and his mind from the much too much. The reemergence of his own personal demon, John C. Miles, and the afterimage of that impossibly white paper surrounded by blood swam nauseatingly through his belly, paisley flowers prickling the corners of his sight.

"This is happening," he muttered, and shook his head hard to keep his vision from tunneling. "I've got to get up on this. I'm not on top."

He slid the binder back into his backpack and started in fright at a sudden noise, before realizing that it wasn't gunfire but an air conditioner kicking to life.

Rosemont walked over to the long, narrow floor-to-ceiling windows that flanked the front door and looked out. Two men were stepping away from the Volvo, walking toward the stoop and the blue door. Rosemont stepped back from the window, retreating into the warm shadows of the house, but kept his eyes on the men—one hunch-shouldered and canine, the other balancing an ugly cinder-block skull on a thick neck—until he was sure they were coming to this house. Which they were.

Rosemont hunched down and, barely aware of what he was doing, scooped up the many paisley flowers that had scattered from the bandana's floral print and then lunged to the bathroom door, shutting it a moment before the front door opened.

"It's not here," said a high, tense voice. They were in the foyer now.

Japanese, thought Rosemont, standing in the bathroom. The woman on the floor looked Japanese to Rosemont and her makeup was beginning to stand out garishly against her blanching skin. Rosemont was unable to step over the woman's body, unable to move or pull himself away from the voices in the foyer.

"Not here?" said the other. "What do you mean?"

"I mean, look. It's gone. So's his bandana. Gone."

Hide, you idiot, Rosemont told himself as the sounds of mad rustling and crumpling of paper came from the foyer.

The bathroom was actually quite large, with a sunken bath, a pale blue bidet, and a shower. Gold appointments everywhere, and a small plaster statue of a cherub reclined next to the tub. A large linen closet looked promising as a hiding place, but the hamper inside would have to be removed, and there was no time for that. To the left of the bathroom door was the shower stall with a sliding door. Once inside, standing under a drip from the showerhead, he tried inching the sliding door shut, but it grabbed in its track. Rosemont jerked his hand back, terrified that touching the door might make too much noise, and clutched his backpack to his chest.

"Fuck. Fuck!"

"The Iranians must have doubled back after they threw him in the trunk," said the deeper, calmer of the two voices, "and—I don't know. Somehow—"

"But it was right here!"

"Bene. Relax. No sense crying over it now. The Iranians or the Blackleafers have it."

"Fuck!"

"But we have Miles. Look, I said relax. We'll get it out of him or he'll lead us to the monk. We have something else to take care of."

The more high-strung voice let out an exasperated sigh. "Let's just leave her."

The deeper voice laughed, and then the sound of the bathroom doorknob jiggling sent a shock through Rosemont's heart. The door was opening.

"At least we stopped one." The high, tense voice seemed calmer now, but the nearness of it, reverberating in the bathroom, shook Rosemont. "That's worth something, isn't it?"

Rosemont's whole body went stiff. He pressed back hard against the wall of the shower and tried not to think about the woman and her normal, everyday sneakers. The strange code written upon the plank. The nail. *The guys who did this. God, they're right here in the room.* They'd find him in a second, and then, and then, and then.

"As long as the connection isn't fused yet," the deeper voice said. "Yeah, that's good."

"Okay. Let's do this thing."

Rosemont shut his eyes and listened, half expecting the sound of sawing or dismemberment. But it sounded like the men were hunkering down or sitting on the bathroom floor next to the woman. A moment later, they were whispering. Rosemont strained to hear what they were saying, but they whispered together in a rush, both of them, speaking so low and fast as if racing to some finish. Rosemont couldn't make out individual words or even the language, and the whispering carved little patterns in the air, symbols that also seemed to speak in little whispers to Rosemont. Like the muttered prayer, say, of a remote tribesman hunkering in the desert, examining day-old caravan tracks, and wondering if they were the footprints of gods; an echoing temple, with robed eavesdroppers huddled beneath a ceiling painted lavishly with boats, listening to the dark-skinned tribesman pray, far away, on the sands. Their words, which were not words as Rosemont thought of them, seemed to speak to him on their own accord. Free us from this place, the eavesdroppers' words begged, this abomination to loam and water, this spy house of whores. Free us from the diseased prisons of your masters and carry us—

Just then the wall at Rosemont's back gave.

Glancing over his shoulder, Rosemont saw that the shower wall had gone transparent, insubstantial, and dark. He looked again. *Is an animal's body moving in the shadows of the wall? A horse. No, there's fur. Wool?* Rosemont gave a small gasp.

The whispering in the bathroom stopped.

Rosemont looked up. Listening. Eyes scanning the scene outside the shower, nothing in the bathroom seemed to have changed. The lavish room looked just as it had, with its sunken tub, plaster cherub, bathroom sink, and vanity mirror.

But in the mirror he could see the two men, and one was looking up at Rosemont in the mirror, crouching, as if ready to leap.

Rosemont started back in fright and his back hit hard against the wall.

"What is that?" asked the shorter of the two, everything about him small and blunt. "Is that real?"

Through the mirror, Rosemont could see that the body of the Japanese woman was gone, the tiled floor was clean, and the larger of the two men, while staring intently at Rosemont, looked glassy-eyed, drunk. "Could be," he said. "Can't tell. Is that John C. Miles?"

"Are you John C. Miles?" the shorter man said into the mirror.

Rosemont was stunned silent, bewildered by what they were asking.

The shorter fellow stood, and his vicious little eyes flashed between hate and perplexity. Rosemont waited for the man to lunge at him in the shower stall, figuring he could use his backpack as a shield if the short fellow had a knife. But both men continued to stare at Rosemont's reflection as though peering at something miraculous through mist.

"It's a doppelgänger," the shorter man said, backing out of Rosemont's view of him through the mirror. "It's a projection from Miles. Or someone more—"

"Lemures can't *do* that," the larger man said. Staring balefully up at the mirror, he scooted backward too, showing Rosemont the crown of his great white head. "I've never heard of a lemure doing that," he said when he was out of view. "We go. Let's go. *Now.*"

A moment later, the bathroom was silent. Rosemont listened but he didn't hear the door open, nor were there footsteps in the foyer. Nothing. He peered through the mirror but could only see the wall to his right outside the shower. After the wall had seemed to give way and go dark, Rosemont had no idea if he was truly safe, if he could trust his eyes or his senses. Had the wall really given way? Had this really happened?

Finally, he stepped out of the stall on unsteady legs, holding on to the shower screen and looking down where the body of the Japanese woman had been. There was nothing there but clean, rose-colored tiles. Rosemont listened a bit longer, and then opened the door to the bathroom. But there was no one in the foyer, either.

Rosemont closed the door and lunged across the bathroom to the sink, needing to feel something real. Water. Cold water on his hands and face. He was about to turn on the faucet, but he froze and panic jolted through him as he stared into the vanity mirror.

A gathering of many colored planes representing the

angles and curves of his face stared back at him. The face in the mirror, though, was not Rosemont's, not remotely. It seemed reptilian, and it opened its mouth independently of Rosemont's mouth and his other movements—or lack thereof, for Rosemont stood perfectly still, gripping the sink, staring at the turning image in horror and disbelief. One moment, his reflection looked reptilian or birdlike, but then, as the face turned, it seemed suddenly simian, and then the polychromatic mosaic of planes and surfaces frowned into a yawning circle of flower petals, before the light in the bathroom shifted, and the visage became reptilian again.

It was incomprehensible, all of it. He could feel the muscles of his face spreading, contorting in abhorrence at the tortured woman's body, her disappearance, and the vision of the animal in the shower wall, but his reflection would not mirror him. He wished he would faint so that he could stop staring at the thing. Where was *he*? Where were his own brown eyes? His backpack hit the floor but his legs stayed strong, and Rosemont and the reptile-man opened their mouths in dread at each other.

6

Midcigarette, Boy King stood outside Dona Mia's front door. He hadn't smoked in years, but he had a fresh pack in his book bag, and he was puffing this cigarette down to the filter. He watched as a party of twelve snaked its way to the maître d's podium within, bumping against a party of eight that was leaving brunch in a giddy haze of mimosas and Bloody Marys. A man at the tail of the entering queue nodded at Boy King, then reached into his own suit coat pocket for a pack. Cigarette suddenly between index and middle finger, he gestured with it, just a lifting of the cigarette. *Light?*

There was no wind, so Boy King held out his lighter, stiff armed, and flicked it. The man slipped the cigarette into his mouth, leaned, and pursed his lips at the lighter.

He and Boy King exhaled together.

"God, I hate birthday parties," the man said.

Boy King flicked ashes with the man, agreeing, then dropped the lighter back into the pocket of his baggy pants. He used to smoke without a thought to such vaults past overture, the sharing of kind silence, and smoking's cabal of hands and breath. But he was back in the real world now. And all of it was coming back. "Why'd you come?"

The man said, "My friend Lara told me there was a fortune-teller."

Boy King didn't look at him. "Okay."

The heavy silence that followed told Boy King that he'd be hearing more, very soon, so he dropped his cigarette butt and stepped on it with the ball of his foot. He gave the man his farewell by way of a glance, got a curt nod in return, and then stepped inside the restaurant.

The atrium cleared as the waiting party filed toward its brunch table, and Boy King entered, stood alone at the podium. He could feel people turning to watch him. He was dressed in a black turtleneck beneath the double-breasted suit he'd Dumpster dived. Along with his burned-tan face, beaten posture, razor-hewn black hair, and pin-striped suit, he knew he looked more like a hobo in search of a gangster film than anyone who belonged in a restaurant like this. But it was as close as he was going to get to passing.

Which was important; it was a nice restaurant now. Not long ago, Boy King had ground-scored organic strawberries from behind this place, which, until recently, had been the last hippie café on the West Bank. But what had once been unfinished wood benches, chalkboards, and a sign that read U.S. Out of [Fill in the Blank] (with a nail to hang words like *Minnesota* or *My Uterus*) were now white tableclothes, Italian baroque menus, and warm yellow walls sponged with maroon paint. The crowd was a promising mix for Dona Mia's grand opening too. Lots of gray ponytails falling over Ralph Lauren suits sitting beside new suburban money that had ventured into the city in pleated pants and fine black leather. The restaurant was loud with bubbling conversation, three band members of Boiled in Lead stood on a little stage, unpacking their guitars and mandolins and uncoiling black cords, and orange mimosas sparkled in flutes on passing drink trays.

From the kitchen, Lara appeared. "Enter the dragon," she said and chuckled under her breath at him.

He realized he was gawking. In a purple silk blouse with oriental collar and clunky black shoes that seemed more Uptown than West Bank, she had transformed.

Lara flipped a neat sheet of brown hair off one shoulder. "What?"

"You're wearing long sleeves," teased Boy King.

"Yeah? You're wearing a suit."

Boy King bowed.

"So we're both incognito. In the old place, I probably could have showed tat, but not here," she said with a bent, ironic grin.

"I guess this is what you'll look like on Sundays from now on."

"The family biz." Lara rolled her eyes. "Come on, I'll set you up."

She led him across the restaurant to a standing screen in the corner and as they walked past a bank of decorative mirrors by the kitchen, Boy King saw his reflection standing there, glaring at him with arms crossed. He averted his eyes quickly and followed Lara.

"You hungry? I asked the chef to put goat cheese omelets on the menu today."

When she'd told him several weeks ago that her father was getting her a job at the restaurant, Boy King pictured Lara washing dishes with her tattooed arms bare, shit kickers wet with suds, her hair in a frizzy bun. But she had control over the menu and could hire a tarot reader. He felt naive. "Goat cheese, huh? No. I don't need anything."

A sign on the screen in Lara's handwriting said Tarot Readings. In the corner, two chairs sat at a small table with no tablecloth. A standing wooden screen provided privacy and a tall altar candle burned next to an ashtray. Lara said, "Good?"

A hook on the wall showed that whatever had been there had been removed. Boy King blew out the candle and handed it to Lara. "Good."

She shook her head and took it. "I didn't think you could be a gypsy *and* a minimalist."

"Thanks for the ashtray." Boy King put down his book bag, which contained his cigarettes and a tarot deck wrapped in silk. "You look rough today."

"Feeling pretty rough. After Dream Machine, we cruised over to the Wiggle Room to see Garbus. Shouldn't have done that." Lara leaned a hip against his table and slumped a bit. "Thanks for doing this, Boy," she said. "Remember, you got people here. Gitana's waiting tables. Did you see her?"

Gitana was flirting with a thick-shouldered busboy, a standing-room-only crowd fizzing in the café section around her. This was good. Having even a small nest of goodwill like this would be crucial if Boy King might need to protect himself. The crowd seemed innocuous, but if a tyro *were* here, Boy King might never detect it. A Chaldean tyro had once masked himself as an entire seminary of alchemists when local mobs came to kill him, after all. He'd heard that the Blackleaf occultists could mute whole cities, knock them into heightened dream states for generations. But the cults of the ram-headed Khnum were the most frightening tyros of all—their powers had never been fully documented, so a spy, hook, or drain could be hidden in this dense mass for all Boy King knew.

"Hey. Incoming transmission." She snapped her fingers to get his attention. "Are you okay?"

He chuckled at himself. The new policy of fearlessness wasn't gelling yet, apparently. "I'm here, ain't I?"

"By the way," she said, putting on an overly enthusiastic voice, "there's a cheap apartment across the street. Did I tell you this at Dream Machine?"

"No."

"The landlord is an old buddy of my dad's. I could get him to waive security deposit, and, geez, in two Sundays, you'd have first month's rent and then some."

Wonderful. I'm her "project" now. The Boy King glanced at the sunflower-faced clock over the bar. Five to ten. The deal was that Boy King would throw cards from 10 a.m. until 3 p.m. for anyone who wanted a reading, and the restaurant would pay him five hundred dollars cash. Plus tips, it was a princely sum for Boy King, and he couldn't deny he'd been thinking about an apartment. But he didn't like Lara's babysitter routine, the note in her voice that made her sound like a cheerleader at the Special

Olympics. "I don't know, that might interfere with my plan of blowing the wad on hookers and crack, Lara."

She laughed, which helped, and after she retreated to the maître d' station, he fished out his cards and unwrapped them. He stared down at the deck for a moment, trying to conjure the old thrill this deck elicited. Nothing. Time was, he had felt about tarot the way some felt about a good, hard pharmaceutical, one that reorganized and simplified life around itself. He'd once welcomed all the little sacraments and ceremonies that came with the cards back then—the silk cloth, the wooden box in which the deck was kept, and the necessary music (disc two of Miles Davis's *Bitches Brew, Maggot Brain* by Funkadelic, or nothing). But tarot had not kept pace with the traditions and obsessions learned later in his life. Looking at the cards now, idly flipping through his deck, Boy King felt certain that tarot had been concocted with sheer optimism that anything hidden might be revealed. Tarot was designed as if the artist understood tarot's lame optimism, too, with its cartoonish approximations of the mystic (The Magician) and the profane (The Fool). For his gig today, Boy King had chosen the Rider-Waite deck; the stark line drawings and bold colors of this deck worked well on people who didn't know tarot. For Boy King, though, this deck was light fare. What had been Miles Davis now felt like Steve Miller. Smack into beer. Tarot didn't scratch the itch anymore.

Boy King picked up his deck, shuffled it once, then flipped over the top card. It showed a king in red robes holding an ankh scepter, with rams' heads on the arms of his throne. They weren't Khnum's rams as depicted in the symbol he'd found, but even the inexact radar of tarot got things right sometimes. In fact, once in a blue moon, tarot could be mockingly accurate in its messages.

The Emperor. King of kings and lord of lords. For a homeless man on the first day of his new job.

You're watching me, again, aren't you? he said to the cards.

The day began with a handsome woman in her fifties. She appeared at his wooden screen with sky-blue eyes, white hair in a French braid, and no ring on her hand. The neckline of her sundress plunged quite low for a woman her age. Generalities could be made from these details, and Boy King had learned which details were truly telling.

"I've never had a reading before. Are you psychic?" she asked. "Is this part of your belief system?"

"Go ahead and shuffle the cards."

When she was done, he took six off the top and tossed the cards on the table. Without really looking at them, he said, "Your question is about love, and there's a lover you want to know more about. He's younger than you are."

The woman smiled enigmatically, but her eyes flashed, telling him he was on the right track.

As the morning sped on with no Egyptian gods in sight, Boy King let himself relax. Soon lumbering deductions unhinged from mere physical detail (scent of an unsmoked cigar and a hospital wristband with the words *birthing center* on it; deeply tanned hands but white where a wedding ring had been; jittery fingers, tight lips, double checking if the readings were free, followed by a little sigh of relief) and gave way to more stunning inductions catapulted from the business end of metaphors. That's how a tarot reading worked, if it worked at all. Keep talking in metaphor until you found the vein and truth spilled out.

("Ten of Wands reversed is like cancer in remission"—and the client's cancer was *in* remission). All the while Boiled in Lead stirred their Celtic potions. Boy King threw his spreads and knocked back the readings as fast as he could, as though racing their violins and fast guitars.

This was the groove. After the twelfth reading, he knew what cards would appear for people the moment he touched eyes with them. *You have sorrow written all over you*. Nine of Swords. *Cocky little man aren't you?* Six of Wands. As the sun swung past noon, he saw Dona Mia's crowd whole, past and future, like an aerial photograph of a river, where they flowed, where they were flowing, where they would ultimately empty themselves. He saw one woman's legal battles burning with no end in sight after consuming her finances for years. He saw that a man had cheated his business partner, that his guilt would devour him before he saw a decent profit. A reconciliation with a son. A young man bound for Iraq. Luscious affairs and hidden strengths. Psychology, logic, and synchronicity plodded somewhere below Boy King on the paths of pedestrian traffic, while he soared in a jet stream in which he hadn't sailed since Rome.

With his pulse tapping away in his body, effervescent and sharp, he gestured for the next client, and from behind the screen, his smoking pal appeared, accompanied by a woman. Boy King stood and they both ducked their heads at him, like little bows. "Hello, hello," they were murmuring as they took seats at the table.

Boy King sat down too, and was about to offer them the deck when he saw a sudden, sweeping view of their lives, as if someone had snatched back a curtain to reveal a canyon with frightening depths. He tried not to physically recoil. It was like the feeling he'd had before finding the suit in that third Dumpster, but so strong, so dizzying, he wondered if he would black out.

Hands flat on the table, on either side of the cards, he said to them, "Readings are free today."

"We know," said the woman. "That's wonderful of Dona Mia's to—"

"But I want money from you."

The man's expression was somber as a shut church door, and he nodded as if expecting this, respected it. "How much do you want?"

Boy King's nostrils flared. He wondered if they understood what they were doing here or if they were completely oblivious. Either way, it was time to draw some well-defined, protective circles around himself and to feint, buy time, and get a bead on what they wanted from him. "Whatever's right," he said, eyeing the man. "You tell me."

The woman watched her husband as he took out his wallet and put ten twenties on the table.

Boy King stared at the pile of money. Could he holler for Lara?

The man was watching him. "Isn't that enough?"

They were seemingly on a hunt of some kind. By the ease with which they parted with money, Boy King deduced that they'd done this many times before in a vain effort to find answers about the staggering depth of that canyon.

"We heard about you," the man said. He didn't look at the money, didn't appear to care how much was there.

"Lara says you did a reading for her, says you changed her life," the woman whispered, "that you really spoke to her."

"She usually reads for me, actually." Boy King noticed that his own hands were still flat on the table, that he wasn't scooping up the money. If he picked it up, he stood to earn more in one day at Dona Mia's than he'd earned in the last three months of diving.

"She says you're something special."

"We need something special," the woman said.

Braggarts were the ones who got drained. "I'm nothing special. I'm just what I am. I just say what I see," said Boy King. It was coming, whatever it was. If he didn't stop this right now, they were going to spill their guts to him and a continent in the sky would slip, slide down, and crash against him. He opened his mouth to speak, to send them away, tell them to take their money and go to hell. But he couldn't deny it: he felt for them. That view of this territory like a river seen from above—they were in the flow and so was he. He'd hung out his shingle, put out the welcome mat to anyone who wanted a peek at the other side. It was a promise that he'd do it, an intrinsic one. Even though he didn't live by any Code of Card Readers, he didn't break promises, especially not to people in need.

"We have a question that we have to ask you," the woman said. She wasn't pretty but she was all put together in a jade necklace, green fingernails, and green pumps. A slight green tint to her eye shadow. Expensive watch matched expensive earrings. Boy King wished he would stop noticing. She said, "Do you recognize us?"

It wasn't a question he was anticipating. He looked at the two again. The man's nails were manicured, his teeth were capped, which was odd, because he wasn't good-looking enough to be an actor or a movie star or a news personality, and there was a casual carelessness about him that said such efforts and looking this good didn't really matter. "No, I don't," Boy King said. "Should I?"

The man nodded with approval. "No."

It didn't matter. This school was strange, but everyone was so nice to her. She could go by this name now. It didn't really matter.

Boy King flinched.

"What is it?" the man said.

"Quiet," the woman said, "he knows."

"Shh," Boy King hissed at her angrily, sitting down finally and leaning forward and low on the table as if bullets were tracing over his head. "I don't 'know' anything."

The man inched forward to the edge of his chair, and the cool smoking rituals of understatement and silence evaporated in a panic. "You *know* where she is?"

Boy King leaned back in his chair now, feeling sick, wondering if he would lose it all over the floor.

"Can you help us find her? Because if you can do—"

"I don't! I'm sorry, I don't know anything, and I can't see anything," Boy King said, his voice a croak of nausea.

The couple didn't move. They were watching him expectantly, the set of his shoulders, his brow, reading him. "God, Lara was right about you. You have to tell us if you can see her. Come on, you look green."

Boy King snapped his mouth closed. He shut his eyes, shook his head. No, he didn't know a thing, just like they didn't know a thing. He didn't know, just by looking at them, that they carried their guilt and shame like frightened tourists holding valises close to their bodies in a dangerous city they shouldn't be in. That their self-consciousness said more than their eager imploring. That down to the shine on the husband's shoes and the sheen on the woman's perm, they were trying to make an impression first, find a daughter second. One could hardly blame the poor fellow—he was out of his depth and flailing. He didn't know how to grasp the horror, and neither did she by the choice of her mall-bought earrings, as if this was just another Sunday brunch in the city for a suburban couple. Who *could* possibly know how to behave? Were there guidebooks available to tell one how to dress while searching for a child who'd been missing for over a year?

And all that was from the deductions, from simply having thrown a thousand tarot spreads, which put him on par with old therapists and confidence men in being able to read a perfect stranger. How could he say what had induced itself into him from a day of reading cards, his opened senses, and the vantage from which he gazed down on his little realm? How could he tell them that their daughter was gone because of their insipid neglect? Their belts and bracelets and shiny, nice manners said they might be willing to believe anything he told them, that she'd been hit by a car on a dark boulevard and that her body would turn up in a remote culvert or alleyway. His answer was irrelevant; they just wanted him to speak with authority.

The Ellings had been advised to look their best to get invited back on that TV show. It cost a lot to look this good, but they'd do anything, said their tanning bed tans, mortgage anything, said her necklace, and enlist anyone willing to help, even if it only meant ratings to those people at the network.

And Boy King knew. He did know. Little Tanya Elling had been drifting away in a childhood without mooring of any kind and had meandered out. No. That wasn't true. Someone had found a way *in*.

Exposure. Air time. Keep the story in the media eye. Tough to compete with war coverage. Do whatever you can.

He was heartbroken and furious. The nerve. The un-mitigated gall they had to come asking for his help and looking for answers. Leaving her alone by herself at night while they went drinking with friends, or letting her stay overnight with people who were barely acquaintances. They didn't see how their own hands were covered in shit, would never allow themselves to see.

Sometimes the metaphor came first, and details came to him from the other side of it. Blue canvas sneakers and white knee socks in a Dumpster. A receipt for new clothes from Old Navy. A voice sweet and imploring that first night away from Mom and Dad, too sweet for the Boy King to suffer it. But it got easier and easier the longer she was away. That's how it worked with kids.

Leave me alone. Don't show me this, is what he wanted to say, but then he realized what was happening.

Someone *had* gotten in, gotten at their daughter, yes, but someone got inside the parents too, inside their very hearts. A master, one of the powerful ones, did this terrible thing, or at least allowed a monster to exploit a weakness. But the tyro had yoked Mr. and Mrs. Elling with a sly, omi-nous force that suddenly made the Boy King feel as though the very walls of Dona Mia's were teeth of a shutting trap, and these parents and their unignorable tragedy, the bait.

"I'm so very sorry," the Boy King said. He slumped into his chair, feigning exhaustion though he was wired and jumpy and wanted to sprint from the restaurant. "All my spirit-sights have gone misty. No totems or crystals have come to me. I need to do a guided candle meditation or something. It wouldn't be right to take your money."

The man nodded sympathetically. They'd clearly heard this sort of explanation before.

But the woman was buying none of it. "You," she said succinctly, "saw something."

Boy King picked up the two hundred dollars and handed it to the man.

"Not until you tell us," said the woman, taking the bills from her husband and slapping them back down on the table. "You're a good man. We both see that. You can't not tell us if you know where Tanya is."

The man, following his wife's lead, leaned across the small table and put his hand on the Boy King's shoulder. Boy King felt severe pity, compassion, regret—but knew he couldn't show them any of that. It wouldn't help, would only serve to encourage them. Instead, he shoved the man's hand away.

The man ignored the gesture. "Do you know where her body is?" he said.

Such a willfully stupid question, Boy King thought. As if humans didn't have a single volt of instinct left, as if the animal in this man couldn't sense what had happened to its young. They were better off in this pretentiously saintly state, not knowing what they had allowed to happen. Whoever yoked these people had them tuned to a snowy channel, and in his anger, he wanted to psychically yoke them himself and frog-march them to face their own role in this, face how it had been their own pathetic weakness that carried them to this moment.

He was about to yoke them, about to steer the two of them, together, side by side, beneath the ancient arch, the place humans—kings, beggars, sinners, and gurus—could be leashed like dogs, where these two had obviously been yoked already. He was ready to make them his for the purpose of setting them free, could even hear the crying hue of the mysterious gathering that was ever drawn together about that dreadful arch.

But he couldn't. Not even to help. No yoking ever again. He wanted no more broken souls on his soul.

Besides, there were other ways to snap the bonds of power.

"As if you don't know," Boy King hissed at the Ellings in his most menacing voice. "As if you hadn't been bleeding over that poor girl her whole life."

Both faces went blank. Not even a note of horror or bewilderment on their faces. The man's cell went off but he didn't move.

"That's right, send yourselves away. Some *more*," said Boy King. "But listen. You won't find her. Not anytime soon. New last name, new city. New school and new friends. It's all normal now." Speaking truth in mockery. It was the only way, though it was like a jagged edge across his own heart to even say those words. Then, to make sure the man would stand, help his wife to her feet, and quickly make for the door, Boy King added, "Want to hear the kicker? She tells her new dad that she loves him."

Just as the Boy King hoped, the man stood. But instead of helping the woman to her feet as he predicted, he leaned on the table, lunged forward, and, faster than Boy King could block the punch, a supernova of pain exploded in his face.

Boy King spilled from his chair, arms flailing like limbs falling from a broken mannequin. Slumped on the restaurant floor, feeling his nose open like a faucet, he thought a long time was passing, but then he realized the wife was still staring at him in furious astonishment. The man was still straightening from throwing the punch, rubbing his knuckles in pain.

Boy King smiled up at him drunkenly, his mouth wet and warm with blood. "That's the spirit."

"Crazy motherfucker," the man hissed at the Boy King.

The wooden screen concealing them from view suddenly teetered, toppling to the side, and a second later, Lara and Gitana were hauling the man back from the little table by suit jacket and belt. Frog-marching him, Boy King noted.

"Crazy motherfucker!"

Lara was telling him to shut up, while Boy King experimented with getting to his feet, but it felt like he was on a listing ship. He seized the table as if it were about to slide across the floor, but a second later, the busboy that Gitana had been flirting with came rushing out of the gawking crowd and tackled Boy King, knocking the wind out of him hard as they hit the floor.

"Winn! What? Get off!" Lara was shouting.

A sharp blow jerked Boy King's jaw to the left and scrambled his mind into nonsense and randomness. More screaming, some four-letter words, but it was all drowned out by the workmanlike grunting of the gorilla on top of him, raining blows on Boy King. What the hell was this guy doing?

"The hell are you doing?" Lara shouted. "What the hell? Stop!"

Distantly, Boy King was aware that the voice of the lost girl was still in his head, singing the song she'd sung to soothe herself that first night. All he wanted was to get it out of his head, get away from it, away from the beating he was taking, and a second later, he was standing next to her, the lost daughter, an ordinary girl with stringy auburn hair. They were standing together in a farm field, with swaths of white snow on black earth, and the tan stubble of cornstalks poking through. Prairie wind whistled at them, and her sailboat-print pajama dress wasn't nearly enough to protect her from its bitter bite.

"What's happening?" she asked Boy King.

A red-winged blackbird chirruped in the marshy distance.

He touched his nose. It was straight and unhurt. "You must have brought us here."

She hugged her elbows and bent her knees, shivering. "Geez, it's freezing."

Boy King could hear church bells echoing across the flat land. "I had a different thing. Tarot. I used to make up tarot stories at my grandparents' house."

He looked over his shoulder and could see two figures, small in the distance, running at them in a menacing, straight line. Their whipping, lion-colored robes shot fear through Boy King. He'd hidden from them for twelve years, and they'd found him, here of all places. Trackers. Desert sprinters. Murderers. They needed very little water or rest when hunting down rival cults to rub them out and could bound across time, through dreams.

The girl was suddenly across the field, standing with an isthmus of snow between her and Boy King, her voice low in his ear. "You better go."

He didn't think this was a dream, or anything "real," but felt certain the desert runners were quite real. "Yeah, I think that's a good idea. But how? How do I 'go'?"

"Thanks for trying to help my parents," she whispered. "Are you going to be okay?"

From the other side of the restaurant, looking at the backs of the bystanders and listening to the clattering of silverware on the floor, the cries of confusion, Boy King began walking backward toward the front door. Each step left a blazing red footprint on the pretty ceramic tiles of the restaurant floor and it filled him with misery to look at them.

I hope so, he thought, answering the girl. *Do whatever you can to get the hell out, Tanya Elling.*

No time to do anything about the footprints. He was lucky to be out of that melee in the corner.

"Where is he? I fucking had him!"

"Winn, would you snap out of it? Christ, what's wrong with you?"

None of these people would see the tracks anyway, so before the trackers found him here, he moved quickly across the Dona Mia floor, leaving a line of fire-engine red steps and then, finally, turned and sprinted, barreling out the front entrance.

7

It was above and behind him. He could feel it, there, like fire crawling up the bathroom wall. Rosemont sat on the toilet with the lid down, his head bowed almost to his knees so that he couldn't see the mirror, and wished he were back in the Hostelry of the Tyros. The house outside the bathroom was silent, and some small part of his brain that was still his, still rational, scolded him to get out while he could. But he wasn't certain he could stand, wasn't certain that the mirror-thing wasn't staring down at him, right now. If he looked over his shoulder, would it still be there, waiting to meet his eye, gaping its ugly mouth at him? How did it get in there? Was it really there? Did it come from him? It wasn't him. *It's not me. It's not any part of me.*

Something else was happening, he told himself. It was happening and he had to clear his head, think this through.

The two chanting men had thought the thing was John C. Miles, but why in the world would they conclude that?

Rosemont jerked his head to the left and stole a look over his shoulder at the mirror, but all he could see was a fish-shaped water stain on the ceiling, reflected from across the room. He sucked in a breath of relief and let it out. With the thing gone for the moment, Rosemont blocked the mirror's view of his backpack, hunching over it with his body, and removed the red binder. His hands were still shaking terribly, but he flipped open the cover and thumbed past *The Refutation of Rosemont,* looking for clues about what Miles might have to do with the thing in the mirror. But the binder simply held copies of old documents, photocopies, and even a few mimeographed sheets. Thready fibers in old manuscripts tended to stand out with an almost sandy quality, Rosemont knew, when photocopied; some of the copies here had to be of primary, original documents. Did John C. Miles's name on the cover mean that he had compiled these documents, or that they were compiled for him, or *about* him for some reason? Other pages in the binder looked like simple letters; there were even handwritten notes on hotel bar napkins, though none in Miles's jabbing, childish hand. Nearly all of them were copies. Is this what those two men were willing to kill and torture for? *Copies* of old documents?

Rosemont had forgotten about the mirror for a moment. He threw a frightened glance over his shoulder. Just ceiling. Nothing else. Maybe it never happened. Maybe the men had been hallucinations, tricked by another hallucination. Rosemont sighed. He told himself he might be safe now and continued flipping through the binder. It calmed him to feel the dry paper in his fingers.

After the copied texts, he found what looked like an interview that Miles had conducted with a woman named Priscilla, some medical transcriptions, a few news clippings, and then an article slipped out from the back pages. There were no hole punches and the pages looked clean, new. It was titled:

```
Chemical and Fiber Assay
Dr. Johanna Ingebretsen
Guelph Institute
```

A fiber assay. A simple, dreary-as-dust fiber assay. Rosemont gratefully fell upon the familiarity of academic routine, the logical rhythm of the report, the scientist's workaday prose. The organic composition bar graph showed considerable deciduous and coniferous tree matter. Infrared chemical analysis revealed a high rate of copper. The pH balances were lovely in their boring simplicity. As he absorbed the graph on decay rates, he noticed his hands had all but stopped shaking.

Guelph was a premier lab; whatever was being examined was getting gold standard treatment. The eccentric John C. Miles wasn't necessarily that brand of academic, though. Miles was more your drink-all-week-and-call-it-research scholar for an analysis of this caliber.

Wiping sweaty hair from his brow and scanning the report again, Rosemont tried to determine what was being authenticated, but he still couldn't tell. Carbon dating showed that the inks (were they from a text, a painting?) were just over one thousand years old, placing them somewhere between AD 925 and 950. Probably sourced from the apothecary/artist guilds in northern Italy at the time,

Rosemont surmised, looking at the high amount of copper in the inks and paints. Fibers in the provided sample were consistent with the mashes of crude, early papermaking in Europe, and the mashes—the wet pulp that eventually became paper—were traced to hard deciduous wood of varieties typical of northern Italy too. The assay placed them at the same age as the inks: AD 950.

For the art historian in Jeremiah Rosemont—that part of him that he'd abandoned, left for dead in Texas years ago—this was as baffling as a letter in the Managua night, or startling visions in Roman mirrors. The carbon date was way too early. The question about what was being tested was secondary to the mere fact that someone had discovered anything made of paper in 950 Europe. The Chinese, who'd invented the art of papermaking, had kept it a secret till late in the first millennium. The secret only slipped out in one place, when Muslim Persia had sacked a western Chinese city and a few Chinese paperers were taken hostage. But 950? In northern Italy? At that time, the secret was just arriving in what is now Iraq, with the first papermaking facilities appearing in Baghdad in—

Rosemont's teeth clenched, biting down on a thought. The word *tarot* had been sprinkled throughout Miles's letter to the editor, and Rosemont had seen it in a few of the other transcripts too. Was this a tarot? A deck made in 950? If so, the ramifications would ripple beyond tarot scholarship. Paper wasn't manufactured in Europe until 1150. The game of Tarocchi, for which tarot cards were specifically designed, wasn't played for three hundred years after that. It was like finding an automobile in Shakespearean England.

An argument with John C. Miles from three years earlier came back to Rosemont. More, huge swaths of his life snapped, by degrees, into crystalline focus as he considered how that rather characteristically odd argument might relate to the Guelph report and disappearing corpses, chanting men, desert visions, and disturbing, disorienting reflections. Maybe this very concussion to reality that he'd just suffered was causing new thoughts to sprinkle from Rosemont's mind, forcing him to reconsider that the random fight at the conference on Albanian Renaissance art in Atlanta was not random at all, nor were the events that sprung from it. Had Miles been trying to tell him something back then? He might have known that something was up at the time, but so much about Miles had always been haphazard, from the way he dressed to the way he walked into a room that, at the time, Rosemont had simply regarded his old friend as too much undergraduate and not enough grown-up, someone who'd failed to shake off the waywardness and defiance of a youth spent in the overindulgence of Austin, Texas. Miles's mortician's tails. His yellow-lensed sharpshooter glasses. The stalking, Groucho-esque walk. The immature contrarian streak. His seeming inability to tell time when even important dates had to be kept. "Sorry!" His loud, sudden entrances were nearly always made with an apology, whether entering a dive cowboy bar or a conference room filled with colleagues. "Sorry! Couldn't be helped. Sorry." Miles was already muttering when he entered Conference Room A, where some fifty people and a consortium of Renaissance art historians were waiting for him. "A Nazi. Sorry. There was a Nazi, though."

From the panelists' table in Conference Room A, Rosemont watched Miles track through double doors practically at a run, circling the audience and making for the panelists' table with his black messenger bag bouncing on his hip and one hand making excuse-gestures in the air. "Right outside the hotel! Can you believe it? A real, live Nazi." The waving excuse-gesture became a thumb that jerked over his shoulder. "A cop, I mean." The hand went back to waving at the crowd. "I was innocently buying jumper cables from a guy, but it turns out you shouldn't tell a cop he's interfering—oh, you didn't start without me! Hi. Hi."

Back when Miles was merely five minutes late for the panel, the moderator, one of the conference organizers, had asked the audience if they wanted to begin without him, but it was just a rhetorical question. This audience had come to hear Miles fight with Rosemont, so after a murmur of no's and some general head-shaking, the crowd had settled into arm-crossed waiting. Now that Miles was here, many smiled or rolled their eyes at crazy ol' John C. Miles, as though they were in on a delicious joke, and it irritated Rosemont. As if the man weren't already over-indulged. As if this debate would be of any consequence. Even Dr. Vincent Abernathy, who'd been sent by a French museum to make Rosemont an offer that he had no intention of refusing, seemed eager to be entertained.

From the dais, Rosemont glowered at the smilers, willing them not to encourage Miles, then slid his microphone closer. Rosemont's dry voice boomed in the room. "Oh, good, the floor show has finally arrived."

Miles was waving at the three panelists now. "Look, there's Harvard. Hi, Sarah Lawrence. Hi, Jeremiah. Look at you. You're already pissed at me."

"Thank you for making it, John," the moderator said

happily. Rosemont gave him a dirty look. He was probably the one who arranged this little tête-à-tête.

Miles stood behind the open chair and the paper tent with his name on it. "Down here?" Then he pointed at Rosemont, touched the tip of his nose, pointed again. "Would people mind?" He looked at the moderator and the other two panelists—Ted Fitz from Sarah Lawrence and Denise Olivetti from Harvard, both of whom flanked Rosemont—saying, "I should really have been seated next to Jeremiah."

The moderator frowned. "John, let's get started. We're twenty minutes into a sixty-minute slot. Let's—"

"Harvard. Hup! Swap with me!"

Denise gave him a pained smile, but a moment later, she lifted from her chair like a marionette.

Meanwhile, Ted Fitz was organizing his talking points on the Shadow Caliphate's influence on tarot. Rosemont smiled. *As if he's actually going to get a chance to speak.*

"While our scholars get resettled and reacquainted, let me remind everyone that the name of this panel is—"

"Do you need water? Jeremiah? Thirsty?" Miles lifted the pitcher of ice water after filling a glass for himself. "Don't get up. I'll just bring it down." He smelled the pitcher and shrugged. "You know, man, I read your paper on Moakley in *Orbis Tertius Hermeticus,* and there's a few problems that we really have to go over." He and Denise passed each other behind the moderator, Miles raising his glass and pitcher high. Denise continued to smile, struggling to look game.

"What did you need jumper cables for, Miles?" someone in the back shouted.

Miles filled Rosemont's glass. "They were so cheap. I

don't think the guy knew how cheap he was selling them for," he answered, shielding his eyes from the ceiling lights and peering into the crowd. "Was that Everett? Hey, man."

Great, Rosemont thought. *He's got a posse.*

Arms were uncrossing. Bodies were shifting forward on their seats. The world of art historians was not a world of artists, though most of them embraced what Miles had labeled *faux-hemia.* This Renaissance-obsessed sliver of the art history world was small, well heeled, and unobtrusive, a well-tended copse of polite little trees. In Austin, Texas, a loudmouthed dude in mortician's coat barely turned heads among fey punk cowboys, Butthole Surfers, Texas separatists, neo-hippie Zendyks, and other desert-scorched freakery. At the conference on Albanian Renaissance art, however, he was a marquee event, ready to thumb his nose at straight academic Jeremiah Rosemont—hence a crowd of fifty in a conference of only two hundred total participants.

Miles leaned his elbows on the table and, looking at Rosemont to his right, said sidelong into his microphone, "Let's have a show of hands. Who here read Jeremiah's article in *Orbis Tertius Hermeticus?* The one where he body slammed me."

"God," Rosemont sneered, "no one body slammed you."

About two thirds of the audience raised their hands.

"Miles," said Rosemont. He knew that the exasperation in his voice would make him the heavy, but he couldn't help it. He wanted to body slam Miles now. "I referenced you, I didn't attack you. I admired your research into the *triumphus*—"

"Admired? You teed off on me! You didn't even address my thesis about occult origins."

Rosemont couldn't believe that's what this was about. "And?" he said. "So? My article was about the correlation between Mardi Gras and tarot, Miles. I specifically said that I didn't see any occult origins for tarot. I never—"

"Aha!" A long, bony finger appeared in Rosemont's face.

Rosemont flinched. "What?"

"You admit it!"

"That there are no occult origins?"

"That's right!" shouted Miles.

"Of course, I admit it. What is your *point*?"

"My point?" Miles rolled up his sleeves and wiped his mouth. Rosemont knew that gesture. It meant Miles was nervous talking to Rosemont about this, and Rosemont's heart lifted to him, wished he could say something to calm his old friend. But this was a boxing match, apparently, not a chat between pals, not a lively exchange at Trudy's or the Circus of Infinite Wow. Rosemont was on the wrong side of Miles's line in the sand; his old friend wouldn't hear friendliness now. Miles dropped his hand from his mouth, and the moment passed. "I agree with everything you said in your tidy little turd of an article," he said. "Yes, tarot has its roots in Renaissance Lent parades, which in turn have roots in ancient Rome and the triumphal rites honoring victorious generals."

"As does modern Mardi Gras," Rosemont said, looking at Abernathy. "The floats built by soldiers for Titus's triumph in AD 71 after his Jerusalem campaign and—"

There was a resounding thump. Miles feigned nodding off on the microphone, and then his snore thundered through the room. "The *problem*," he barked, head snapping up, "is that you can't have it both ways. You can't mention the triumphal rite without mentioning its occult purpose."

"Occult purpose?" Ted said, his slight English accent creeping into the Monty Python register. "A general? Returning to Rome to gloat? What occult purpose could there possibly be in a military parade?"

"Well, I sure am glad you asked," Miles said, face spreading in a big Texan grin. "How did the *triumphus* end, Ted? What happened after the triumphator marched clockwise through the streets of Rome, driving the enemy in chains before him?"

"Great sex?" Ted mused. The audience laughed appreciatively.

"You don't know? It's okay to admit it. It's only a jury of your peers," Miles said, hand waving at the audience.

Ted cleared his throat, lifted his chin, and scratched his throat. "My expertise is the Egyptian influence on tarot," he said, "actually."

"Egypt. If you didn't have tenure," Miles said, voice soaked in contempt, "that would be *adorable.*"

"John, that's enough. As facilitator here, I need to ask you to refrain from—"

"Blood sacrifice!" shouted Miles into his microphone. "A blood cult! A spilling of blood, and boy was there a bloody lot of bloody blood. Did I mention the blood? Why? Anyone? God, this panel is falling to pieces." He stood, mic cord snaking through his other fist, a singer ready to rock. "Everett? You still here, man? You take a swing at why they conducted a blood sacrifice at the end of a military parade."

"For the continued glory of Rome," Everett yelled, his

voice sounding a thin counterpoint to Miles's shouting through the mic.

"Wrong! I mean, sure, that, but, come on, let's take 'em to school," Miles said, voice calling out like a preacher. "Who else was there? Who was waiting for that victorious warrior at the climax of this show, at the Temple of Jupiter? Go! Say it!" said Miles, pointing into the audience.

"A haruspex!" Everett shouted back.

"Yeah. A goddamn motherfucking haruspex," shouted Miles, spitting on the P and making the crowd jump as the consonant exploded in the room.

"And what's a haruspex? Ted? Everett? Never mind. This is where it gets good." Miles said, stepping up on his chair. "They read entrails, Jeremiah!" Miles yelled. Then, with horror-show relish, he growled down at Rosemont. "*Livers!* They were 'reading' the bull's red-hot liver. Get it? Not unlike tarot *readings*? Well, they were taking this 'reading' because every Roman secretly believed that their mighty city was on the verge of plunging into eternal chaos. Someone ask me why Rome believed that. Why did Romans think they were on the verge of plunging into eternal chaos?" Miles said, eyes on Rosemont. He paused and watched him expectantly as if Rosemont might ignite and burst into gorgeous flames.

At the time, Rosemont hadn't understood Miles's significant look or the hidden implications of the rant that followed, but thinking back now, from the Roman bathroom, with the binder open to *The Refutation of Rosemont* on his thighs, he knew. He knew.

Everett shouted from the audience, "Rome's foundation myth *said* they were doomed!"

"Goddamn it!" Miles shouted into the crowd, irritated. "Everett, shut up! Yeah, okay, that's totally right. But why were they doomed?" He paused, as if to give Rosemont one last chance to speak. "Because the city, according to its own creation story, was born from a crime—a horrible murder. So occultists were on hand to read the signs and see if divine justice would finally come falling on Rome."

"Murder?" Ted said. "Who was killed?"

"Rosemont knows," Miles answered, eyes still consumed with Rosemont. But when Rosemont refused to respond, Miles answered, "Remus."

"Remus?" said Ted. "Of Romulus and Remus?"

Rosemont shut his eyes tight. Miles's argument, his preoccupation with those days in Austin, his mortician tails, and Romulus and Remus—it was all so damn agonizing in its childishness.

"Romulus killed his own brother in cold blood," Miles continued. Rosemont thought he could feel Miles looking at him. "Did you know that? Most people only remember the she-wolf that suckled them. But Romulus killed his brother and claimed kingship over their new city, even named it after himself. That's how Rome was born, and Remus was all but forgotten." Seeing nothing like flames or even comprehension from Rosemont, Miles had seemed to deflate, his head of steam dissipating away behind him. "That's what the rite was for. To remember that lost brother."

At the time, Rosemont the panelist had simply returned Miles's stare with dead eyes, letting him see how unimpressed and angry he was with his friend for showboating and making a mockery of him. Especially in front of Abernathy, who held the keys to a future of influence and status for Rosemont in European circles. *How could he do this to me?* Rosemont the panelist had thought, looking up at his friend standing on the chair like a drunken boor. *Why doesn't he shut the fuck up?*

But the Rosemont still trembling in the bathroom, struggling to make sense of what he'd seen in the mirror, felt he finally understood the odd fight that Miles had picked with him all those years ago. *God, that was our myth, his and mine,* Rosemont thought. The name Remus in Miles's voice, pronounced correctly as *Ray-moos,* should have sent a shudder through him back then, as it did now recalling how passionately Miles had spoken. *I didn't give him squat. I just stared at him like he was insane. Like I didn't know what he was talking about.*

Best friends. They were so tight, back then, they could finish, hell, *start* each other's sentences, could hold whole conversations just by showing single tarot cards to each other—the Calvino Method it was called—and one fortune teller would throw a spread for a client, while the other interpreted it blindfolded. There was no border between their minds. Drawing a dedicated clientele of forty-year-old housewives, lost girls looking for strangeness, and hipster fans from the burgeoning cool class of Austin, Miles and Rosemont became minor celebrities. But how to explain the genuine strangeness? How to explain the fortune tellers' telepathy to people who wouldn't take "love" for an answer? Miles and Rosemont didn't understand it themselves, but, lo, a story came unto them after consulting the Oracle of Shiner Bock, a story of two cosmic babies, one carried down the Colorado River in a reed basket, the other down the mighty Pedernales in styrofoam, each wrapped in tiny Republic of Texas flags. Some said they'd come from the clan of archangels who'd built the railroads, while others said their parents were time travelers who'd abandoned the children here before escaping into the Forty-second Dimension. Regardless, the babies were saved separately and raised together by Mexican free-tailed bats, that's right, raised by bats in the wilds beneath the Congress Avenue Bridge. These two young boys learned the arcane language and secret mysteries of the bat colony, Miles told clients waiting for their readings, an occult knowledge that fated the boys to become the greatest prophets since the Alamo days. Romulus and Remus were their top secret names, and though an older story was often told that another Romulus killed a different Remus for leaping across the unfinished walls of Rome-to-be, the better story was that the twins were alive and well and dwelling in the sacred light of Austin's Moon Towers.

Bullshit. Silliness. It didn't even matter anymore—lies told at a maniacal postmodern circus, that's what Rosemont the panelist would have thought, if he'd managed to remember the story at all. *A link between tarot cards and Romulus and Remus? Please.* That's as much thought as he gave Miles. Down the panelists' table, Denise and Ted were performing a duet of eye rolling. A few audience members were too. Some had zipped up briefcases, making for the door at the end of this absurd performance. Abernathy looked ready to fall asleep.

Rosemont smiled blandly and said, "It's a very interesting idea, Miles."

But Miles would have none of that from Rosemont, apparently, and stepped off the chair with a scowl. "Are you even listening to the words coming out of your mouth? You see that they were occultists? You see the roots that tarot has in the occult, in *that* story, and that's all you can say? 'Interesting'?" The look on Miles's face was one of betrayal, but thinking back, Rosemont imagined there was probably sorrow, too.

Rosemont had wanted Miles to shut up so he could go have a drink with Abernathy.

"God, you won't even let me agree with you?" Rosemont had said. He didn't feel outraged or incredulous. He simply wanted to get away from Miles. Rosemont glanced at the crowd as if checking a clock.

"It's just 'interesting' to you? You used to be a different person. This isn't just a story, a myth—it's so much more." He gave Rosemont a pleading, angry look. "See what I'm getting at? Something was preserved. Almost three thousand years old. It's what you and I were looking for back in Austin when—"

While Miles spieled, Rosemont's eyes had drifted to Abernathy, who was looking decidedly unimpressed with this panel. He was politely stifling a yawn while simultaneously eyeing the door, and suddenly Rosemont feared the man would leave without bringing Rosemont the offer from France, a lucrative deal to consult on an exhibit of early playing card industries in Renaissance France. Voice hardening, Rosemont cut Miles off. "So write a paper."

Miles stared dumbly at Rosemont. "A paper?"

"It *is* interesting. So refute me. Find a publisher and get your great big idea in print." Rosemont slipped his notes into his briefcase. "Until then, this is just so much mental masturbation."

Miles gave Rosemont the same contemptuous head shake that he'd given Ted when he mentioned Egypt. "I can't believe you. I thought if I laid it out, if I handed it to you, you'd at least wake up enough to remember what you—"

Rosemont flicked off his mic and stood with a sideways glance at Abernathy. "Ted, Denise."

Miles muttered at Rosemont, looping the strap of his bag over his head. "Keep pretending you're normal, Jeremiah. Keep rejecting yourself. But this isn't just about tarot, and there's more where this came from."

In the Roman street fair, a tuba chugged outside the quiet house. Before him, the showerhead dripped in the stall. Rosemont hadn't given too much weight to that argument with Miles subsequently, or those last words that at the time had seemed to be a limp, parting taunt. Another random scene with John C. Miles that went nowhere.

But something had changed. It was all different. All rearranged somehow, he knew, looking up at the gleaming mirror.

There's more where this came from.

Rosemont now figured that Miles was the one who'd sent the letter to him in Managua. Miles couldn't have known where Rosemont was, but the two chanting men seemed to attribute powers to Miles far beyond tracking down old friends in other countries. *Doppelgänger. The thing in the mirror. They thought it was Miles. Was it?* Miles had been trying to tell him something, convince him of tarot's occult origins for some reason. It wasn't enough that Rosemont simply agree with him. Rosemont knew it must have something to do with their old hunts and haunts in Austin, days that he'd simply put behind himself for a career, status, and a name. But Miles hadn't. *This isn't just about tarot.* Something had happened to Miles, changed him into something that Rosemont didn't understand.

Rosemont opened the red binder again and thumbed back to *The Refutation of Rosemont*.

You curators and collectors are too busy bidding on moldy bones, so you probably aren't familiar with my work at Ligget & LaSalle University, where I created the Department of Urban Mythology. To be clear, I don't use the word "myth" to describe calcified morality tales, Joseph Campbell's self-help bliss-chasing, or cute fables.

Though Jeremiah Rosemont used his authority and status to liberate me from my tenure at Ligget & LaSalle, and the burden of the salary that went with it, my life's work is still a search for living, modern myths that make sense of the world—but more, that literally *make* the world. To not tell a "true myth" is to submit to madness, and conversely, to tell a true myth is to work one's fingers into the warp and weft of reality. You used to agree with me on this, once upon a time, Rosemont.

"The stupid narcissist thinks I got him fired," Rosemont said to himself. Bender after bender on the university meal ticket and he blames me? Selling psilocybin mushrooms to his students? Rosemont scanned the article until he found this:

Jeremiah, I can just imagine your lips tightening in anger. I can just see you saying, "Perhaps, Miles," which would actually mean something vicious like, John Miles is a bipolar freak who shouldn't mix his meds with alcohol. Maybe you've abandoned your investigations into awe and passion, but as for me, I can see that you're holding these very typewritten pages and sneering down into these as-yet-unpublished words. You're wearing the shirt, the brown and blue shirt I bought, the one with the mustard yellow stripes. You're sitting in a bathroom, aren't you? There's a mirror behind you. Currency from a Central American country is in your jacket pocket. You need a shave.

Oh, look, you just read that last paragraph. Don't look so stupid. I made the jump we dreamed about in Austin, while you chose static safety. In your world, the academic world, I'm a disgrace. But in mine, I'm up and over and out and away.

"Hello?" came a man's voice.

Rosemont started in fright. With the bathroom door open, he was sitting almost in full view of the foyer, he realized. He closed the binder silently and slipped it into his backpack.

"Jeremiah?"

Any steadiness that he'd received from sitting quietly and reading was shattered hearing his name called from the other room and reading Miles's words. How had Miles known? Mirror. Bathroom. Central American currency. Rosemont's whole body was quaking again as he looked down at his brown and blue shirt with mustard stripes.

Rosemont leaned forward to look out of the bathroom. The man in the atrium was a tall fellow, standing with his back to Rosemont, craning his neck to look into a far parlor room. The man from the trunk. It had to be. He had short-cropped black hair, and his voice was surprisingly welcome to Rosemont in the battering strangeness of recent events.

Rosemont stepped into the bathroom doorway and realized that someone else was there. Deathbed haggard, with flashing dark eyes in sunken, waxen sockets, the woman looked like something from a 1930s Universal Studios horror picture with her killer widow's peak. "Miles," she said, noticing Rosemont.

The man turned, and there indeed was John C. Miles in his yellow-tinted sharpshooter specs, his long curly hair shorn stubble short. He was jowlier and more tired looking. But there he was, whatever he was.

Rosemont was still feeling rattled deep in his blood by what he'd read and everything he'd seen, but he managed, "In all the Volvo trunks in all the towns in all the world . . ."

"Not bad." Miles laughed. "You recognize me now? You don't look so great, buddy. What just happened?"

Rosemont could tell his eyes were darting as his brain scurried for an answer. "I'm not sure."

Miles and Vampirella looked at each other in concern. "This is Priscilla, Jeremiah. She's okay."

It hadn't truly occurred to him that she might not be, but now he wondered. For that matter, was Miles "okay"? With people being maimed, killed, and disappeared, was *Rosemont* okay in any sense of the word? He could scarcely trust his own mind in this situation, let alone other human beings, but he swallowed hard and said, "There were two men. In the bathroom, there. They were chanting something bizarre and the wall—"

"Here?" Miles took a step toward Rosemont. "You saw them?"

"Through the mirror," Rosemont said, stumbling a little on the word.

Both Priscilla and Miles recoiled slightly, as if in sympathy. "Mirrors. None of us like looking in mirrors," Miles said.

"But who were they?" said Rosemont.

Priscilla visibly relaxed. "They're gone?"

"Yes. They took—they and a body went..."

"A body?" said Miles. "Was there a, um, nail?"

Rosemont blinked rapidly and turned his head as if from the sight of that body before him. "Yep."

"They killed another authenticator, then," Priscilla said. Then she whispered, almost imploring him, "We're down to you, Mr. Rosemont."

Rosemont looked at the woman, at her cargo pants and black T-shirt. Just another budget road traveler? An artist slouching in Rome, maybe? He thought she sounded resigned, rueful, but her accent and manner were pronounced, so he couldn't read her very well. Was she Pakistani? Afghan? Rosemont said, "What do you mean, she was an authenticator? Am I an authenticator?"

Priscilla stepped toward him, as though prepared to hand him something precious. "You, Mr. Rosemont, have what—"

"Wait," Miles said. "First things first. Did you get the binder? It's not on the desk."

Priscilla's shoulder straightened and she glanced at Miles with a look of contempt that dissolved into a nod, appreciating his words.

"No," Rosemont said, hoisting his backpack. He looked at the desk too. "No, I never found it. They—"

"They have it?" Priscilla said with venom in her voice. Her eyes were slicing Miles to ribbons. "They have your binder, and all your work." She laughed and it sounded metallic like coins falling on steel.

Miles all but collapsed against the front door. He looked helplessly at Priscilla. "I couldn't do anything about it. The Iranians jumped me. I'm lucky they didn't—"

"Stop," she told him. Her cold laugh softened into a chuckle.

"We have to get it. It's everything I've worked for," Miles said. "Everything I wanted to show Marni. The Guelph report."

"Look, you're a complete idiot, as I've pointed out before, so it'll be easy for you to forget it," Priscilla said, pushing him away from the front door and grabbing one shoulder in a friendly but domineering way. "We have Rosemont. We have an authenticator. That's all we really need."

Rosemont watched the two carefully, feeling so shaken that he couldn't be sure this wasn't an act for his benefit. But, no. He knew Miles well enough to see that he was truly overwhelmed, confused. Rosemont felt awful for lying to him, but he'd give the binder back as soon as he'd read some more, learned more about what was happening, and what Miles had become.

"We have to get to the *templum*. It's almost nightfall, Jeremiah Rosemont," Priscilla said. It sounded stilted in her voice as if she'd been waiting to say his name for a long time. "We are going to run very, very fast now. Fast by modern standards, anyway. Are you well enough to run?"

Rosemont got his backpack into position over both shoulders. "Yes."

But Miles looked ready to vomit.

"Miles? Come now. Come. Time to let it go. It was only half a decade's work. Put it in perspective."

"I know. This is the game. I knew it was going to be like this."

Priscilla put her hand on the doorknob.

"It's just words," Miles was saying in his quick murmur. "They've been trying to rub out our proof for years. Just one more kick in the mouth, eh? Okay. I know we should go. I'm ready."

"As soon as I open the door," she looked at the two men in turn, "run like devils are behind you. Because they are, and they're coming for us."

Then she flung the door open.

8

The leather feet of his ghosts were padding about the upper stories, again, pacing and chasing each other, nails scritching on the stone and wood. He could hear them, their ambling gaits, their bouncing playfulness cut short by unnerving shrieks and howling. Boy King sat curled in a shadow on the bottom floor of Bryce & Waterston, a night rain falling in straight, thick sheets outside. He'd invited the ghosts for protection, but they were given to bursts of violence, so he stayed down here in the dark, drinking himself numb.

The first night after the debacle at Dona Mia, a member of the Hmong family next door had followed Boy King into Bryce & Waterston to see if he was all right. A normal person would hear nothing, see nothing but a frightened man with a broken nose cowering in the nooks and crannies of the warehouse. The graffiti was just graffiti and the rain was just rain. With blood sprayed down the front of his suit and his nose sagging against his face like a scrotum, he clearly needed help. "You need me to call a doctor?" the fellow, James, asked Boy King.

Boy King had reached into his pocket and pulled out the last of his money, two twenties, and held them out to James. "Get me all the booze you can get."

James was a kind-faced young man who looked worried for Boy King right now. Fingering the bills, he said, "I know a doctor."

"For forty dollars?" Boy King said.

"Maybe. It's my uncle's best friend. Military doctor, but he won't be shipped out. He sees us on Sundays free of—"

"No. Sunday? No, no. Gotta fix my nose tonight. Gotta get drunk fast. Please, just whatever's cheap, okay?"

James had heard far stranger requests from Boy King— fencing the pound of hashish Boy King had found in a Dumpster; going to the cops to tell them about that body by the river—so a trip to the liquor store for medicinal purposes must have seemed downright reasonable. He even stayed with Boy King while he sucked down the rum as fast as he dared, but James politely made his apologies when Boy King declared he was finally drunk enough for the "straightening."

After that, Boy King remained submerged in a pool of drunkenness, and he was grateful for it. Pain hovered in the periphery of consciousness as he slowly whittled at the rum, and he kept the pain at bay the next day too, breaking into the second bottle of four. No food. No water. Just rum and fear. He'd been on these benders before so his body snapped into the rhythm of it like a dancer picking up an old number. Nursing bottle number two for the better part of the day, he began to see that ecstatic, mad place where the magic was, like a ceiling he was floating toward. So he kept going, and by the second night, he'd busted into bottle number three.

The rain was welcome. It wept from the booze-fog in Boy King's mind and washed the city in a mild confusion so that beat cops steered the wrong way down familiar one-way streets and kids forgot the rules to games they loved. Where his rain fell, he could hear the splashing footsteps of those desert trackers as they stalked through the city's abandoned, mislaid, and broken corners, the dead rail yards and mills, the weedy waterfronts, and baseball fields turned gravel lots. Boy King drank some more, listened for them, and arranged his traps for the desert hunters. The priests of Khnum, Khemet's creator god, searched for random fires of magic to snuff out. In the days when humans were barely human, Khnum's hunters had continually extinguished the earliest glimmers of clans becoming something more than clans, when pre-Egyptian culture sparked in its first and faultiest quickenings. Eventually, the fire had raged out of control, according to their cult, and they regarded the contemporary world as dead, thoroughly burned. These hunters were adepts at making certain the embers, the Boy Kings of the world, didn't reignite into anything uncontrollable. His traps were for them.

By the time he hit the third bottle, Boy King was past mere mortal concerns of hangovers, headaches, and the throbbing pain of a broken nose that he'd straightened himself. So when it came, the phantom, a slight figure, androgynous in fitted black that rendered it all but invisible in the night warehouse, Boy King couldn't even be certain if what he was seeing was real. Stepping into the window frame that Boy King always entered through, just a few feet away from him, it might have been another ghost. Boy King caught his breath. He froze and waited for it to make a sound, to be certain it wasn't a hallucination or one of his own traps.

Black against an iron-gray sky, the silhouette's head turned this way and that, but did not seem to acknowledge Boy King, who stood in full view, close enough to see the visitor's creased and dusty black leather shoes. Black gloves. Little black backpack like those carried by fashionable young girls. His Cardin jacket.

Oh my God. It wasn't a desert tracker. It was worse. *How did you find me here?*

Boy King's left hand wanted to touch his right, to protect it all over again, so palpable was the memory of the raised hammer, the sour breath of his torturer. This man wasn't the one who'd hurt Boy King, but he was there that day, and while Boy King knew this man only as Transom, the man's gait and the hang of his arms were as familiar as the comforting pressure of the tight black glove on Boy King's own hand.

Through Boy King's snarls and misdirects, Transom stepped lightly across the warehouse floor, nosing, ferreting. Boy King dared not move for fear of calling attention to himself, so he stood still as the steel door beside him and followed the visitor with his eyes. Transom came to stand within three feet of him, so close that Boy King could see Transom's doughy face.

"This has to be it," Transom said quietly, speaking as if to someone standing behind him. "The desert men, that's who. Their tracks led here and then vanished."

His mind had been turned inside out by so much rum for so many days, but even Boy King could appreciate the cleverness of that ploy, tracking the trackers. Maybe he could steal a page from Transom's playbook. He stood, experimenting with balance. Transom took a step forward, and Boy King followed on unsteady feet, the two walking across the old loading bay of the warehouse together.

Upstairs, a ghost screamed but Transom didn't react. His cult was immune to the cries of the ghosts of Remus.

"To the teeth," Transom was saying, sounding nervous. "So, no, I don't intend to tangle, believe me."

Brazen with rum, Boy King matched him step for step. He imagined that Transom was speaking to Visconti, the hammerer. Visconti was probably listening from a safe, remote location—a Denny's maybe, having crappy coffee and listening in on Transom. As long as Visconti stayed away, Boy King felt he could handle this situation. The bully was probably ready to appear at a moment's notice, though, and the very thought sagged into Boy King's stomach, made his left knee wobble.

Transom stopped and turned as if he'd heard a footfall.

Boy King stopped. He crossed his arms over his chest, embracing himself, and inhaled his fear, hiding it from Transom deep in his body.

"He might be," Transom said, "but I don't think so. Not for a while."

Transom adjusted his backpack and walked to the stairs. Boy King followed, still hugging himself. As Transom passed the syllables that Boy King had spray painted on the walls years ago, he touched them with a ring finger, ever so lightly.

"Yes, but it's just graffiti."

Boy King nodded. *Just graffiti. That's it. Keep walking.* But to Boy King's dismay, when Transom passed these sigils and signs, the power in them dimmed and blinked out.

The second floor was where Boy King kept his second-rate Dumpster scores; items he might need, sell, give away, or eventually junk. The gardening tools, antique kitchenware, bikes with bashed-in spokes, broken printers, a bookshelf. Boy King had been careful to make all these things look like they'd been thrown about haphazardly over years, and he kept a judicious amount of real trash heaped about too. Transom began rummaging through the collection, and Boy King realized that he wasn't looking for general evidence of Boy King or even clues about who lived here necessarily. He seemed to be foraging with a certain verve and purpose.

Oh, shit. He knows I have it.

"How should I know?" Transom said, after kicking over a box of old teapots. "It's a landfill in here."

Boy King's bedroom, so to speak, was on the third floor where the howling ghosts were, accessible only by taking the hooked pole that lay under a water-stained mattress on the second floor and unlatching a trapdoor in the ceiling. In his years of squatting here, he'd seen many visitors wandering downstairs. A few homeless folks had broken in through the old coal chute, as he had originally, and a troupe of teenage kids got high up here several times a week for about six months straight. But no one had ever discovered the third floor.

Transom inclined his head and looked right up at the trapdoor as if it had called for him. "There. Up there."

Boy King picked up one of the broken bricks that cluttered the floor everywhere in Bryce & Waterston. He hefted it till it felt good in his hand, till he could imagine opening Transom's skull before the bastard ever knew that Boy King was there. He had vowed long ago never to manipulate, control, or yoke another human being again, and in light of that, he wondered if he could instead kill a person—even this loathsome specimen. Yes, he decided. He could do it easily. Transom had been the one to lead Visconti to the Boy King, after all. All those years ago, he'd guarded the room while Visconti hammered the spike through Boy King's right hand. Killing was far better than merely yoking him, and best of all, Boy King was drunk enough to actually do it.

Transom kicked through the heaps of trash, scanning for something with which to reach the trapdoor. Then he found the mattress and pulled up one corner. "Here we go," he said, finding the hooked pole.

Transom fished at the ceiling for a moment, swaying back and forth trying to catch the leather strap. When he got it, he gave a little shout in surprise as the trapdoor opened and the ladder ratcheted down loudly into place. A moment later he was clambering up—the Boy King right behind him, still holding the brick in one hand.

When he reached the top of the ladder, Boy King saw the circle of ghosts, gold eyes burning in the light of Minneapolis's skyline, backing away as if in obeisance to

Boy King's arrival. Quite a joke, that. Three years ago, they'd arrived at his call and pounced him in his sleep for three nights, their leathery pads and claws tearing real wounds in him. After the violent afternoon at Dona Mia's, Boy King had invited the ghosts here again, for protection. But their loyalties were tenuous at best.

Transom turned away, and when his body seemed to rear back with an almost startled lift of his shoulders, Boy King knew what he'd found. So did the ghosts. He could hear their scuffling, their urgent grunts.

The stack of cardboard boxes.

Transom stood before the cardboard boxes while the Boy King scrambled up the ladder, getting leverage on the brick to swing himself unsteadily into the room. There were hardcover books piled atop the treasures within each box, to say nothing of the lead crystal ashtrays he'd stuck there too. He hoped it was enough.

"Maybe?" Transom was whispering. "Maybe, there. I'm nervous to go poking all of a sudden."

Smart man, thought Boy King. *Now just go. Get on and get.*

But Transom was always more curious than smart, and he put his hands on the top cardboard box, bent his knees, and hoisted it from the stack.

The brick felt deadly in the Boy King's hand. *If I do it, then there's a body. But if I only knock him out and drag him down to the river, then he'll just come back. But if I kill him, then someone follows to find out what happened. If I set the ghosts on Transom, though, then—then Vis—... the man whose name begins with V will know that Remus's disciplines are practiced here. And he'll bring more than desert trackers—and more and more.*

Boy King had only yoked three people in his life, and the last yoke had cracked the mind beneath his hand. That yoking had filled Boy King with such horror and guilt it had shot him from the last fringes of sane civilization and into these nether zones, hiding in the fringes where he could remain neither himself nor a danger to others, to dwell in the silent contemplation of getting away with far more than murder. But this. This agent of whimsical horror. This mome rath, this slithy tove. Here he was, Transom, rifling closer and closer to the dusty cardboard boxes, and death wasn't good enough to stop him.

Putting down the brick, Boy King stood behind Transom and placed his hands on the man's shoulders so there would be neither disconnect nor retreat, and then they both raised their faces to the high stone arch that appeared before them in the roofless, indigo sky.

"See that?" Boy King said, slurring.

Transom's chin bobbed upward and his eyes almost globed from his head. "What in the name of fuck is that?"

Keeping one hand on the man's shoulder, Boy King stepped forward and marched Transom toward the marble arch, the bright red veins shooting through the white stone. The ghosts fled in a scampering retreat, and very near, beyond the structure, they dissolved into a deafening crowd that cheered and jeered in so many different languages that the tumult was nonsensical. All Boy King could see beyond the arch, though, was not the crowd, but his own back as he marched Transom forward.

Boy King nodded solemnly as they walked. "So simple," he said. "Socks me in the face how simple."

A moment later, Transom was sitting cross-legged before the cardboard boxes of Boy King's hopes and horrors.

Yoked. His eyes were empty pools, and he sat with the backs of his hands on the floor. City light shone against clouds and illuminated this upper floor, and Boy King removed Transom's backpack.

"I need that," Transom said absently.

"Shh," scolded Boy King. "No, you don't."

"Take it, then."

Inside, Boy King found what he was looking for—a simple three-ring binder. It held the errata of proofs and corroborating documents that validated a tyro's irrational beliefs. Little bibles for madmen, a tyro had explained to Boy King. All tyros carried them and Boy King had seen several, had even attempted to keep one of his own a number of times. In the end, though, his concern had always been to divest himself of power, not to amass it. Besides, the obsession for citation, notation, and authority was lost on him after years in straight academia; that all seemed like posturing on this side of the rainbow. Evidence? Proof? He had all the proof he needed that the world was lousy with the inexplicably gifted, the insatiable, and the stupefyingly wondrous. Nonetheless, most tyros swore by these collections, needed them to justify their premeditated forays into madness. Some, the No Lanterns, descendants of the rag-and-bone men of London, made their way in subterranean urban mazes of ducts and utility ways, surfacing only to steal documents from "sunlit tyros" and retreating to absorb and digest the stolen knowledge. Boy King supposed he fell into that camp now.

There were whole schools of thought too on whether documents should be placed chronologically, alphabetically, by subject, by author, or by systems that the tyro created for him- or herself. Flipping open the binder, Boy King found that Transom ordered his documents with the most recently acquired on top: a transcript dated two months ago in this case. He skimmed through it, ready to rifle through the thick sheaf of documents within, but then he saw his name, so he doubled back and read more closely, his drunken gaze bumping over the words.

Medical and Psychological
Transcription Services, Inc.

Date: 3/3/02
Patient Doe. Admitted 9/3/92. No records previous
   to admission. Ward of state.
Interviewer: Dr. Dale De Vore, consulting
Cherryvale Institute

PT: I can't fend it off forever. The drugs actually
   help. I think I need them back.
DR: What are you fending off?
PT: A terrible— You—you don't know me, right?
DR: Should I?
PT [laughs]: I don't know. I just had a flash of
   doubt.
DR: It's this holiday from the drug regimen.
   Normalcy is an altered consciousness for you.
   Impressive. Quite a med schedule they have you
   on. Never mind. I'll represcribe after our
   meeting, don't worry.
PT: Makes it hard. Where is President Bush? I'm
   fencing.
DR: I don't see a sword in your hand.

PT: All up here. And in my gut. It's always knocking on my heart and I can feel its knuckles. Bump-bump. Bump-bump. Bump-bump. Bump-bump.

DR: What is? Can you tell me? What is it? . . . Your primary tells me you believe that a god is after you.

PT: I never said that. Not me. Not a god.

DR: You don't think a god is after you?

PT: I mean it's not—no, I don't think that.

DR: Good. Might feel like a god, but . . .

PT: You know, I really don't like this lack of control. You need to kill me or put me back on the drugs.

DR: No, no. Don't talk that way. Come on. You were about to say that they're not after you, right? They're after someone else, aren't they?

PT: . . .

DR: And they won't stop until they get it. Is that it? Is that what you wanted to say?

PT: . . .

DR: Do you have any idea how many different powers you're up against right now? How many powers you defied in Rome?

PT: You said Rome never happened.

DR: Really? I didn't say that. Your primary may have said it, but I didn't. Come, let's cut to the chase. Where's the Remurian? The lemure. The lemure? No? Okay, then, where's the prophetess? Come on. Who is helping you?

PT: This shouldn't be, right? Is this happening because I'm not on my pills?

DR: I want to help. I know all about you. I know about Priscilla. I know she was close to her goal of re-creating her city in Madison.

PT: ...

DR: Ah. You didn't know that. Revolution was in the air, back then, but no one knew what sort. Heh.

PT: This can't be. You're a part of me.

DR: More than you know. We all want the same thing. We all want Our Lord the Spinning Wheel's lessons. We all want to avoid his cattle slaughter. I don't know what you want, but I can help. I need the paintings to help protect you.

PT: I've been protecting myself.

DR: I know you have. You made a deck with pictures cut from magazines. Your primary sent me color copies. They are exquisite and you are very resourceful.

PT: I've been shielding the warehouse where he squats, but then someone got to him, I think.

DR: Warehouse? Warehouse? What warehouse?

PT: ...

DR: Is he a tyro finally?

PT: I don't know. The Boy King—but he's hidden. Even from me now.

DR: A boy king? A pharaoh?

PT: He's too frightened to leave.

DR: ...

PT: I shouldn't have—

DR: Shouldn't have what?

PT: ...

DR: Are you okay?

PT: ...

DR: You know he has the deck. You know he's got it.

PT: ...

DR: You didn't know that, did you? He does. He stole it. Do you remember any of this?

PT: ...

DR: Where is the warehouse?

PT: I'm ... I'm not.

DR: Where is the goddamn warehouse?

PT: What warehouse?

DR: The warehouse you told me he was in.

PT: I told you who was in a warehouse?

DR: You said that a boy king was—

PT: ...

DR: Was in a warehouse.

PT: Oh. Ah—

DR: What warehouse?

PT: No. No. I don't remember saying that. Where is Bush?

DR: Son of a bitch. You said warehouse! Now *concentrate*!

PT: It's all. All George Bush. All this fencing.

DR: I'm going to order you back on your regimen and then we'll try again. Son of a bitch.

Boy King slumped down on his rump, hard. He sat cross-legged facing Transom, binder open in his lap, the little wet mouths of the ghosts smacking nearby. A breeze had picked up and the whole warehouse smelled like the rain, clean for a change. The cardboard box of his hopes and fears was at Boy King's back, and simply reading a reference to its contents made him want to open it, gaze again upon the images there, recharge them with a human spark, and learn, learn, learn. But he hadn't done so in years, and it would be foolish to attempt without months of preparing, masking, hiding. Masters, slaves, and lunatics all over the country now knew of his whereabouts.

Boy King reread the transcript, but his reeling mind slipped and slid across the words, until finally he lifted his head and said, "Is that you interviewing the Patient Doe?"

Transom was sitting primly, yoked, ready to attend Boy King's every whim. "No. That is Duke Visconti posing as a psychiatrist."

Boy King's mouth tightened around the name. Tarot's original financier and the Etruscan Discipline's great Judas. "Visconti." More to the point for Boy King: the hammerer. "Is he coming here?"

"As soon as I report back, he'll be interested in speaking with you. As will others. Probably. I would guess." Transom gave his vampire grin.

"Others? What others?"

"I can't say."

Boy King felt like he'd been slammed in the nose again. "What did you say to me?"

"I said," Transom said, sounding dead and afraid now, " 'I cannot say,' Exalted One."

"You know I can strip you down to nothing. Like you just did to my warehouse, and I'll laugh while I do it."

"Yes," Transom intoned. "I know. But sadly for you there is a greater power..."

Oh my lord, thought Boy King, staring at Transom's slack expression. He'd never come across this before, didn't know how to handle such a thing. *He's refusing my yoke?* "Who is it?"

Transom shook his head in one forlorn shake. "Three letters."

"What do you mean? You received three letters?"

Transom closed his eyes, shook his head.

Boy King wanted to do it. He wanted to strip Transom's personality down to nothing. He felt certain that by yoking Transom, he'd grabbed a monster by the tail, because now he couldn't simply release him, couldn't let go. The entity that had yoked Transom, the three-lettered thing, was thrashing and turning toward him, out there, somewhere in the dark.

"Does Visconti know you're yoked by someone else?" said Boy King.

"Yoke him yourself and ask," Transom said. "Exalted One."

"Okay, well," the Boy King mustered. "I need you to go to Visconti, Transom, you heinous little fuck. I need you to go to him right now, and as soon as you get to him, tell him that you found nothing here. You got that? Do everything in your power to convince him and your other master that I'm not here and don't hold back."

Transom nodded, eager to please, now that he was satisfying Boy King again. "Anything else, Exalted One?"

Boy King looked down at the transcript, scrambling for any information that might help him. "Yes."

"What, oh my glorious and exquisite dark lord?"

"Stop that. This shit about Priscilla," Boy King said, glowering down into the big binder. "Was that true? Or was that Visconti bluffing?"

Transom's quick grin was like a snake slithering out of a hole. Boy King was fighting two other yokes to maintain control of Transom. "Oh, no. Very, very true," Transom said, apparently enjoying Boy King's discomfort.

"What was she doing in Madison?"

Transom eyed him suspiciously. "You didn't know she was there? I wonder why. Madison was a pivotal point in the reemergence of your disgusting religion."

"It's not a religion."

"Oh, I'm sorry. Your 'Etruscan Discipline.' I was there, you know. Visconti was charged with tracking down a lemure, Rebecca, and anyone that she—"

"Who?"

"Rebecca Goldblatt. She went by the name Thyme back then."

Boy King caught his breath. "Thyme Goldblatt?"

Again, Transom gave him his evil little eye. "You knew her?"

Boy King was about to answer, but simply glared at Transom. *Jesus, they didn't know I was there.* He'd said too much. He'd told Transom something key, that he knew Thyme, and there was no sucking the words back into his mouth.

The ghosts' laughter snicked in the dark.

Priscilla had been watching Madison. Thyme was somehow connected to the Etruscan Discipline. It all rearranged his view of his childhood and himself. It was as if he had just transformed into a different person and could now look into two pasts, at both the person he'd imagined himself to be and the person that Transom said he was. It felt oddly comforting. Almost a relief. The Etruscan Discipline would call this *divining*—not telling the future, but finding one's self in accord with the forces of the universe. He had the odd sense that in his life being reorganized this way, he was seeing it as it should have always been seen. Not "true," per se, but directed, funneled, and bent upon an end. *Divined.*

But he had to be sure. He glanced at the cardboard boxes that Transom had come frighteningly close to opening.

"Time for you to go, Transom," Boy King said, getting unsteadily to his feet. "I got something to do." He steered the man down to the first floor and toward the doorway. Then, much the same way that he'd marched Transom beneath the white marble arch, he gently pushed him forward, got him walking toward the dark wall of rain before them. Boy King had him thoroughly subjugated, now.

Transom nodded thickly, about as fuzzy-headed as Boy King was. "Ask a question?"

"Go ahead," said Boy King.

"Why were the ancient throngs deriding me?"

Boy King said, "They weren't." He wondered what the ghosts would do now that he, an agent of Remus, had acted as Romulus, subjugating an enemy like this. "They were deriding *me.*"

"Oh. Okay, then. Is there time for soup?"

Boy King could feel that the evil little weasel had snapped for good. The cockiness and the evil grin were gone; he felt surprisingly distressed to see them disappear.

Boy King was just protecting himself—Romulus's famous excuse.

"Yes. Go get soup," he said to Transom. "Hurry. I bet you're starving."

"Sure am. Some soup. Good gosh, it's bright today."

9

The roving blur of Rome's Aventine Hill neighborhood spiraled around Rosemont in great smears of buttressed walls and domes, cupolas, blue shutters on crimson facades, and crumbling slices of the great city, here, on the lesser of the two central Roman hills. In that shifting, dissolving run of hers, Priscilla took Miles and Rosemont through the tableau of the festival, frozen in place as it was so that here the blob of a man's dripping ice cream hung like a pendant in the air and there a pigeon's wings seemed ready to applaud or pray for the runners as they skipped like stones across this still lake, stepping in and out of Rome and across it too.

Until finally Rosemont came to stand next to Priscilla and Miles in a curious little piazza, where three cobblestone streets emptied into a chapel's courtyard. The chapel had seen more ecclesiastic days apparently. It was now a coffee shop, or perhaps a private apartment—judging by the gentle casualness of the woman drinking espresso at the lone table. There was a line of garbage cans, one at the end turned upside-down. Candy-striped awnings leaned over flowered vines spilling from windowsills, park benches sat at the four corners of the piazza, and a modest fountain with a little gargoyle spurted water from thick, pursed lips. A whiff of sewage was on the air. "Here it is," Miles said. "The center of my universe."

Rosemont stepped with him. He liked feeling Miles near after all the whirling confusion in the apartment. "This?" Rosemont said. "Seems too quaint and cheery to be the center of *your* universe."

"Yeah, not exactly Oil Can Harry's in Austin," Miles drawled. He watched as two cats pounced on something behind the garbage cans on the other side of the piazza. "It doesn't live up to its history, that's for sure."

"What is it?" Rosemont asked.

Priscilla said, "There's Marni. Let's go."

As they walked across the square toward the older woman drinking espresso, she stood and embraced Priscilla. "I've missed you intolerably," she said, but her face remained impassive, as if she hadn't spoken. She was maybe in her eighties, but very hale, with an aristocratic, angry posture that said old age was an inconvenience that she wasn't bearing well. She wore a blue peacoat with a sauce stain on the lapel. Like Priscilla, this woman Marni was hard for Rosemont to place. Was she Iranian? Miles had said something about Iranians. Or Russian? She said to Priscilla, without looking at Miles or Rosemont, "Who are these men? Which one is John C. Miles?"

Miles raised a hand in greeting. "Hi, I'm Miles. I'm very honored indeed, ma'am."

Rosemont looked sidelong at Miles. He'd never heard him sound like Eddie Haskell before.

"I just saw the Moroccan walking through on his way to the celebration. I think it's official, now," Marni said, still without looking at Miles. She flicked at the dried stain on her coat's lapel. "You have every major sect after you."

Miles nodded, then grinned his best smile at her. "Not every one."

Now Marni looked at him straight on with glinting brown eyes. "Oh?"

"There's still you."

Her face never broke its stiff blankness, but she laughed. "Ek tariana ek coo."

"I'm sorry." Miles shook his head. "I'm still learning your language."

"It means, 'That's the problem about *my* skull,' I would say," she said. Her hands slipped into the pockets of her dark blue coat.

Miles frowned, apparently decided he was supposed to laugh, and forced a chuckle, but he sounded mystified. "All right, then."

"We're almost ready," Marni said. "Sit with me. It will just be a moment."

They sat, four around the table, but no one came to serve them. The silence was awkward. Rosemont wanted Miles or Priscilla to introduce him to Marni, discuss the contents of the red binder, or tell this Marni person about the chanting men and their disturbing lusts and powers. But Priscilla and Miles remained quiet, staring down at the table, as if waiting for Marni's permission to speak.

A moment later, Rosemont inadvertently caught Marni's eye. The old woman pointed her gaze across the piazza and then looked back at Rosemont. He followed her eyes and saw two men in white coveralls hauling between them an unconscious Italian soldier, recently home from Kuwait, judging by the desert fatigues. They dragged him past the gargoyle fountain, his combat boots making a stuttering, scuffing noise on the cobblestones, and placed him on one of the park benches, folding his legs up on the seat before marching off.

Miles and Priscilla didn't seem to notice.

Another pair of men in white coveralls arrived from one of the other streets, dragging an unconscious woman. They seemed more aware of the strangeness of their situation, looking this way and that for reactions from people in the square. But passersby kept about their business, walking past the little fountain as perhaps they did every day, to and fro on their well-worn trails. Were these men in white invisible to them? Or was this just another day in the big city with experienced Romans avoiding unnecessary eye contact?

Finally four unconscious people were lying on benches at the four corners of the piazza, and Rosemont recalled the dormitory through which he'd passed in order to enter the hostel. He said to Miles, "Do those sleepers form some kind of boundary?"

All three people at the table turned their attention on him with such ferocious, urgent expressions that Rosemont slid a hand over his mouth.

"Too smart for his own good," Marni said to Miles.

"Or," Priscilla said, "he's becoming sensitized." Her brow wrinkled in apparent worry beneath that dramatic widow's peak, and again she gave Rosemont a stare that made him feel she was about to hand him or tell him something.

Miles whispered to Rosemont, "Just hold tight, buddy. I think you'll get some answers in a sec."

Marni took a deep breath, nostrils flaring, and nodded as if she were enjoying sweet music that she alone could hear. She actually smiled then, and was quite stately and beautiful, Rosemont thought, when she did. "This *is* delicious," she admitted, eyes drifting about the square. "This is very delicious, friends."

Miles sighed heavily, seemingly in stunned relief, and looked across the table at Priscilla. "I was hoping you'd think so."

Priscilla nodded, watching the older woman. "Documentation is lacking. But I told Miles that shouldn't matter."

"You say how old?" Marni asked Miles after a long pensive moment.

"It's a guess," he said. "But I think it's almost three thousand years old." Revealing this information seemed to lift a weight from Miles's shoulders. His voice was lighter, happier. "Does it feel familiar to you, Marni? Bring back any memories of the, er, old country?"

Maybe it was the recent war in the Gulf, but she looked Kuwaiti to Rosemont. He looked at her again closely. *Arabic? Armenian?*

She breathed in through her nose, seeming to revel in the mysterious ocean breeze or meadow or mountain rain that she alone could smell. "It's a terribly strong *templum*. It reminds me of places where our watermen used to scry the minds of previous generations. You can still feel the sharp edges of those invisible squares, if you know where to walk." She glanced around at the awnings. The popcorn stand. The stray cats eating now. "Here of all places. Who built it? Do you know?"

"A descendant of yours," Miles said.

"Of mine?"

"Of Wilusija's, yes."

Rosemont almost jumped as he recognized the name. He'd wondered how it was pronounced when he chanced across it in the red binder, scanning a transcript of an interview between Miles and Priscilla. Were Marni and Priscilla from the same place? This Wilusija? Was it a country? A city? A castle? He'd never heard it before.

"Who built it? Who are you talking about, Miles?" Marni said. Whatever she had experienced with the *templum* seemed to have softened her. "How on earth did you find it?"

Miles was all but crawling up on his chair with excitement. "I've been eager to meet you and discuss it. Priscilla helped me. She had certain information that I didn't have, while I had information she didn't have. We met in Sarajevo a few years back."

"Sarajevo?" Rosemont said. "You were in Sarajevo?"

Miles looked at Marni. "Do you think we're safe to talk about this?"

"Oh, we're very safe here," she said, looking at the sleepers. "Besides, I think it's good that he knows."

Priscilla said to Rosemont, "I met Miles while he was in Sarajevo, gathering evidence for his theories on urban mythology."

"Specifically, I was studying a twelve-step Alcoholics

Anonymous occult sect," Miles said to Rosemont. "I was researching it for the—for an article I was writing."

Rosemont swallowed a smile. He felt certain Miles had been about to say that he was researching *The Refutation of Rosemont.* "An occult twelve-step program?" Rosemont laughed through his nose, then realized Miles wasn't kidding. "Are you for real?"

Miles returned Rosemont's stare, but then his face broke into that grin. "None of your lip or we'll take you back to that bathroom and leave you in there with the mirror."

Marni chuckled.

"I had the same reaction you did, Rosemont, when I came across this sect. But the twelve steps are thoroughly occult, if you think about it," Miles said. " 'Admitting one is powerless before God as you understand Him.' " He raised his eyebrows, cocked his head, selling the idea to Rosemont. "Or how about this? 'Made a decision to turn one's will and one's life over to the care of God.' But here's the big step, the most supernatural of the twelve where I was concerned. Step number three: 'Came to believe that a power greater than ourselves could restore us to sanity.' "

Rosemont was about to say that if those were occult maxims, then born-again Christians were palm readers. But Priscilla spoke first, saying to Marni, "That's how Miles discovered me. The founder of the Sarajevo Alcoholics Anonymous understood what Miles was after and brought him to me. We came here six months ago, looking for the lost twin. Remus."

Priscilla kept talking but Miles suddenly turned to Rosemont and whispered, as if not to disturb Priscilla. "Rosemont."

Rosemont blinked at him in confusion. "What?"

Priscilla watched the two of them out of the corner of her eye as she spoke to Marni, shifting into a language that Rosemont didn't recognize.

"Hey," Miles said, kindly. "Hi."

Rosemont narrowed his eyes, scrutinizing him. He chortled. "Hi, Miles."

"I'm glad you came," Miles said. He sighed deeply, a shiver in his breath, and put his hand on Rosemont's leg. "Isn't this the best time you've ever had?"

Overly familiar and inappropriate as always, and always welcome. Rosemont put his hand on Miles's hand. "This surreal shit? Dead bodies? People vanishing into thin air? You can't be serious."

"Yeah, it's so fucked," Miles said, smiling, nodding. The hand slipped out from under Rosemont's and the odd, affectionate moment blinked out. "Fascinating shit, that dude in Sarajevo. He was the one who told me it was ancient, didn't even call it twelve steps, even though their gatherings were meetings where raging alcoholics and long-recovered addicts get together and they're free to talk about whatever they want. But all in this language of 'defending the city' and 'raising walls of protection'—the language of a discipline that had come out of a destroyed Bronze Age city, I came to realize, was a myth and a rite." Miles was quoting their old formula for whether a story was a true myth or just an old fairy tale: story plus ritual equaled myth. Miles laughed. "A living goddamn myth."

So often, talking to Miles was like trying to hold eight conversations at once. Still trying to parse the meaning of Miles's hand on his leg, Rosemont said, "Are you serious? You found a cult that had survived since the Bronze Age?"

"Preserved in the twelve steps like amber." Miles grinned. "Man, I've been wanting to talk to you about this for years."

Rosemont felt himself give a frowning smile. "What's the rite?"

"Disciplina etrusca. The Etruscan Discipline. The Etruscans built reality out of the smoking heaps of a chaotic world because the city they survived from had been destroyed. That was the Discipline's expressed mission—a postapocalyptic rite, you know? To create a place for the culture, the *city* to survive. Twelve-step meetings are now where their creation story is told person by person—a creation of self, sanity, and shared reality—which is what every creation story *is*. And what I was *after*. And I found it in the modern disciplina etrusca. But, oh, that's not all, boy, because—"

"Wait." Rosemont put his fingertips on his brow, concentrating. Miles had this effect on him. Rosemont didn't know where to begin questioning him about what he'd just said, how to backtrack and seize upon the thread of Priscilla's comment *(Remus? They were looking for Remus? Our Remus?),* or to eavesdrop on Marni and Priscilla who were definitely speaking the language that Marni had spoken previously, or how to interpret Miles's sudden show of affection, and then the disappearance of it. Walls of protection? Shared reality? A postapocalypse in the Bronze Age? It was like meeting Miles for the first time all over again, in the sideshow tent at the Circus of Infinite Wow and that swift engine of Miles's fecund theories, supernatural ponderances, surreal musings, and rambling asides, and Rosemont realized he had to grab on right now, jump aboard, or get left behind. So he grabbed on for the second time in his life. "Wait a minute. Bronze Age city and Etruscans?" said Rosemont, glancing at Marni. *Good lord, he can't mean what I think he means.* "What city?"

Miles smiled in appreciation. "You always zero in. It's like talking to a bird of prey, talking to Jeremiah Rosemont. That's right. E-truscans," whispered Miles, breaking up the syllables. "Ex-Trojans. Romulus and Remus were *ex-Trojans*. Descendants of them anyway. Descendants of Marni's culture. Charged with the task of rebuilding her city after the Trojan Diaspora, and that rebuilding effort is alive and well in Sarajevo. The wall-spell has been recovered. The city is still waiting to be built."

Hearing the names Romulus and Remus in Miles's voice shocked Rosemont into silence. Was Miles talking about their ridiculous myth, with babies saved from Texas rivers? No. He seemed completely serious. The names of the twins paralyzed him as if he'd been caught naked in a spotlight, and he immediately faced Priscilla to see if she'd heard what Miles had said. Priscilla had stopped conversing with Marni and sat listening to Miles, nodding, eyes cast sidelong at the older woman. He realized that Priscilla was gauging Marni's reaction, the way Rosemont was gauging hers.

Maddening, thought Rosemont. If it weren't for the two other people at the table who clearly regarded his old friend as an authority of some kind, Rosemont might have taken a deep breath and let loose on Miles for his absurd, soft-brained fantasy. Romulus and Remus were ex-Trojans? He might as well have said they were raised by bats in the wild, descended from highway-building angels. But Rosemont couldn't speak, couldn't challenge, ask, rant, nor mock, couldn't move his own mind to respond, because he couldn't explain anything that had happened to him since arriving in Rome. Of all things, why should Miles's irresponsible scholarship outrage him?

What is that? Is that real? the shorter of the two men had said, crouching, looking up at Rosemont's reflection in the mirror. He'd seen it, both men had, and they'd fled, not understanding what they were looking at, seemingly no more aware of what was happening than Rosemont. The only person who seemed to think they had a grip on this situation was John C. Miles.

Just hold tight, buddy, Miles had said a moment ago. *I think you'll get some answers in a minute here.* For the love of God, if these were answers, Rosemont thought he was better off running blindly into the streets to get away from this gibbering maniac.

But Marni obviously liked what she was hearing from Miles. She was warming to him. He had this magnetic effect on people—they either loved him or were repelled by him—and their decisions often turned on a dime. Rosemont knew because it was the same effect Rosemont had on people.

"I think we should drink a few drinks and eat while we discuss what Miles has shown us. Wouldn't that be diverting?" said Marni.

"Hell, yeah," Miles muttered, upper body bobbing in agreement.

Rosemont's stomach bobbed in agreement too. He still didn't know what to make of Miles's wild theories, but he hadn't eaten since the plane ride. "I'd like that."

"Um, *ekta*?" Priscilla said, crossing her arms. "It's not a good idea." Her eyes were on Miles. "No drinking."

"I get this from the twelve-steppers," Miles said, making

a wild-eyed face at Rosemont. "I apparently give off an 'addict vibe.' "

A waiter arrived just as Rosemont was about to ask if he could borrow some Italian currency from Miles. Everything about the waiter, even his mustache, looked pinched and irritated. On his tray were four plates of plain pasta and Collins glasses full of Campari. "The cheapest meal on the menu," he sighed, "all around."

Marni put her hand on the younger woman's arm. "You have been outvoted, apparently."

Priscilla smirked and picked up her fork. "You'll see."

For his part, Rosemont didn't care how the waiter knew to bring the meals or what drinks to pour. He pulled the plate close, twirled his fork in the pasta, and the rosemary-flavored olive oil drizzled over the plate smelled nourishing, fine.

Marni took another deep breath of the *templum* and said, "Before I agree that my traditions may have roots in Priscilla's and yours, Dr. Miles, I'll need proof. If it's as old as you say, how could no other tyros have seen this *templum*?"

"Because it was hidden in plain sight. That's the unique power of Remus, the magician who created it," Miles said as he picked up his fork, "and if my work hadn't been stolen, I could show you hard evidence of that." Miles bared his teeth in a frustrated smile, and then went on. "But there are three proofs that this *templum* is Remus's. The first is the Lemuria, which—"

"That was a Roman ritual honoring the dead, *ekta*," Priscilla said.

"Ach. I know what the Lemuria is," snapped the old woman and she put down her drink. Her gay mood had flipped on itself with Priscilla's comment, and her wrinkled face seemed to darken with anger. "But how can that possibly be a proof? It's not a ritual anymore. Just a quaint custom."

"The name itself is a proof," Priscilla said. "L's and R's were interchangeable. Lemuria is Remuria, meaning, *that which belongs to Remus.*"

Marni's creased lips pursed as she sipped from her glass. She set it down with a nod. "You called me from Istanbul for this?"

"But it *was* a ritual, once," Miles said. "This piazza was an ancient site of the Lemuria for honoring the dead twin, because it's the place where Remus read his augury for—well, in my notes, I have collected archaeological reports from the Museum of—"

"You have no *proof*?" said Marni with a disappointed scowl. "I'm supposed to simply believe you that there's a connection between Roman, Etruscan, and Trojan traditions? Because of etymology? What next? Genetics? My dears, evidence of cult and ritual are what I want and all that matters."

Staring at the old woman, Miles's jaw worked like he was chewing.

Priscilla caught his eye and rolled her hand in the air as if to say *Get on with it.*

They're looking for a cult? A Remus cult? Rosemont feigned total, famished absorption in his pasta, but he was hanging on every word in this conversation. He wondered if this was what Miles was trying to tell him in Atlanta, that he'd found something powerful, unexplainable. A cult. An occult practice of some kind. *There's more. There is so much more, Jeremiah.*

Still staring at Marni, Miles coughed, swallowing a snide comment, Rosemont imagined. "Well, I suppose that brings me to proof number two," Miles said. Seated on the corner of his chair in a pose of beseeching, Miles faced Marni with one knee up and the other bent, almost like a medieval ambassador entreating a powerful queen. Rosemont had never seen Miles so conciliatory, so appeasing. The smart-ass at the Atlanta conference, battering down his colleagues and grandstanding, was long gone. He was appealing to Marni for some reason, wanted her confidence, and obviously didn't like her scowling at him. "Do you know the story of Romulus and Remus, *ekta?* Or more specifically, how it ends?"

"Yes. It was told widely by the Romans themselves," Marni said in confusion and disgust. She lifted a gnarled hand as if offering something ridiculous to the air. "They used to *brag* that their founding hero killed his own brother. Immoral, from the beginning." She wiped her hands on her napkin. "The Greeks especially couldn't understand why Romans chose to tell such a horrible story about themselves."

"The best stories are too painful to ignore," Miles said. "Romans told this one because something strange happened the day Romulus killed Remus and they puzzled and worried over it for centuries."

Marni lifted her chin. "What happened?"

He hooked her, Rosemont thought with a smile.

"It happened the day of Rome's birth," Miles said. "Romulus and Remus were augurs, diviners, and they had held a contest to see who could determine the best place to build their new city. Romulus won the contest and began building a perimeter wall by cutting a circular trench around the tallest of Rome's seven hills," Miles said. "Well, Remus crossed that trench. He deliberately jumped across the trench that his brother was cutting with a plow."

"Yes," Marni said, "I'd always heard they were arguing about where the wall should be built."

"But, *ekta,* listen again to what Miles is telling you," Priscilla said, leaning forward and steepling her fingers. "A city founded by divination. A plow. A circle cut in the earth by a magician."

Marni's eyes remained impassive, but then they flashed. "Oh my." The old woman looked thunderstruck, fingertips lighting upon her chin. "It never occurred to me. I can't tell you how many times I heard that story. It never occurred to me what Romulus was doing."

"No one did," Priscilla said, "because no one was intended to know."

"What was he doing?" asked Rosemont, noodles draped over fork tines.

"He was casting the same spell cast the day that Wilusija—Troy—was founded," Miles said. "Romulus and Remus were members of the same occult sect that Priscilla belongs to, the Etruscan Discipline, which preserved the city-building magic of Troy, a cult dedicated to the construction of gates, walls, streets, and sewers," Miles said. "Romulus was resurrecting Troy."

Rosemont imagined he could feel mountain air, for a moment. Cool, invigorating breezes. *The templum,* he thought. Rosemont looked across the piazza at the sleepers on their benches. *I feel it.*

Marni nodded in appreciation, but then her scowl returned. "You still haven't told me. What is the strange thing that happened to Remus?"

"The strange thing that happened?" Miles said. "Nothing happened. When Remus jumped that magic circle, it should have killed or cursed him. But he survived."

"But neither did he destroy the Wilusijan spell by crossing the circle," Marni said.

"That wasn't his intent," Miles said. "Remus was simply showing his brother that he was protected by this *templum*." Miles hooked his finger and pointed at the ground. Then he crossed his arms. "He was showing him that he was the stronger magician."

"All right," Marni said. "I'll eventually want to see proof, but I'm stirred by your claim."

Rosemont couldn't believe it: Miles was bowing. He was bowing and averting his eyes. "Thank you, *ekta*," he said.

Rosemont was beginning to see it. It had all been rushing past him, at first, too fast to organize it in his mind. But now he was beginning to see a piece of this whole mad conversation, because he understood how Miles had come to this conclusion. It was their story of Remus. The Remus who had found a way out. In those days, Miles and Rosemont were seekers, looking for a peek behind the curtain of reality, unsure if they ever really could, but seeking, throwing cards, imagining—and Remus was the hero they invented, the would-be magician who'd leapt from this stifling world and into the unknowable beyond.

Rosemont understood what Miles was getting at when he'd said that tarot's imagery and structure had its roots in the occult purpose of the ancient triumphal parades of Rome. Those parades were all for Remus. Remus was being remembered, whether Romans realized it or not. Remus was being remembered in tarot, too, whenever the cards were shuffled, whether New Agers realized it or not. It all made sense now.

More, Rosemont had the distinct impression that Miles was standing on a cliff, a brink, and, with one step, he'd fall away from this mundane world. He was certainly further along than Rosemont, who'd run from the strangeness that followed him his whole life, seeking normalcy, not mysticism, not mystery. Miles was offering a hand to Rosemont, offering to pull him along, despite Rosemont's denial and embarrassment as a Very Important Scholar.

"So. How did you find it?" asked Marni. "How did you know the *templum* was here?"

Miles coughed uncomfortably and glanced at Rosemont. "I'm an occultist. I live with my eyes wide open. Always."

"Many do. That doesn't explain."

Miles said, "That brings us to my last proof. What I have to tell you now should really be kept confidential. Between us three," he said, pointing to Marni, Priscilla, and himself.

Rosemont sat back in his chair as if shoved. "What is this? Why?"

"Look," said Miles, "it's nothing personal, but you're here to be an impartial authenticator. It would defeat the purpose if I told you everything I have to tell Marni."

Rosemont had just been about to come clean. He'd finally felt he was getting some answers, and he'd been getting ready to reach down to get his backpack, remove the binder, and hand it to Miles finally. Now he felt betrayed, pissed, vindictive. "Sure. I'll just go powder my nose, is that it?"

Priscilla said, "Why can't he stay? We're all going to see the deck when—"

Miles shushed her. "Because the Monk asked me to be discreet."

"What monk?" Rosemont stared at Miles in disbelief. "What if I refuse? What if I stay here? What then?"

"You will eventually be vulnerable to Visconti and his toady Transom, the men who came for you in the apartment," Marni said, glaring at Rosemont, "because the sleepers will wake and the sacred *templum* will go back to being a little corner of Rome. We'll all be unprotected then. Let's get on with this."

Rosemont gave Miles his dirtiest look and then his chair scraped loudly as he stood up fast. "Unbelievable. Un—believable."

He took two long strides away from the table when he heard Marni hissing at him. He turned back and saw she had picked up his backpack and was offering it to him with a pointed look.

"Take this with you, while we discuss the Monk?" she said, and when he grabbed one shoulder strap, she held on just a little longer and said, "Thieves everywhere, you know."

He smiled at her. "Yes. There are," he said. "Okay."

The cardboard boxes of his dreams and horrors were open. Boy King had opened them himself, but after twelve years sealed, simply seeing the boxes undone quickened his pulse and jumbled his brain with fright.

Rippled sunlight fell around Boy King, cast down through antique glass. He'd let the rain go, let the morning sun come. A car door slammed—Farah coming home with a client (he could tell which one by the sound of the car door: the middle-aged introvert with the acne scarring. "Born to Run" would begin its nonstop cycle soon). For a long time, Boy King sat listening, making certain the wooden stairs hadn't squeaked, that no one was below the third-floor trapdoor, trying to open it.

A few moments later, when the E Street Band started its classic crash, Boy King decided things were normal, and from a leather bag produced a mirror and a red-and-black Mexican wrestling mask. Even touching mirrors made him nervous, but it was time to look at last into the crystal ball. Time to clarify what Lara couldn't, and do it before Visconti came knocking.

Boy King placed a chair at an angle, facing the wall, and then leaned the mirror upright in front of the chair, so that he could see the ground at a right angle through the mirror. Then he sat down and rested a wooden Art Deco poster for Riemann Hardware against his knees and dragged the cardboard box of his dreams and horrors in place on the other side of the poster. Deep breath. Deep breath. Then Boy King tugged the mask over his face, fabric stretched painfully across his broken nose. By reaching around the poster with both arms in a sort of embrace, he could look at his hands in the mirror and see the box. But he couldn't see the contents with his own eyes, not even in his peripheral vision—only in the reflection. The poster was in the way, so he couldn't see his trembling hands, and he was careful not to look at his own face, his own reflection.

Across the lot, Farah was shouting over Springsteen. "Dude! Dude! Aw, dude! Dude!"

Boy King removed the first small painting, hermetically sealed in its clear plastic casing, and showed it to himself in the mirror.

The workbench. The baker's hood. The unformed dough.

Or, from another point of view: the con man's table. The swooping hat of a deceptive foreigner. A piece of cloth covering something before him.

And from yet another: a ram-headed lord with long, wavy horns and two half-formed wads of soon-to-be-human clay on his potter's bench.

Boy King removed more paintings, also sealed. A hunter with his orange dogs; the skygazer and her beautiful twin stars; the delirious horseman—each still blazing in Boy King's mind from the day the Mad Monk had shown them to him.

Boy King raised another painting and looked at it through his angled mirror. The Arch. This image was the most terrifying of the thirteen ancient paintings, because whoever had painted it *knew.* Maybe the painter knew it from the *triumphator*'s vantage, passing beneath the arch into his city, or from the point of view of the trumped, that is, the captured enemy driven before the victor in abject humiliation. But the artist knew what it meant to yoke and be yoked. Red veins shooting through the arch's white marble like an old man's skin. Cruel, imperious sun overhead. Romulus's trench, dug by his plow for the spell and the wall to be. The raised shovel. The fallen brother. Spilled, innocent blood.

But what of the potter? How did that fit?

The con man?

Your consciousness can march only one thought at a time through the luminous doorway of your mind. To live, you assume that you must eliminate some thoughts or make a smear of them all into one manageable thought. One person with a single file of thoughts. One arch. That's the way of the human mind. But it's not our way.

Boy King kept the paintings in the cardboard box and gazed at them through the mirror so that they were framed within a frame. Narrowed. Controlled. Each painting was a point of power, a "lifting of the plow," to quote the Monk, a spot in the furrow where Romulus's wall would not be but a doorway would. These paintings were doorways, breaks in the ancient spell of Romulus the conqueror. Each painting, each card, was an image gazing out, just as Boy King was an image gazing in through the doorway at an image of himself gazing out—as a nine-year-old boy.

Madison, Wisconsin, is what he saw. He could see a woman walking up Broom Street's row of duplexes and flophouses, a nine-year-old boy in hand. Boy King knew those houses. He knew that street. He'd been hoping for answers about Visconti's plans or the whereabouts of those desert trackers, but this was welcome. Boy King hadn't known this woman as an adult, so to slip through the door of the ancient paintings and the doorway of this woman's mind was a precious gift. A treasure it was to scry his mother's mind.

She was holding her son's hand, praying for Vacancy signs, and Boy King could tell that Anita was absorbing how Madison had knuckled under. A tension seemed to be in people's bodies, she was thinking, not in the streets anymore. That curious mix of hairy veteran and hairy freak used to galvanize even casual encounters on the street corner back in the day, when his mother used to come here on weekends from Racine. She longed for that, he could tell. The students she passed now were altogether tidy, walking with purpose and edge, looking at the sidewalk before their feet, and never meeting her eye. The people here seemed less wild than the Madison she remembered of

1968, and the wildness was why she'd come, Boy King could tell.

Boy King sat staring in awe. He realized now that he hadn't had a mental image of his mother. He'd looked into her thoughts before, but not into her eyes, her face. Boy King liked how fierce she seemed, as she stood in front of a sprawling 1910 house holding her little boy's hand, reading a hand-printed sign.

COME TO VALHALLA COMMUNE. WE'RE A HOUSE OF 20–25 MEMBERS (AND 3 RADICAL CATS!) DEDICATED TO ALTERNATIVE LIFESTYLES, SMASHING PATRIARCHY, ANARCHICAL FOOD SYSTEMS, TOTAL GENDER EQUALITY, AND KIBBUTZ-STYLE LIVING.

"What's a commune?" asked her son, reading the sign. He was known as Finn back then, but he would have twenty different names before his time on Earth was done.

Anita pulled Finn up the stairs to the front door before he could ask about *anarchic* or *kibbutz* too. "It's a place where people work hard to change the world."

Finn sounded skeptical. "Here?"

For Boy King, this was the only place that ever truly felt like home and to see it now, feel it through his mother's pores as well as his own, was delicious. A playground within a playground, Valhalla was a beacon for dedicated nonsense and for young people seeking, like Finn's mother, to shuck off the pinching uniformity of their childhood homes. A child in this world was unique—not freak show unique, but cherished, fawned over. And Boy King could feel it, even from Bryce & Waterston. Young Finn had a never-ending supply of playmates who saw in the boy an avenue into pure whimsy that Madison's grown-up strangeness of toga parties and goofball, collegiate alcoholism only lamely approximated. Thyme was his favorite. She was an earnest young feminist who played "tarot stories" with Finn, making up involved, rambling tales about characters depicted in the cards.

As for Anita, her studies kept her busy to the point of exhaustion, and Thyme willingly took care of Finn in her absence. But, as Boy King watched, Anita's afternoons of reading Chaucer at Helen C. White Library eventually stretched into evenings of throwing pots at the campus art lab (after quick calls back to the house to ask if someone could put Finn to bed). The grown son, scrying his mother, hated and admired her for it. She was getting ready, after all, readying to take her next step: Racine, Madison, then away. Why shouldn't she? Why should this strong young woman tie herself down when late hours at the art lab could be allowed to stretch into real camaraderie like she'd never experienced before? Cigarettes and bottles of Point beer at the 602 Bar or the State Street Infirmary were waiting for her. Fellow students called her talented, praised her artwork, her politics, and asked her opinion on matters of the day, and part of Boy King felt that, after a decade of being chained to a cash register and a son in Racine, Anita *should* walk through whatever doors opened to her. But his brain was a blur of fury and panic watching her retreat unfold, as she followed bands on short road trips to Iowa City and Chicago, sleeping with the more tender morsels that came her way, and leaving her boy behind. On those trips, when she rode alone in her dilapidated Maverick, chasing a van or pickup loaded with amplifiers and drum kits, Boy King saw that she sometimes passed a figure on the darker highways, a character carrying a khaki backpack that she repeatedly saw on the hem of her headlights, standing still on the shoulder of the road.

Was it a ghost? A man? Was it waiting for her? If so, it wasn't clear why. Understanding these events and images in the ancient paintings wasn't like watching a DVD. To simply comprehend who the lurker along the cornfields was, Boy King had to stare through the painting's doorway until his brow and face dripped with sweat and the wrestling mask clung like a vise to his broken nose, making his whole face throb in agony.

When the truth came to him, finally, he saw, striding forward in the blast of light from his mother's headlights, Priscilla. The black V of her widow's peak was unmistakable, and she looked no younger than when he'd last seen her in Rome. Headlights blinked out, engine silent, Priscilla threw her backpack into the footwell and slipped into the passenger seat, the two women side by side in the perfect darkness of the car.

"It's over. The ram has found Valhalla," Priscilla said to Anita. "It's only a short while before they realize it's not Thyme who's at the center of things, Anita. You have to get out of there."

Anita cracked a window and lit a cigarette. "Anyone watching me thinks I'm a boozing student. It's perfect cover in that town."

"Good. But they've an alliance with federal agents who—"

"The circle is being cut, Pris. A couple biodynamic

back-to-landers out in Blue Mounds started it two weeks ago." As Anita spoke, she exhaled smoke through her nose. "Do we resurrect Jerusalem and create a place where the messiah will be born? Or hope the messiah will come and help us resurrect the city?"

"I hate your Sunday school analogies." Priscilla said nothing for a long stretch of darkness. Then she whispered, "Finn is watching us right now. Did you know?"

Boy King's hands almost let go of the painting.

Anita's cigarette curled smoke into the air. "How could that possibly be? Has Thyme—?"

"Probably. Or she will. But I don't know how," Priscilla said. She angled the rearview mirror, gazing about the car's interior with her scimitar brows arched, but her eyes never met his in the mirror. "Maybe it's another fragment of his self, but he is certainly here." Her hand drifted from the mirror and settled in her lap. "It doesn't matter. He won't understand the language we're speaking, anyway."

But through these paintings, Boy King *could* understand, and, coupled with Transom's revelation that he'd been tracking Thyme back in the seventies, Boy King realized with a burgeoning dread that his own connection to the Khnum cult was older and deeper than he'd ever known. They'd been tracking him his whole life.

"Do you see what has to happen?" Priscilla hissed. "If this alliance between these federal kings of America and the ram finds you two together, Anita, and determines who you are, they'll understand what he's capable of. Then, everything Thyme brought from Europe will be snuffed out."

Anita looked at the glow of her cigarette and flicked ash out her window. "And if they don't find us together?"

"Then, they'll think they're saving a normal little boy," Priscilla said, as if this were the best and obvious course. "They'll make him into that because that's what they'll think he is."

Anita shook her head in seeming resignation. "Fuck that."

"What they think is immaterial, *ekta*," Priscilla whispered. "Tell me what you think you should do."

Anita's words never came or maybe they were stolen from her by the silent highway's swallowing darkness.

Boy King could count on one hand the number of times he'd looked into these paintings, and every time he did it, his tyro mind was pried open a little more. But every time his mind was so opened by the *templum* and aperture of a painting, flocks of maddening questions flew in, whirling and batting inside his skull. His mother wasn't a boozing student? That was just "cover"? For whose benefit? The Khnum cult's? Boy King's? The government's? And if it was all an elaborate ruse, could he trust anything that he was seeing that couldn't be corroborated with his own memory? So thrilling and baffling, this drama, this world.

The women spoke a bit more about the Czechoslo-vakian plow that the farmers were using to cut the "circle spell," until finally, Priscilla slipped from the car, dissolved into the ponds and pools of shadow that lay across these fields, and Anita drove away as she did from each of these uncanny encounters, returning to Madison, back to class, to syllabi, textbooks, house meetings, and her all-too-real life with Finn. She was changed by these meetings with

Priscilla, Boy King could tell, irreparably, like a chameleon that couldn't quite shift back to her original hue. Until eventually, after one of these departures into the country, she simply didn't come home.

Her son never saw her again. Boy King remembered waking that morning to find her bed still made and no one in it. He'd called for Thyme, who'd become something like a second mother to him, and she came padding in to help him get ready for school. Rebecca Goldblatt, Boy King thought, watching her. Both Transom and Priscilla implied she was something more powerful than the gentle young woman who came in that morning to soothe Finn, lay out their cards and tell "tarot stories."

It wasn't that unusual for Anita to stay out well past Finn's waking hour, but when that first morning turned to night, and the first day became the second, everyone in Valhalla realized that something was terribly wrong.

Meetings were held and unbeknownst to them, the students and members of the house were being worked over in classic tyro fashion. Boy King knew it, understood that Thyme was using them to stonewall the circling forces that were on their way to Valhalla. He had always thought the houseful of wannabe Black Panther and communist students was simply overwhelmed by the task of what to do with an abandoned nine-year-old. But not so. He saw now that Thyme had engineered a tactical stand against the child welfare agents who came knocking with ram's heads embossed on briefcases and yoked police officers shambling through Valhalla's backyard at night. But it didn't take long for Finn's once idyllic childhood to come to an end after that. As if a last wall had finally collapsed, armed federal agents raided Valhalla and stormed through the maze of the old sorority-turned-fraternity-turned-commune—demanding young Finn and threatening everyone in the house with reckless endangerment of a child. To Boy King's own recollection, it seemed like a hazy movie montage, though he had one clear memory of a female agent in aviator sunglasses entering his room with two armed agents behind her, FBI blazoned in white across their blue jackets and T-shirts.

The boy was whisked away and all but airlifted to his grandparents' home where he was given a new name, his first of many aliases—and Valhalla Commune, tarot stories, Thyme, the Everybody Room, and the little candle of his Madison blinked dark.

Boy King wasn't quite ready to let his mother go, though. He understood her now less than he ever had before, so he turned his mind to a last comforting image of her, an image he enjoyed, at any rate. He presumed it was the night she was thinking of leaving. She was young and stern-looking, a serious woman sitting in the Crystal Corner on Willy Street, alone at the bar in a cocoon of cigarettes and pensiveness, "Interstellar Overdrive" by Pink Floyd thrumming on the house system (hammering drums, hammering drums), eight C.C. Riders in leather regalia just outside the front door, loudly hassling a passerby. That's the last Boy King could ever see of Anita, through the reflection of the painted Arch, a somber, quiet woman, nodding her foot to Floyd on the night that she just didn't come home to her boy, and never would again.

"You're still there," Boy King said into the mirror, to the Arch. "I can feel you through the plastic frame."

As Boy King watched, the colossal presence that dwelled in these paintings rushed toward him. He hadn't beheld this presence since Rome, hadn't dared to let it see him. Was it a god from the place where that arch had been constructed? Or perhaps a city loaded with gods, all of them yearning toward him now, with the swelling of a forward flowing tide? His mind wanted to scurry away and hide under something dark and heavy, but there was no retreat from this. He would see it finally. The presence had followed him his whole life, followed the golden thread that seemed to draw Boy King forward—to here and this. *A boy that the world had discarded, sitting as a grown man in a hidden, forgotten warehouse,* the waxing presence seemed to say. *But I never forget, and I never discard.*

"Are you Khnum?" Boy King said. "What are you?"

The great salvager. The mighty junk pile. Lord of recycling and reminding, in a world that prizes neither. I equalize your rubies with rubbish, raise your rubbish to rubies. Your world despises me. En ego dimidium vestri parsque altera voti.

"Who is coming for me?" Boy King asked in desperation. "Do you know? Someone more powerful than V? Can you tell me without symbols and metaphors and riddles?"

Boy King leapt at the sound of a clash, as if cymbals had crashed here in the third floor of his warehouse. The ghosts skittered back from him, retreating into the damp shadows and then, out and away.

Like that, it was gone, the presence in the old paintings washed away, a storm blowing itself into disquieting silence.

Boy King sat in the ghostless dark, wondering what had

happened and how safe he was, wondering over the vision he had just seen. Broom Street and Thyme. That Madison was so gone, and he longed for it, but he wasn't certain why, he realized.

Because it wasn't his.

It wasn't his Madison.

It wasn't his childhood memory.

Like a house painted upon a glass, that memory had been in his foremind for so long, but it didn't take much in the jarring, crashing wake of that enormous presence to see the transparent image for what it was.

Lies. Madison didn't happen to me. None of that. My mother's name wasn't Anita. Where did this painful, pretty childhood come from, whose was it, and why do I think it's mine?

He tried to see past the painted glass, but he couldn't see his own parents or childhood friends. How had this happened? Had his look into the paintings all those years ago cracked his mind and created this false childhood? Had Rome done this to him?

It wasn't completely false, though. There was something, someone familiar in this vision: Priscilla, the woman he'd last seen in Rome over a decade ago. But what was she doing, haunting that Illinois highway like a figure from an old Midwest ghost story, talking to that false mother Anita in her car and then vanishing again? The familiar face wasn't reassuring to Boy King. The image of her standing along dark cornfields was unsettling and put a quiver of anxiety in his chest. A piece of Rome here. The vision of a strange childhood there. It was all jumbled and scrambled like too many jigsaw puzzles dumped together.

Boy King looked at Transom's oversized binder, wondering if the stack of paper within held remedies, possibilities.

"Christ," he said, opening it. "It's like Rome all over again."

11

Rosemont sat in the restaurant's restroom stall, backward on the closed commode, facing the cracked-plaster wall. He had Miles's red binder open on the tank, using it as a little desk. Presuming the *templum* protected him from the two men whom Marni had called Visconti and Transom, Rosemont took time to absorb information from Miles's binder. Marni had mentioned that she, Priscilla, and Miles would discuss someone called "the monk" while he was gone; so Rosemont thumbed through the pages until the word caught his eye in a translated journal. It was accompanied with a fax marked by four coffee cup rings.

FAX

Prof. John C. Miles
Room 648
Hotel Garibaldi
5 pages to follow
February 6, 2003

Miles,

I found this document in an archive dump that Ligget
& LaSalle acquired from Milan's Biblioteca Mansutti
(a library devoted to the history of insurance in Italy!
Amazing what gems Europe has in its collections of
garbage). I think you'll find this one especially interesting. As you suspected, Visconti betrayed the Mad
Monk (whose name is di Trafana). This is also the
earliest reference we've found regarding di Trafana's
deck.

In this fax you'll find copies of both the three original diary pages written in April of 1425 by a contracted officer-for-hire (*condotierre*) and a translation
conducted by Dr. Rita Boris at the University of
Nottingham.

By the way, your last letter arrived opened. Future
correspondences should be faxed if possible.

Sincerely,

Everett

THE CONDOTIERRE'S JOURNAL

April 8—I have come to believe that the astrologer, di Trafana, is plotting some hardship upon our beloved Duke. Chiefly, I believe di Trafana is the papal spy that F. warned me about.

I cannot convey how suspecting this warms the cellars of my cold, old heart.

April 17—The astrologer received my gifts and letter, as I'd hoped. My plan is to seek his advice about a costume for the Duke's approaching March of the Triumphs.

No one knows very much about this foreigner with a Milanese name (di Trafana), though I have asked about him extensively among Duke Visconti's other *condotierri*. He apparently comes from Rome, but he does not share a Roman's typical love of the Vatican.

April 25—The astrologer has agreed to help me with my costume for the March of the Triumphs, which is a great ease to my mind, since he has actually read Petrarch, whose poem *Il Trionfi* will be the influence for this festival, and I cannot stomach modern poetry. But more important, he has the complete confidence of Visconti, and I must ingratiate myself to the Duke.

Questions before me: Does the Duke suspect this di Trafana of intrigue as I do? The astrologer is the logical candidate, as he is a foreigner. If the Duke does not suspect him, why does he not? Perhaps the Duke knows nothing of the Holy See's moves against him. Could I be so fortunate?

April 26—Last night di Trafana received me in his chambers—in the very Citadel of Milan where dwells Visconti himself, and I experienced a most startling evening.

My first indication that the visit would proceed strangely was the complete absence of halbardiers or partisans. We would be speaking alone—a highly unusual occurrence in the Citadel, the Duke's castle of a thousand eyes. Di Trafana's chambers were filled with books and charts, but also works of art, blocks of wood for making woodprints, pots of paint and ink, and other such frivolities.

He is indeed a curious man. Petulant and easily annoyed, di Trafana could turn in a moment and wax Jovian the next. This irregular demeanor was apparent from the start. When I arrived, di Trafana invited me to ingest an intoxicant that he called simply *murm*, but I declined. Then he asked if I might like to dance while he sang. Again, I made an excuse. I wondered if this were madness, but as our initial conversation progressed into more familiar matters, I determined this behavior indicated military genius, conducting himself with unpredictability in order to keep me, a rival in the Citadel's game of influence, unbalanced and unsure.

When matters turned to the ball and *Il Trionfi*, di Trafana said that selecting a costume would say as much about me as selecting armor or heraldry might. Parlor games for women and bored courtiers, to be sure, but I yearn to impress, so I bid him tell me more.

At this juncture, he interrogated me: "Which is more important, wisdom or power?"

Thinking that he was either seeking to flush out a traitor on the Duke's behalf or interviewing a potential conspirator, I decided to test him. "Power leads to wisdom as a course of nature," said I. "One need only examine a line of men like the Viscontis for proof."

At this, di Trafana grew agitated. "The most powerful are typically unknowing and darkened of mind, I have at last come to understand."

I asked him if he were referring to Duke Visconti.

Di Trafana said that the line of the Viscontis was weak, that the current Duke was revealing himself to be a shortsighted man. I found it extraordinary that the astrologer would unveil his mind to me thusly, as he was a foreigner and his position in Milan precarious, even if he currently enjoyed the love of the Duke. Seeing a potential ally against our common benefactor, I asked him if he was considering leaving the Duke's service.

Di Trafana said no, he hoped to yet convince the Duke to embrace what di Trafana called "the legacy of Rome."

I thought that at last, here was the conspiracy, so I asked if this "legacy" weren't a papal scheme. "Has an infiltrator from the pontiff arrived in the Citadel, then?"

A conspiracy of the order that di Trafana then described, I had never dreamed upon. "You think power sits in the Vatican," di Trafana said to me. "Even as you rebel against that office, you northerners hand the pontiff power. But I refuse. I refuse to see that office as anything but mine."

The statement was incredible. "You wish to be the pontiff?"

"I *am* the pontiff," said he. "The pope is nothing but an impostor. Long before the coming of the Christians and their Hanged God, I was pontifex—'the sacrificer on the bridge'—and I was responsible for reminding Rome of its legacy. I threw little boys made of bulrushes down into the Tiber River so that all might remember what we'd lost, what we'd become. Do you know who was thrown? Do any now recall?"

I said that I knew the old nursemaid tales as well as any. "Romulus and Remus, the babies who were saved from the Tiber River and nursed by a she-wolf." To show I understood the significance, I said, "The founders of Rome."

"Romulus," di Trafana said in contempt. "He was in no need of being remembered in our rituals, for his name is synonymous with Rome. But the other boy—Remus. He we gave back to the water in memory. He was the greater magician, reader of lightning, and seer. Even in death, he proved himself so. To embrace this legacy is to upend the Vatican, the pope, and to rock the walls of Romulus."

But the breadth and scope of this endeavor, a conspiracy to break the twin lock of Rome and Vatican upon the northern city-states, left me breathless in my contemplation of it. "How might we 'rock the walls of Romulus,' astrologer?"

"By finding the lost twin who hides in plain sight. There lies our power and wisdom." Di Trafana then removed from a richly carved, dark wooden box a small pile of cards, neatly stacked. I know cards for playing games of chance among my Turkish mercenaries, of course, but there seemed to be a mere fifteen or so in total. What game could be played with them? They were drawn with almost a cleverness that one might call artistic, I suppose, and exceedingly beautiful, or so it would appear to my eye. "Behold, the legacy of Rome. Remus is here," he said, holding the cards facedown, "and fools and magicians are made with a mere glance, herein—and new humans too."

I presumed he meant that in the cards a code for communicating with conspirators had been secreted. F. told me last month in Venice that the Holy See fears Duke Visconti's control of water (fresh supplies and ease of navigation, both) in northern Italy, so di Trafana's open slander against the Duke and the Vatican made sense to me, but I was ruminating over his claims of long life and "creating humans" too. Had he spoken metaphorically when he said that his life and this secret society were ancient? Perhaps he did not mean himself literally, but the cause, the endeavor. Though it also could have been that the astrologer was making sport of a doltish *condotierre*. I decided to ignore that part of his story in hopes of learning what resources di Trafana had at his disposal for accomplishing his titanic plot.

"I have been looking for unleashed, free humans all my long life in a thousand cities that have risen and fallen. And I thought it would be now, in this lawless era, one of the Dukes or daughters of this line, the Viscontis." The astrologer said that he prized fearlessness, a certain darkness of spirit, and an unfettered joy in life that years ago the Viscontis exhibited to the astrologer but that has been otherwise bred out of humankind. "This duke," he said, and I realized by the way he slurred his words that the astrologer was perhaps intoxicated by the *murm*. "This

Filipo Maria. The only thing dark and unfettered about him is his unchecked lust for murder. He has joined with a wicked cult of foreigners, the Chanoume, who seek to erase the legacy of Rome." Di Trafana then showed me a profane symbol carved upon an old piece of wood and that dangled from a necklace.

I was being swept up into something larger than I had ever imagined, a conspiracy older than the Vatican, older, it seemed, than Rome. "Perhaps I could be a student of yours," I said, using what I assumed were his code words for conspirators. "I wish to be a magician in the service of the legacy of Rome."

Di Trafana looked at me hard and laughed. "You are ridiculous. You don't have any notion what such a statement might mean."

I bared my mind to him and I said that I was prepared to move against Visconti, that I had partisans who could be called up at a moment's notice. If Visconti had foreign allies, I had stout Italians to face them.

Di Trafana laughed again and said, "You are absurd. You elect to see what's remembered in the cards? You want to see why Romulus slew Remus?" I assured him that I did, that I was worthy of his secret society's confidence. He laughed at me again and turned the top card over, showing me the first pictorial message, that of a shepherd gazing at a star. I found it potent, as if the lines with which it was drawn were etched upon my mind as I looked. But then I saw that it was not a shepherd as I'd first thought, but a picture of the pope in his red robes, holding keys and standing before two acolytes. I asked the astrologer what trick this was. He said nothing and simply watched my reactions like an old soldier watching a younger try his first ale. But now that I write these words, I am struck anew. I wonder now if what I saw were not a completely different picture, that of a ram standing upright like a man with horns not unlike the one that the astrologer had shown me.

If this was the power of the legacy of Rome, then I was convinced, I told di Trafana, and I was dazzled, and I told him that if any attempt to stop us were...

April 27—Fowl, the very smell of fowl. Herein to be the uppermost then. Teas of loss and shipwrecked faith. Will that penis pierce the sun? If only I could see you once more in your capes of wanton lizard scales. Suppress the olive trees and lay flat the canals and undo the word as it was spoken then to Carthage and Jupiter and wafts of castles washed over with milk and orange.

(What follows are seven or eight entries written over one another in different colored inks over many months, all in the same handwriting as the earlier entries. So the *condotierre's* journal ends.—Everett.)

Rosemont wanted to keep reading, but he was beginning to feel conspicuous about how much time he was spending in the restroom. Oddly, looking at the one page of scribbling, mad journal entries that Everett had sent Miles made him feel for the first time that he had a grasp on the situation, slight and shaky as it might be, that he at least understood what these people believed was at stake with the Mad Monk's deck: the legacy of Rome. He didn't completely understand the ancient grudges, why Miles had asked him to leave when talk turned to the monk or whether the Visconti in this centuries-old journal was the same Visconti whom Rosemont had seen in the apartment. But the deck in question sounded wondrous, ominous, and he understood why these people would be intrigued by it. Now Rosemont felt like he had enough of a peek behind the curtain to go back, join the table, and play dumb if he had to. He wanted to see this deck of di Trafana's, if that's what they wanted him to see. He wanted to see how this puzzle fell together, if it did at all.

Hoisting his backpack onto one shoulder, Rosemont stepped out of the stall and moved toward the door, holding up one hand to shade his eyes against the twisted thing that continued to seethe and stare at him from the mirror. He considered pausing to wash his hands, but didn't want to risk looking in the mirror over the sink, and instead fished in his pocket for change to leave in the basket.

A moment later, the restroom door opened, and distantly, the festival's cacophony hummed louder for a moment, and then went quiet as the door swung shut.

Rosemont didn't see who'd entered. He was turned at a ninety-degree angle, looking at his change, a handful of Nicaraguan coins. He couldn't leave those. They were worthless.

"Pardon me. Are you Professor Jeremiah Rosemont?"

Out of the corner of his eye, Rosemont saw a stocky little fellow all in bright green. The body of a Kermit the Frog costume. No mask. "And you are?"

The man reached under his frog-green shirt and said, "Drop your backpack."

With a strange sense of disconnect, Rosemont realized

a gun was being yanked out from under the ridiculous costume and pointed at him. Coins in his flat palm, he looked at the man from under his brows. "What?"

"Put down your backpack and please open it."

Rosemont glanced at the door and saw that the man had locked it. No hasty exits, then. Rosemont closed up the coins in his hand and unshouldered his backpack, setting it on the floor between them. The walls of the restroom simultaneously expanded and contracted, but Rosemont felt surprisingly calm. The fistful of coronas was growing slick in his hand, but he was otherwise keeping his panic at bay.

"Please," said the man, stepping forward, gun still trained on Rosemont, "open your backpack—now. Quickly."

Rosemont did as he was told, squatting and unzipping the pack. "I haven't had money for laundry for a few days, so you better stand back. It's a little ripe in here." Beneath the shirt, socks, and pants, the red binder was stashed. "My socks don't match. Is that a problem?"

The man glanced into the open backpack. "No book? No collection of historical documents? No diary?"

Rosemont stood, shaking his head no.

"Empty it."

Rosemont looked down at his clothes. "You don't believe me about the socks?"

"Empty the backpack, Professor Rosemont. Hurry."

Now that the shock of seeing the gun was wearing off, his breathing even, Rosemont realized he had nothing to lose. It was the very same sensation he had when anyone shook him down for money on highways in Central America—a quiet, smirking invulnerability.

So he reached out with the hand holding the coins,

as if to pick up the backpack, then, while grabbing the man's eyes with his own, let the coronas slip through his fingers.

The coins hit the tiled floor, loud and musical in the little bathroom, and Kermit flinched, his eyes dropping to the clatter.

As soon as Kermit lowered his gaze, Rosemont slapped the man's gun hand, but he failed to loosen his assailant's grip.

Gun barrel pointed off to the right, Kermit looked up into Rosemont's face. But he didn't look furious or cold-hearted.

He was scared.

So Rosemont backhanded the man's face and sent him sprawling against a square garbage can. Then he immediately pounced on Kermit, prying the gun out of his hand and delivering two quick blows to his mouth. Rosemont backed away from him, gun aimed at the man's chest.

Slumped against the garbage can, which leaned askew against the wall, the man kept dabbing at his lip with fingers, looking for blood. "The fuck. They told me you were a fag teacher."

Rosemont snapped, "I'm *not* a teacher."

"Okay. Well. You're not a tyro, either."

"And?"

The man looked up at Rosemont with aggrieved curiosity, his combed-over black hair sticking up like a bird's crest. His eyes lowered to the open backpack for a moment. "So why would you risk me shooting you over your clothes?"

"I knew you wouldn't shoot," Rosemont said. "You aren't desperate enough to shoot."

The man struggled to his feet, looking down at his fingers as if he now felt betrayed that he wasn't bleeding. "That's probably true. But I didn't think you'd attack a guy with a gun."

It surprised Rosemont too, but bandits who'd jump a *norteamericano* on a desolate mountain road or raid a small coffee farm for cash made this little interaction seem downright civil. "What were you looking for?"

The man had soulful green eyes that couldn't seem to mask a single thought. They now gleamed at Rosemont with confusion and wonder. "Are you for real?"

Waiting for Kermit to remember he had a gun trained on him, Rosemont stared.

"Visconti and Transom sent me looking for your collection, of course," said the man, warily. "That is—"

"*My* collection?" Rosemont thought Kermit was after Miles's binder. What other reason would Rosemont have had to be in that apartment? What did they think was happening here? "What are you talking about?"

"Unless..." Kermit's glance skimmed over to the mirror and his moist eyes widened slightly, then back to Rosemont.

He sees it too. Rosemont could feel the supernatural reflection staring at him from the mirror. He allowed himself a peripheral glimpse, and a hulking, fractiled animal face was there, panting.

"Unless you didn't *know* you're a tyro," Kermit said, a vague smile on his face.

"That thing just started appearing in my reflections recently," Rosemont whispered. "What the hell is it?"

"Some of us have been waiting years to see our tyro selves. You see it, but don't even know what you're looking at. Are you here for the Watts deck or not, faggot?"

Rosemont's fury and confusion of the last several days came swooping out of him, and he pressed the gun barrel against Kermit's brow. He pushed until the man saw something frightening in Rosemont's face that wilted his posture. "You keep calling me that."

Kermit was backed against the trash can again, eyes scrunched shut, and his face turned away from the gun barrel.

"But *you're* the one in the lime-green onesie," Rosemont said. He pulled back, but kept the gun in Kermit's face. "Let's cut to the chase. Tell me what you think the Watts deck is."

Kermit stammered, his obvious terror bubbling over. "It's—it's too—there's so much. I can't even answer that, there's so much."

"I understand it's thought to have roots in, um—Wilusija. Maybe it's an Etruscan item?"

Kermit's eyes fluttered in perplexity and searched Rosemont's face. "You've already been in touch with Dr. Miles or Priscilla, then." His eyebrows furrowed and his face twisted in a sneering, derisive smile. "Well, I suppose they told you their asinine theory. Dr. Miles is such a loudmouth, debating with you about tarot in public forums, disclosing ancient mysteries to the grant boards of Ligget & LaSalle. Moronic. He's lucky he wasn't put down like a rabid dog years ago."

Miles has been on this hunt longer than I realized. "You don't buy his theory?"

Kermit laughed, then stopped and looked at Rosemont as though to see if it was okay to laugh. "His Magicians Anonymous bit? Occult self-help? No, I don't buy that any more than I imagine you do. Not that I'm paid to think," he said almost arrogantly. "I'm the gossip."

"So let's gossip," Rosemont said. "What do others say about this deck?"

"Oh my God," said Kermit. "You don't know?"

"No."

Kermit stared up at Rosemont in disbelief. Finally, he seemed to decide that Rosemont wasn't toying with him. "That idiot. Can I have been so lucky?" said Kermit. "He was probably too eager to gush about his own theories, right? Monologuing on and on about mystical drunks in Sarajevo? Christ. He hasn't told you anything about the war?"

"What? With Iraq?" said Rosemont. Even coffee farmers had news of Desert Storm.

"No," said Kermit. "I mean the disagreement over the Watts deck."

Rosemont tightened his grip on the gun. "What are you talking about?"

"There is great disagreement over what the deck might be, no matter what Miles and Priscilla might have told you," Kermit said, as casually as if they had a couple of cappuccinos between them, not a gun. "Those accounts that are remotely credible say the deck is a bit like a mirror, an echo of the mind. Tyros see what they want to see when they look at the deck, so they must be very careful not to make too many assumptions, or they start seeing their own selves, their own desires and fears bounced back at them.

And the real challenge is to see the mirror, the deck, not the reflection."

"So that's why they want an authenticator?" Rosemont said. "They want someone without presumptions to come and look at the mirror, see the deck for what it is, if they can?"

"Yes, I think that's the plan. But everyone has presumptions," said Kermit with a derisive toss of his head. "Over the last few centuries, tyros from various traditions have sought audience with the deck's owner, an insane monk, in order to see it, to make a claim to it, if they might. The Spanish Moors, for example, say Watts was created by their occult mathematicians in the glory days of the Alhambra. The Coptic tyros say it's a gnostic Christian curio. Miles and Priscilla now say it's an artifact of Trojan and Etruscan divination, maybe Hittite too, and whatever else Miles has in his junk-drawer brain. But the Muslims, Nubians, even the Iranians—forgive me, the *Ayurvedic Babylonians*—all stake their claims to the Watts deck. All so predictable and childlike, really. But then there is the eldest." Kermit gave him a knowing look. "Have you ever heard of the Khnum?"

"The Khnum?" Rosemont shook his head.

"Oh, this is too much fun."

"What is the Khnum? A person?"

"No one knows. But it's drawn as an imposing figure, maddening in its strangeness. Tall, stately," Kermit said, "a human with a ram's head."

"What?" Rosemont scoffed. Kermit almost had him with his foreboding preamble. "Are you fucking serious? Like goat man?"

Kermit gasped and shook his head once, hard. "I

wouldn't joke like that if I were you. We're talking about something older than anything *named*."

Rosemont tried picturing this, a man with a ram's head. "Is this a god? You don't mean the Egyptian god Ammon, do you?"

"No. Ammon was drawn with the typical curved-horn ram's head." Kermit made a spiral in the air with his index finger. "Khnum is so old that the species of sheep drawn upon its head is now extinct—the flat-yet-wavy-horned ram." To illustrate, Kermit held out index and middle finger horizontally, fluttering them.

The symbol that the condotierre *drew,* Rosemont thought. The foreign cult that di Trafana talked about, that this person Visconti supposedly joined, was a Khnum cult.

"It comes from the Upper Nile," Kermit said, and he was speaking now with a scary eagerness, "but long before that region was farmed or fished. Khnum created humans. He wanted men to be more than herd animals. He didn't want to see them diminished by becoming cattle trapped in civilization or, worse, a race of fools, led astray by deceivers. Like the Ayurvedic Babylonians, the Blackleaf 23 addicts, or John C. Miles."

"I don't get it," Rosemont said. "This is just a total right angle from everything that—"

"It's not a right angle. I'm telling you about the source of all the strange occurrences you've no doubt seen since coming to Rome." Kermit's eyes darted to the restroom mirror and back to Rosemont. His tone shifted from that of an eager, incorrigible gossip to a babbler. "The strange events that have perhaps followed you your whole life? The helpers who are drawn to you in your time of need?

The people who bend to your will without you even trying? The fires, the disappearances, and then, the very same helpers who loved you turning on you in ways you can't control?" Those expressive green eyes glowed at him.

Rosemont couldn't hide his surprise. "How do you know about all that?"

"Because that's the way of Khnum's best creations. I see it in your reflection, one as powerful as you. The creator god stole for the strongest of us the ability to control the elements, dreams, and other human beings. That's humanity's ancient gift from the Khnum. Lesser humans are susceptible to the powerful, like me speaking now. It's not the gun making me talk. I can't help it," said Kermit, placing a hand flat against the wall behind him as though to see if he were still cornered. "You, in turn, are compelled by that which is more powerful than you whether you know it or not. The Khnum coaxed a strong one like you to come from very far away."

Rosemont was confused. The Khnum sent the messenger to Managua? "How did it compel me? With a letter?"

"No. It compelled you with the Watts deck, of course. It may be in the hands of the Mad Monk. It may be the obsession of John C. Miles. But that deck was created by the Khnum."

Rosemont didn't trust this man who'd come looking for him with a gun, had no reason to believe this story over Miles's—but he couldn't deny that the fellow offered semi-tangible explanations of all this bizarreness, where Miles, Marni, and Priscilla offered only more bizarreness. They offered intriguing stories and demonstrations of extraordinary strengths like Priscilla's shifting run through Roman streets, but ultimately, the elements of the mystery only deepened the mystery. Was Marni born in the Bronze Age? Was there a line between the "legacy of Rome" and what seemed to be a legacy from Troy? Did it involve the Watts deck? Kermit's explanation squared with the *condotierre*'s story—Duke Visconti had abandoned di Trafana's Remus cult for a foreign cult of some kind, presumably because it was more powerful, or power-centered—and it squared, more important, with Rosemont's own experience. Somehow Kermit seemed to know about the kind of events that had eroded the last vestiges of a normal life in Austin, explained Rosemont's strange life to him. Marni, Priscilla, and Miles barely explained anything, let alone why it involved him at all.

"Do you know why it's called the Watts deck?"

"No," said Rosemont.

"It's named for the tyro whom the Mad Monk allowed to look into the deck about a century ago," Kermit said, "a man whose mind was shattered and who spent the rest of his days in a sanitarium."

"I guess all tyros aren't created equal, according to the Khnum," said Rosemont.

"No. And frankly, no one cares if you lose your mind, either, Mr. Rosemont," said Kermit, smiling up at him. "In fact, they're counting on it. Even John C. Miles is."

"What do you mean?"

"They're assuming you'll go mad when you look at it, and wisely so," Kermit said. "Look, long ago, civilization was just a collection of campfires seething along rivers like a line of fever blisters. The Khnum succeeded for millennia in keeping civilization small, interconnected with one another through dreams and what we would now call madness. But civilization is a virus that his creation contracted. It spread out of control, and Khnum couldn't stop it, try as he might, and now there are more humans than Khnum ever thought there should be. So the Khnum continues to shape humanity and discard the waste like a potter's hand shaking off unneeded clay. Finding the beautiful, the strong. That's what the Watts deck is for. Of those who look into it, the deck separates the momentous from the superfluous—magicians from fools, as the Khnum once said." When he finished, Kermit examined Rosemont carefully, as if weighing what impact his words might have had on him.

"What if I keep my marbles?" Rosemont said.

"Then your ability to authenticate it or debunk it is icing on the cake," Kermit said, "as far as they're concerned."

It seemed cold and calculating for John C. Miles. Erratic and wanton, those were Miles's words. Sending a friend into the dragon's maw, to prove a theory, didn't seem like Miles's style.

And, yet, wasn't this whole escapade erratic, wanton? Hadn't Rosemont been brought to Rome as part of some capricious fling, like getting roped into one of Miles's cross-country benders or epic parties? *Isn't this the best time you've ever had?* Maybe. Or maybe he'd get tortured and killed. Who knows? It all seemed to be the same to Miles.

Why *was* Rosemont here, why had he been called, and how much of these various competing mythologies were just bullshit, anyway? Did Kermit the Frog believe a word of what he was saying? An Egyptian god with an extinct sheep for a head? Impossible to tell what was true, what was a lie, and what was intergenerational paranoid schizophrenia. Simply because unexplainable events were occurring didn't mean that there wasn't room for deception. Let alone self-deception. Or madness.

"I just don't understand why it makes a bit of difference what I think," said Rosemont. "I mean, I'm a friend of Miles's and an old colleague. But why me?"

"For whatever reason, you are the authenticator, and authenticity," said Kermit, dabbing a spot in the air between them with his middle finger, "is power. Historical documents. Letters. Scraps and snatches of history that most historians dismiss or discard. An artifact like the Watts deck is too luscious to ignore, try as many of them might to simply forget or discount. But every few decades, it rears its head again. So your opinion about it will matter more than any other." Kermit peered at him. "Assuming you haven't been swayed by Miles already."

"I can make up my own mind," Rosemont said. "I'm not Miles's slave."

Kermit shrugged. "Good, then my mission wasn't a total loss, as I first feared. At least I managed to taint the impartial judge with doubt."

Rosemont laughed in his throat. "I'm not your slave, either."

"No?" said Kermit, and his demeanor changed again, now sounding bemused, harsh. "I beg to differ."

Wary of this shift in tone, Rosemont raised the gun. "What do you mean?"

"Don't think of a ram's head. Right now," Kermit said in a voice dripping with sarcasm. "Stop thinking of a ram's head, Professor Rosemont. Go on. Ram's head, ram's head, ram's head. Get it out of your mind, if you can."

Each time Kermit said the word, Rosemont saw a Dodge truck logo. Or a St. Louis Rams helmet. Or a nature show snippet with mountain rams raring to bash each other's heads in. He couldn't help it.

"Oldest trick in the tyro playbook," Kermit said, edging sideways toward the door. "I'm in your head for good now."

Rosemont felt a wave of panic that he was being bested in some way that he didn't understand, and as Kermit flicked the lock open on the bathroom door, Rosemont raised the gun. "Stop."

Kermit's eyes met Rosemont's for a moment, and then he seemed to see something that made him smile. He reached over and lifted the hook out of its eye on the door.

"Stop," Rosemont shouted, again pointing the gun in Kermit's face.

But a second later, the man in green was darting out the door.

Helplessly, Rosemont watched him go. What was he going to do, fire indiscriminately into the café? Kill him? No, Kermit had seen what he'd seen and Rosemont couldn't deny it: he wasn't going to kill the man.

Well, that wasn't entirely true, he thought, scooping up the backpack. He had gotten through the would-be shake-down with Miles's binder still in his possession, and a gun, which he stuck in his waistband under his jacket, and he now had more information about what was happening than he'd had before.

Reaching out to open the restroom door, Rosemont noticed his hand was quivering slightly on the doorknob. He lifted his hand and angrily made a fist. "Get on top of this," he scolded himself. "Get on top."

12

Boy King rubbed his eyes with his fingertips, careful not to touch the orbital bones of his brow or his cheeks, and then went back to reading Transom's collection. He sat with his back to a central chimney, reading in a dim pool of light from one of the high windows, a little splash of light from Minneapolis's skyline, and he could actually see his nose pulse as he read. He wished he could put down this book. Sleep. His whole body needed rest, from his nose to his liver, and he was hungry too. But his last dollars had been spent on numbing himself through the worst of fixing his broken nose, and in any event, he couldn't run off to get more booze, even if he had the money. There wasn't time to sleep or eat. It wouldn't be long before Visconti or someone scarier came searching to flush him out of his warehouse. Boy King had to read this collection fast and find any advantage he could against his hunters.

But he felt like a mouse peering through fangs into the predator's maw, reading the text before him. The cult of Khnum was so old in comparison to Boy King's Etruscan Discipline, that even the oldest citations from this collection talked about the cult as ancient. Many of the documents referred to other members of the sect, some of whom were apparently older than Transom and Visconti. Visconti had been born late in the fourteenth century, Boy King knew, and his strengths were far beyond his own imaginings. It frightened Boy King to think of the mastery of a tyro who might have been born when the cult was young and Egypt was not yet Egypt.

In a letter regarding something called the Westcar Papyrus, Boy King read about an account of Pharaoh Cheops (known in Egypt as Khufu: "Khnum Protects Me") who witnessed a challenge between magicians, one of whom was the ram-headed god in disguise. Afterward, Khufu abandoned his kingship in order to seek the long-lost "father of Khemet," and the text seemed to imply that Cheops-Khufu was still alive today. This was followed by a translation of a Greek diplomat's stories of Khnum haunting the Library of Alexandria as something of a god of censors, building the collection there as a librarian-priest while destroying evidence and citations of rival sects and creating secret paths for the "open-eyed." A footnote from the translator claimed that the god himself still found archives sacred, still haunted them in Washington, D.C., and London.

Boy King found himself getting sucked into the more "modern" accounts, however. He liked reading about the

lowly observers after the Renaissance who began provid-
ing accounts of brushes with the god or his tyros in
Europe, when an emerging Enlightenment and pounding
normalcy should have quashed such observations. In the
seventeenth-century journal of a *coureur de bois,* a woodsman and pre-voyageur traveling in "New France," a brush
with the ancient cult was described. The woodsman had
been found guilty of gambling at Fort Frontenac in what
was now Canada and had been sent home to cool his heels.
He was working the shipyard taverns and waterfronts of
Marseilles, seeking passage back to the Americas, when he
found a man named Baron who wanted to hire a *coureur
de bois* to guide him to a certain New World river.

The Dakota called it the Meschasipi and its length had yet
to be measured by Europeans, I told him. Baron asked if I
knew its source and were there cataracts? I did not know,
but I'd heard that the famous explorer La Salle was interested in finding the Great Water's source and, after garner-
ing another round of drinks from this exceedingly ugly
fellow, I told him that if he could purchase our fare to
Quebec, I could get him an introduction with La Salle.
This was a lie, but as it turned out, I did make this happen. So in hindsight, it was the truth. May Jesus have
mercy.

I asked Baron why he was concerned with the Great
Water, and he told me an alarming tale. He said he was an
astrologer and that he had determined in his charts and
calculations that a creature called le Cannoume could be
found in the New World. This was a secret that he alone
had determined, that others who sought le Cannoume
were looking for it in Egypt and among the Turque in

Anatolia, the sultanate of l'Orient. But these others did not know the power of astronomy, as it had come to be called, a new science that these ancient charlatan magicians knew nothing of, and Baron alone had determined that the search for the Cannoume was being conducted along the wrong Nile. When Baron heard that there was a Great River coursing through the center of the northern Americas, it fit his own calculations of where le Cannoume might appear. That is how I came to Fort Crevecour in January of this year, enchanted by Baron's promises of deathlessness and magical powers bestowed upon us by le Cannoume here in the land of Louisiana.

Transom and Visconti were hunting for more than a homeless tyro. They were hunting for their god, Boy King realized. They and their cult had apparently been hunting for the Khnum for centuries. Millennia. Across the planet.

Out of the corner of his eye, Boy King saw something stirring. A ghost, no doubt, edging close, testing him. Without looking up, he hissed at the lemure to back away and kept reading. In the diary, the *coureur de bois*, Baron, and their companions were being taken hostage by a tribe called the Issati.

So when this morning by our fire in this great Issati camp, Baron told me that a certain secret college among the Issati was making for a waterfall in order to conduct a religious rite, I knew we were at last about to consummate our quest. Baron said that the savages told him that it was the only cataract along the Meschasipi, and Baron was convinced, after consulting his charts and astrolabe again, that this was the location where le Cannoume would appear.

The "Meschasipi" was obviously the Mississippi, and the Mississippi's only cataract or waterfall was right here in Minneapolis, Boy King knew. Was "le Cannoume" the Khnum? Was Baron Visconti? Did he meet the ram-headed god here, on the banks of the Meschasipi?

Boy King looked up, holding between his fingers the page he was about to turn. It wasn't a ghost there, in the dark, but a little fluttering of light. Just a piece of metal capturing a gleam. Boy King looked up at the night sky through the high windows, the rain falling in, and dense cloud cover over the city. No bright light to capture. He put down Transom's binder and stared into the shadows. What was it? Boy King crawled across the floor toward the flickering.

On the shiny fender of an old bicycle, there was a twinkling and a flashing. Very small, like the reflection of light through a ceiling fan.

He started back when he realized it was his own reflection.

The reflection was waving something, which had caused the flickering. It was holding a small collage in its hand, with a black-and-white photograph of Charles Bukowski having a beer at the center of it. Boy King leaned toward the fender and could see that in neat black pen below Bukowski's beer-hand was written "Knight of Cups."

The way the reflection's hand held the collage—middle finger on upper edge, thumb on lower edge—seemed more significant than the card it held, but Boy King couldn't quite seize it. This was a game. It was a game meant to be played with someone specific in his past—a significant other. Wait. Not a game. It was a way to converse. Whole conversations could be had with raised tarot cards, sorting through a deck and finding the figure that represented the next turn in the story, the next chapter. How did Boy King know this? Was this an old revelation sparking from the bike and its previous owner? No, it was from Boy King himself. His life. How did he know that this "game" was played with only one other person? And who was that?

Knight of Cups.

There were volumes of associations that went with the cards, associations and definitions that could never be found in a tarot manual, that only that other person would ever understand. But those associations were hidden as if under the weight of an ocean. Boy King had never seen this card before, but Bukowski was one of the old associations with this knight. Allowing that remembering to spread through his mind was dangerous—Boy King felt betrayed and intrigued that his reflection was doing this to himself. He'd kept his whole life boxed up in separate containers and stashed away even from his own memory for so long that he was only ever Boy King now. Twelve years of hiding from hunters who could slip into his mind meant he couldn't allow himself to think about precious things like the Calvino Method—that is, the way he used to use tarot cards to tell stories about his life to this significantly other person. What did it mean that he was thinking these things now? He couldn't let himself think of his previous name, his previous identity. His entire strategy for hiding teetered on the shaky fulcrum that he was Boy King and nothing else.

He was about to back away, shut this out, but the reflection-hand lowered, and Boy King could see his own face distorted along the narrow curve of the bike fender. Then the hand held up the card again. Knight of Cups.

The guards and wards upon his own mind gave, and forbidden thoughts came spilling out. A grand voyage into the ill-charted territories of history undertaken by young men obsessed with mystics who'd gone before—Crowley, Eliade, the Order of the Golden Dawn, and even sham-mystics like Napoleon's counselor, Madame Le Normand, who'd fashioned the modern conception of celebrity fortune-teller—that was the Knight of Cups. Misguided quests conducted with irrational maps and a search for the searchers who may have found the means of escaping the encircling fascism of reality. That was the pledge after all: to peer beyond the occulted doorways of this world, open them, and walk through together. That seemed so far ago and long away to Boy King, pathetically quaint in the wake of pre-Egyptian gods and spells cast with hammer blows. Is this perhaps what the genie in the mirror was telling him? Was a new knight riding to the king's rescue? Or was the knight coming to challenge and slay the king? Boy King?

The reflection held up another piece of paper, but this wasn't a makeshift tarot card. It was a single note card with the ram-head of Khnum drawn upon it, rippling horns stretched behind, just as it was drawn upon the piece of paper in the suit that Boy King had found. The same hand. The same pen. Same paper, even.

"Even I'm after myself?" Boy King leaned over the bike fender and raised his middle finger, saying to the reflection, "Fuck off, all y'all."

Then he collapsed back against the ragged brickwork of the chimney, his brow, nose, and eyes pulsing. He wanted to continue reading Transom's collection, learn ways to undo the damage that Transom had done to Boy

King's defenses, but alcohol dehydration was wringing out his body and he felt nauseous, sick down to the well of his soul. Sick of hiding and dodging and so sick of himself.

In the distance, he could hear Highway 35 rumbling to life. Boy King let the binder slip from his hands and he rolled his head against the rough bricks to look out one of the high east windows. Across the sky was the sad gleam of dawn. He closed his eyes. His mind churned over the ram symbol message he'd found in the suit and the Bukowski Knight of Cups. (Had his willful reflection taken up allegiance with Visconti and the Khnum cult? Was it mocking him? Mockery was a sacrament to Remus whose brother richly deserved it, or maybe or maybe or maybe. . . .)

But, finally, slow silence filled his mind, as if a tidal sea washed toward him, carrying with it a dark fog that took the place of his tossing thoughts.

13

The only sound in the piazza was the gurgle of the fountain. When Rosemont had left the table, Miles was starting to hit a stride and a round of Campari had just arrived. Rosemont had figured Miles would be at a jabbering pitch by now. Rosemont paused in the chapel-restaurant's doorway, staring at the empty table, the dishes that the waiter was retrieving.

"Where did they go?" Rosemont asked, striding up on the waiter. "Did you see?"

The man scrubbed at his little mustache with the blade of his index finger and said nothing, heavy eyelids acting as shut curtains. The waiter was about to scoop up the glasses when Rosemont saw a bar napkin stuffed in one that must have belonged to Miles. The barhopping signaling system of old.

"Hey!" he shouted and snatched the bar napkin out of the glass.

The waiter didn't miss a beat, just turned with his loaded tray and huffed something snide that his mustache muffled.

Rosemont opened the napkin and scanned Miles's jabbing handwriting: *Purple Fireworks = No magic & You're Safe. 3131 via di S. Prima. I'll buy.*

Suddenly, the empty piazza seemed even more sinister to Rosemont, without Miles or Priscilla nearby. The sleepers were gone, which meant the *templum,* with its real or imagined sense of safety, was unplugged. *Purple Fireworks = No magic & You're Safe.* The gun in his waistband, far from making him feel protected, made him feel as if he were on the brink of explosive violence. He started walking up the steepest of the three streets, hoping it was taking him back up to the hostel where he could ask about via di Santa Prima. The whirling run that had brought him was confusing, but it had been downhill, generally speaking, so uphill seemed the best plan now.

As Rosemont drew closer to the hostel, the festival crowd grew thicker, more elated, and eventually he realized he was either following or joining a claustrophobic parade that heaved and uncoiled along this narrow street, with its crack of dusk-lit sky overhead, like a great exodus of painted humans on floats and their attendant creatures of fantasy. Lumpen-headed goblins. Scantily dressed angels. Miner hats shining bright beams into beer cups. A stilt-walker phalanx. Cerberus seething. A weeping, martyred Hannibal. Bejeweled opera glasses covering the eyes of bright blue masks. Burkas made from Sesame Street bedsheets, neon tights, and light-up nipple-studs blinking under sheer T-shirts.

Rosemont walked and gawked and walked. He gulped down two cups of beer rapidly, passed to him from a float of women in grape-bunch turbans and Etruscan tunics, and watched a man in a wide-brimmed hat and another, a wild-looking fellow in animal hides and a spray of feathers in his hair. It seemed obvious to Rosemont that one was Naught, a character from centuries-old Lenten festivals, or a riff on him. The other he couldn't identify.

"Who is that?" he asked a young woman standing next to him. Rosemont pointed to the feathered man he thought was Naught.

She was sweaty with drink and laughing, and she grinned at Rosemont, eager to talk. "Matto! That's Matto!"

Rosemont understood. *The Fool.* "And who is that? The man in red with the hat."

The woman had already lifted her chin, anticipating his question, ready to answer. "Il Bagato."

The Magician. Matto and Bagato, clowns of commedia dell'arte—one in white, the other in red. Twin tricksters. Schlemiel and Schlamazo. The dupe and the duper.

"Have fun!" Matto shouted up at a cluster of drinkers in a balcony. "This is all going to be over soon, you know!"

"Who's hungry?" shouted Bagato. "I got everything you need." He held his closed hands out to a stumbling passerby, who leaned over them. A burst of flowers appeared and water spurted in the drunk's face. Broad takes from both Bagato and the drunk.

Lame-ass commedia dell'arte buffoonery, thought

Rosemont. *Like* Gilligan's Island *for the Renaissance festival set.*

"Go home!" Matto shouted at the drenched fellow. "This party is going to end anyway. Just go home now!"

But it hooked him, he couldn't deny, and it caught at him as he flowed with the flow of the festival traffic. It found alleyways to fill and wide porches to slosh against, not exactly sure how he would find 3131 via di S. Prima.

Into the square, behind Rosemont, came the grandest float he'd yet seen, a chariot, with its horses rising up out of the float as if charging through sea foam, and behind, a great spotlight that swept the sky over the rider as three jets bearing the old crest and colors of the empire strafed the Aventine.

How could I have never heard of this festival before? All of Rome is involved. Rosemont wondered at the number of people, the scope, the man painted red, kilt and breastplate, Etruscan laurel leaves adorning his head, and spear in hand.

"That dress makes you look like a hooker!" an old transvestite shouted at the triumphator. It was Roman, certainly, this festival's adoration of the profane pressed against the revered, but its populism and camp didn't seem to belong on the Aventine, one of the most cosmopolitan neighborhoods on the planet. The festival was one enormous mockery of Rome.

Rosemont found himself driven forward with hundreds of others before the red triumphator's float, pushed like spoils of Roman victory. Rosemont passed a corner street sign: Piazza di la Haruspex. He followed the crowd out of the square: towering, slender giraffe necks on stumpy human bodies, girly eyelashes blinking way up high; a blaze-orange devil laughing as a spread of purple chrysanthemum fireworks ignited.

"Okay," Rosemont said. "I'm safe. Whatever that means."

His section of the enormous festival crowd eddied into a courtyard where a giant rust-maroon gear positioned flat and turning, with smaller rusty gears toothed into it, spinning proportionately faster, and in the center of each was a crazed, rearranged mannequin: legs for heads, sitting atop orange traffic sawhorses, and stacked funnels, ropes with toy anchors, where their arms should be. As Rosemont entered the courtyard he could see a stage where a woman was singing a mullah's cadences over industrial beats. Literally industrial. A crowd of men in gas masks were playing sanders, drills, and one man with a whining electric saw was pressing it against an iron slab, sending up rooster tails of sparks over the crowd, all of which turned upon multifold Moroccan rhythms and the singer's reverent, warbling voice.

The parade kept pushing down a narrow street and the crowd became a maze within a maze as Rosemont tried to find his way toward the buildings in order to see addresses better, but he couldn't, really, since the crowd was too dense. It felt artificial, this street, this labyrinthine neighborhood, with golden lamplight falling on too-neat porches and perfect red-brick houses, with the canopy of clouds overhead, a parade held in an enclosed space, a museum's re-creation of an Italian street. It wasn't real.

Rosemont only knew ancient Rome from research, but

here it was—or should have been. The Aventine. Time changes cities, but not Rome, he knew. Rome doesn't change, it only forgets now and then, like an old scholar who'd mastered many disciplines, slipping into senility and losing the edges, the digressions, and the minor, finer details. There were alleys, corners, and markets so old that even Rome could not be expected to remember them all. But the Aventine was not a digression, smothered by teetering buildings and shoved out of mind. It was one of the seven hills—arguably, the *second* hill of Rome, the site where Remus took his auspices and determined that the future city should be built, as the classic version went. It was a static part of Rome's topography—not a neighborhood or transient market. The festival should not have been this sprawling, covered over by so many people and winding, tangling alleyways, Rosemont realized as he broke away from the crowd and stood near a crumbling manse. There were streets below these streets. Not underground, and not streets, but plats. Blocks. Tracts. What were they? Rosemont tamped the ground with his foot as if he could feel them down there below the flagstones. He could not tell what they really were, but he could tell that they were somehow there. *His.*

"Testing, testing, one-two-three," he said to himself, as he pressed the ball of his foot against the ground again, like a man stepping into a boat.

"Jeremiah Rosemont."

He looked up, hand dropping to Kermit's gun, and found three children staring at him from the building, their faces like white moons in the frame of a dark window. Rosemont said nothing, watching them in surprise, as he realized that no one had called his name after all. Something pulled at him from the edges of his awareness. He waited. Triplets. Perfect triplets. As the parade streamed behind him, he watched their beautiful faces watching him. Graceful chins, narrow shoulders, bright eyes. And the three were blinking in unison.

"Come here," the middle child called out.

Rosemont stepped toward the window with great hesitation. Miles had said that there was no magic during this festival. But the triplets felt weird and dangerous, and then there were the girders of force that seemed to hold this city up. Nothing felt right. "What?"

"Come closer," said one of the other kids in the window.

Rosemont stood directly below them. "Hello," he said.

Almost threateningly, the third said to him, "Help us down," and immediately began crawling onto the sill. Before Rosemont could object, the child, wearing culottes and cowboy boots, had leapt into his arms. Rosemont let the boy slip down to the ground and immediately the second was standing on the sill, ready to be caught. When all three had been transferred to the ground, the first one who'd spoken said, "We're ready. We're on our way. We're here. Let's move." Rosemont was about to ask what they were ready to do, when the three literally turned on their heels, like synchronized wind-up dolls, and stalked off down the sidewalk, skirting the street crowd's main bulk.

Rosemont gave one last look at the window, wondered why there wasn't an adult or at least an outcry from within. But then watching them move in perfect unison, he knew there would be no parents in that flat, no family wondering about the curious triplets. He followed them down the street.

"We fracture," the last triplet in line said over his shoulder to Rosemont.

He hustled up to the child and bent toward him as they walked. "What?"

"We are fractured," said the second in line, more loudly.

"We mean that *I'm* fractured," said the leader, almost screaming over the din of the crowd. "And I hate it."

"Do you understand?" said the third, looking at Rosemont.

"I think I do."

"Sometimes the mind is broken, and sometimes the body. In this case, I was in tripled form so I'm stuck this way today. I'm—we're—I mean, *I'm* here to bring you to the viewing. As a favor to di Trafana."

Di Trafana, thought Rosemont. *The astrologer?* "Okay, but what are you?" Rosemont said.

"A god," said one.

"I mean, a kid," said the next.

"No, a hero, a *hero,*" said the last.

Rosemont hurried to keep pace. "You don't know?"

"Not today, I guess. It's this way," said one when they came to an intersection.

"No, it's this way."

"We're—I'm sorry," the third said to Rosemont, "but we haven't been to the maze in Haruspex Piazza for over three hundred years. We're having trouble remembering. This may take a moment."

The eight-year-olds clustered together and screamed viciously at one another and for a moment, the way they leaned at one another with chins out, their skinny chests heaving in anger, fingers arched into talons, Rosemont wondered if they would start clawing at each other.

While Rosemont stood waiting for the tripartite god to get his act together, two men dressed in heavy black Don Giovanni opera capes and matching smiling and frowning masks were speaking nearby. "They platted this neighborhood themselves," said one in a smiling mask, "the two together. But things went wrong, and on this day, one brother murdered the other, so there is no magic during this feast."

The frowning mask gasped. "The oldest of the oldest are just like you and me tonight?"

"That's right. Sitting ducks. It started with the purple rockets. Do you see what I'm getting at?"

The two figures stood staring at each other behind their masks, grinning and scowling respectively.

"It would be possible to kill them all," said the frowner.

The smiler laughed. "Now we might do it pat."

"Wait. You know who I am, right?" said the frowning mask.

"Yeah, I know."

"Are you sure?"

"I just *said* I know who you are."

"I'm Gordon Helfeltz."

The smiler stood still as a tree, smiling. He sounded pissed. "That's my name. *I'm* Gordon Helfeltz."

"No, *I'm* Gordon Helfeltz."

"*I* am."

The frowning mask turned this way and that, seemingly looking for someone. "Oh, shit."

Then the two figures lifted their arms and the skirts of

their heavy cloaks and darted away from each other in panic.

"We're ready."

"We have it."

"It's this way. Let's move," said the triplets, marching off on their too-big strides, the two behind following the first as if stepping into footprints left in snow.

Rosemont hoisted his backpack and hustled behind, trying to keep up with the scurrying triplets in the bump and jostle.

If there was no magic, as Miles and the Gordon Helfeltzes claimed, then how could any of this be happening? How could there be a three-fold child, a god, and how could he feel streets below the streets? It made him suspect that there was something wrong, not with Rome or the festival, but with himself.

"It's a Chi-Chi's," said one of the children.

"Right up here."

"That way. Up ahead."

Rosemont shook his head and sneered. He stopped to castigate them, but the kids kept marching, so he hurried behind. "A Chi-Chi's? You're taking me to a Chi-Chi's? Are you fucking serious?"

The boys lifted their chins and nodded to Rosemont over their shoulders, identical locks of black hair falling on each of their brows. "South side of the Aventine."

"It's where Remus planned to depart from this world."

Rosemont said, "At Chi-Chi's."

"Right there."

They rounded a corner where the tight, strangling street opened into a vista to the south of the wide, flat

Tiber, the magnificently crumbling baths, and the southern stretches of the Eternal City.

And blotting out all that was a pillar sign, with Chi-Chi's flouncy, cursive script in cherry-bomb red.

The festival stopped sprawling this way, coming to the border of this major thoroughfare of traffic and breaking, as if washing back up the hill to history and ferment, away from petty commerce.

Rosemont had just turned back from looking up the Aventine, when the first boy lunged into the thoroughfare in quick strides. Rosemont shouted. Screeching, honking traffic bunched up on either side of the boy as the other two, just behind, made for the far side too. Rosemont followed and waved his hands frantically to prevent himself from being hit by a taxi.

On the other side, the leader opened the Chi-Chi's front door for Rosemont and his two compatriots. "So here we meet."

Inside the foyer, Chi-Chi's greeted Rosemont in a demoralizing wave of faux Mexican decor. *God. Chi-Chi's.* Sad reminders of slipping into a Chi-Chi's once as a young man to get drunk on margaritas with a couple of giddy friends who seemed to think that this was adulthood, that they were stealing into new and untrammeled terrain, here among the crappy premixed cocktails, the black and silver mariachi sombreros, the brightly colored ponchos, the plastic rubber-tree plants. It had all felt like a defeat somehow, as a seventeen-year-old who already knew that maturity was purchased in the failure of adults and from even harder blows, not long-stemmed glassware. Not rims of salt.

"On the Aventine," Rosemont muttered, staring at a velvet bullfight poster advertising margarita mix. "On the motherfucking Aventine."

Obviously, this was a mistake. He'd wound up following the wrong magical creature in taking up with the triplets. Perhaps he should have taken up with the Gordon Helfeltzes? Not many good options here, with the three boys spinning him back into triteness and woe. As he turned back to the door, ready to leave, however, his face prickled with cold at the sight of the two men standing there, barring his way. One was tall, powerfully built, and bald with an ugly misshapen skull like a great cement block. The other was slightly shorter and slim as a spike, in his black, narrow Cardin jacket, staring at Rosemont with curiosity and hate.

"Stay and have one with me," said the shorter man spinning Rosemont toward the bar. "My name's Transom. I have someone you need to meet."

"Wait, wait, wait," said Rosemont, arching his back, his voice breaking in fright as he felt Transom slide his backpack from his shoulders.

Transom opened it and scooped out the red binder. "You were right, as usual, my lord," he said, handing it to Visconti.

Visconti immediately opened it and began reading. "It's here. *The Refutation of Rosemont*." A young couple in matching, pressed T-shirts entered and gave him a dirty look for blocking the doorway.

"What's happening?" Rosemont said. "What's this all about?"

"I hear you have it put together pretty well," said

Transom, looping both arms around Rosemont's waist and casually lifting the gun from Rosemont's waistband. "You're going to authenticate the Watts deck. And once you determine that it is what we think it is, you're going to give the god's deck to Duke Filipo Maria Visconti."

14

Hooks. Fishhooks are shining below this shallow water, waiting beneath your bare wading feet, returning you to shore. Convince yourself that the hooks can't hurt you, because you passed over them unscathed that day. They're just a memory that sinks into your dreams. But these fishhooks rip. A single golden one may shine against a pale blue sky, and it may be so small when it falls that you don't even feel its cold curve brushing the hair on the back of your hand. But a thousand of them, a million, will catch and open you. You'll be peeled apart until your body is turned inside out, and by the will of the eight thousand gods something new will emerge from the undone boundary stones and demarcations of your body.

Time was and what a time. You had a vantage and a scope back then, like none for which you'd ever been prepared, like none your people had ever experienced or prophesied. When the jerry-rigged engine of your cracked-healed-cracked mind is quiet and blind (in black-fog moments like this one), your body remembers that scope, like the vantage of two mirrors facing one another and the emergent telescoping hallway that plunges from flat, two-dimensional surfaces into past and future simultaneously. That was you: a great hallway of many generations, and all their knowing cracked through your gray matter's barricades. Asleep against your chimney, you can almost smell the steely sweat of the runners, pages carrying messages between walled cities of Etruscan kings, folding into the dusty, hot smell of mud bricks cooling like loaves, baked for the first perimeter of Wilusija by visiting priests of Khemet, folding into incense smoke in the market streets of Ur, protecting Gilgamé from the enemies of Babylon. This was the practice that survived the people, the practice that opened, leveled, and raised up your mind: the alchemy of defense, the earliest city magic. In previous generations, *paradise* literally meant "encircling wall"—divine safety—and that's what it was. The promise of a new, safe city was the promise of paradise. But every culture is a paradise lost, in the end. The enemy invades and the homeland crumbles. Tragic, but even magic, you knew, from your new vantage, isn't safe, isn't set forever. Not when the paradise of your mind must crack to gain the vantage, power, and mastery of ancients. That telescoping hallway bored through you, and, in the years that followed, you accepted that the universe and its eight thousand gods accepted you. Tyro. Master. Magician.

But, oh, the price, the *prices* you paid.

Time was and what a time. This vantage wasn't yours,

and the way you came by it was nothing short of criminal, but you sense this truth only in your foggiest moments, when this very voice (your conscience? Remus? An older you?), this scolding, self-mocking perspective comes to whisper cutting truths to you in your sleep. But you never remember. Quite a defense. While events may follow one another in little plotted parades of cause and effect in nature (sunrise, sunset, midnight), it's not so in the human mind. Your mind. Yours leaps forward, stops, recourses, lifts up. It renames, shuffles, and erases. Sunset, swingset, sunspot. Oblivion. Look at you. After all you gained and all you were awarded. Your precious warehouse has been invaded, your machinations shattered and battered, and you are laid bare, flayed raw as the day she disappeared. You'll rebuild, of course, because you have to. But creature safety is not the magician's realm; there's something of the wild dog in your people, circling fires and skirting notice. So now that your stab at normalcy is over, will you "light out for the territory," past your paradoxes and paradises, or will you steal yourself into another cramped kingdom, crowning yourself emperor of an even smaller crab's shell? Maybe get a TV? With a remote? O beautiful for spacious mind. For broken mountain's majesty above the frightened plain. Something and something else. It's hard to remember when you used the power of ancients to forget so much. Well, here's a banister in the mist, something to hang on to, if you can: the betrayal on her babyface. Did you save yourself when you stole what you stole and broke what you broke, or did you save yourself from guilt and remembering? Hold on to this, Boy King, or whatever you call yourself now: Her eyes were locked on yours from beneath the surface, before she sank and sank and sank and the shadows in the choppy lake swallowed her. The fish-hooks waiting for you in the pebbled shore never touched your skin, but she will be two years old forever.

Remember that? Remember that.

Wake up now. Haul yourself up from another floor. What name are you going by again? Miles? Rosemont? Boy King. Oh, right. So confusing, even to you, especially when the black mist retreats and you're alone with your new, stitched-together self. Don't try and remember who you were. It's easier being a self-made man.

Behind Bryce & Waterston, a flock of Canadian geese had landed and made camp on the old rail bed. It was April, so several times a week, a new flock would arrive and scream at each other till noon. This morning, the barking was high-spirited, ardent, and Boy King woke with the sense that something had gone right while he was asleep. At least, nothing had gone wrong. No trackers had jumped him in his dreams. No fifteenth-century dukes had found him while he slept.

Pushing himself up from the floor, his face felt like a great soggy gland, but the sharp agony of his broken nose was gone. That seemed to stoke his optimism. Though the ware-house was now simply bricks and rotting timber after Transom's invasion last night, it felt to Boy King as if life were a blank page. He could do anything now. Go anywhere.

But he was hungry, desperately hungry, and his head thundered with a godly hangover. He counted himself lucky that this was the worst of his pains. Sitting and listening to the geese, he ate an entire box of Saltines that he'd Dumpster dived a week before. Stale, but not too bad. He drank some water from a jug, finished off his last Twizzler from its sticky bag, and felt almost human afterward.

While he ate, Boy King decided this would be his last day in Bryce & Waterston. Transom had successfully convinced Visconti that Boy King wasn't here. Transom had liberated Boy King. Now, Boy King was free to start over somewhere else, and he found himself thinking that maybe he'd been too hasty to dismiss Lara for trying to get him an apartment. Maybe things had calmed down at Dona Mia's and he could talk to Lara about another gig next week. The future was taking shape, like a blessed city coming into view over the horizon.

But Boy King would need to finish reading Transom's collection of documents before any of that could happen. He sat down and opened the binder.

There was little that spoke to him—more copies of hieroglyphs and hand-drawn recreations of ram-headed Khnum—but then he chanced across his own name in a section that had been heavily edited, evidently by government censors. He thumbed back to the beginning so that he could see what the document was.

Department of Justice
Federal Bureau of Investigation
Washington, D.C. 20535
January 15, 2004

Subject: Direct Action and Monitoring
FOIA No. 1014444–9032

Dear Mr. Visconti,

The enclosed documents were reviewed under the Freedom of Information Act (FOIA), Title 5, United

States Code, Section 52/552a. Deletions have been made to protect information that is exempt from disclosure.

The enclosed material is from the main investigative file(s) in which the subject(s) of your request was the focus of the investigation.

One document was reviewed and one document was released.

Sincerely yours,

David N. Laurel
Section Chief
Record/Information Dissemination Section
Records Management Division

Enclosure(s):

From: Indigent and Immigrant Monitoring Division
Re: John Doe, Minneapolis, MN
ALERT: Suspected figure in Case # 98889A-DE-0 (pending)
Date: December 2, 2003

These pictures of John Doe were taken following tips from [   ], who advised that this unidentified individual might be a key figure in a pending case out of the Madison, Wisconsin, bureau. The individual is said to be squatting in the abandoned Bryce & Waterston warehouse in Minneapolis, Minnesota. Length of squat: unknown.

However, Special Agent [   ] used the Forensic Image Analysis team's EigenMatch system, which

[   ] for human identification using eyes, chins, cheeks, ears, and [   ] [   ]. The system employs an algorithmic [   ]

[   ]

[   ] which remains controversial, called "eigenfaces"— standardized facial elements derived from statistical analysis of the EigenMatch database of face pictures using fourth- and fifth-dimensional representations called "auras" that [   ]

[   ]

As a result, Special Agent [   ] was able to determine a 91% match between homeless person John Doe at the Bryce & Waterston warehouse in Minneapolis and the last known photograph of [   ] [   ] taken at the Circus of Infinite Wow in Austin, Texas. In other words, the SA feels 91% certain that [   ] is the Bryce & Waterston John Doe and not the Houston Cherryvale Hospital John Doe as Special Agent [   ] asserts.

Despite this near-positive match, more follow-up is needed. For example, the address of the abandoned Bryce & Waterston warehouse, [   ] [   ] given in Case # [   ] [   ] does not seem to exist in the zip code provided. Follow-up with Minneapolis Police Department found no maps or other records of a warehouse with that name, despite having the attached photograph with warehouse name and logo clearly visible. Sending a beat patrol to the site elicited no hard evidence that this warehouse exists (officer could not find it).

SA [   ] was asked to repeat his EigenMatch findings in real time, which he attempted, but circumstances beyond [   ]

[   ]

for the Bryce & Waterston John Doe's alleged knowledge of the [   ] and its disappearance from Rome in 1991 (Washington office is requesting information of its possible location in US), Visconti's group, known as [   ] (Boston office requesting), the whereabouts of fugitive Leo Burt and other members of the Madison Underground (Madison office), various occult travelers' hostels, connection to Missing Person Tanya Elling, and/or the identity of the Cherryvale John Doe.

As noted in the IIM bulletin, on [   ], Operation Cattle Drive will begin. This coordinated effort between the various State National Guards, Homeland Security, and the Bureau's [   ] will make further homeless investigations in cities like Minneapolis nearly impossible. We advise sending in a SA to Bryce & Waterston for one last interrogation before the round-up begins.

Boy King quickly paged back to the initial letter from the Department of Justice: December 2. That was five months ago, which meant this Operation Cattle Drive was probably still coming—maybe a spring sweep, when a lot of the homeless folks came back to Minneapolis, or at the latest, a summer initiative. He hadn't heard about anyone getting rounded up recently—but it happened every few years, and it was terrifying. People he saw regularly on his Dumpster dives just disappeared, here one day and gone the next. And this investigation had pictures of him, they'd been watching him, and they wanted to interrogate him.

Three letters, Transom had said in describing the "greater power" that yoked him. *Had he received three letters? No.*
FBI. HSA.

Boy King slammed the binder shut and began gingerly placing the paintings back in the cardboard box, imagining special agents parachuting onto the warehouse roof. Could Boy King find Lara? He needed her. He took back all the snotty things he thought about her efforts to help him and wished he had her address, phone number, or any means of contacting her. He didn't know where she lived, didn't know how to reach her except on Dream Machine Thursdays and Sundays at the restaurant. After the mayhem with that couple and the crazed busboy at Dona Mia's, he wondered if Lara would even help him. He had to think of something else. The van wasn't safe, not since the mud replica appeared, so there would be no hasty flight out of town now. Where could he go? He'd gotten soft since finding and building his little castle at Bryce & Waterston. He didn't know the good hideouts anymore, where the cops didn't come searching or where every homeless person in town didn't already squat. He patted the packing tape back in place, loosely resealing the cardboard box that housed the ancient paintings. A homeless shelter might be okay. But getting there, or anywhere, meant walking through very urban stretches of Minneapolis with the objects of so many desires under one arm. If a desert hunter, an eigenmatcher, a Khnum worshipper, or random tyro spotted him...

Boy King picked up the box—easy enough to carry while walking. He couldn't risk changing its shape, not with a dragnet of federal agents and tyros underway. He was just going to have to follow the Mississippi up to the West Bank and see if he could hustle some food and a ride out of town. He took one last look around, then left Bryce & Waterston. He never saw it again.

W ithout the gun, binder, or his backpack, Rosemont
felt stripped nude—so nude that he folded his
arms and hugged himself for comfort and warmth. *Those
idiots,* he thought. *How could they just leave me to wander
on my own?* Transom walked next to him through the
spotlights of a tracklit hallway that hemmed the dining
room and its cheery Tejano music.

"A Chi-Chi's," Transom said. "Can you believe it? The
Romans aren't in control anymore."

Rosemont was shivering. "You're just coming to this
conclusion?"

"By the time you have an American chain invading the
historical, mythological heart of your culture," Transom
said, "the empire isn't just dead, it's *un*dead. This must be
Chi-Chi's of the Damned."

Rosemont glanced behind him as they walked. Visconti was still reading at the door, but he wasn't turning pages. *What the hell would Visconti need Miles's binder for? If he's who Miles says he is, then he remembers the story about di Trafana firsthand, since he was there,* thought Rosemont. *But he said he wanted the Guelph report. Ingebretsen. Now he knows the deck is scientifically proven to be over a thousand years old.*

"I want you to know," Transom said, "that we have Miles."

Rosemont's step hitched and he almost stumbled. "Why? What are you going to do to him?" Rosemont whispered.

"There isn't time to do everything we'd like to do," Transom said.

He's bluffing. "The oldest of the oldest are just like you and me tonight," Gordon Helfeltz had said. *All they can do is scare me that they have him.* And it did scare him. It didn't take celestial command over ancient disciplines to hammer a nail, throw a punch. Passing a line of plastic rubber-tree plants, Transom and Rosemont found a banquet room filled with red Naugahyde chairs and benches. Inside, Priscilla and Marni were seated patiently at a table, the only table occupied of the ten in the room.

"Rosemont," Priscilla said. Almost as if she couldn't stop herself, she lunged to her feet and held out her hand, shooing him toward her.

"Go join your friends," Transom said. "They'll get you up to speed." Then he turned and sauntered back down the hall to Visconti.

Rosemont slid into a seat next to Priscilla and, as she sat, said, "What does it mean that they have Miles?"

THE MAGICIAN AND THE FOOL   219

"They're trying to skew the authenticator's view of the Watts deck," Marni said, hands folded in her lap as if she were simply waiting for a chimichanga. "And it will probably work."

Kermit had done his work well, even with Rosemont aiming a gun in his face. The thought of Khnum was firmly planted in Rosemont's mind, no doubt about it. And the very idea that Miles was somewhere, right now, getting the snot knocked out of him? In a Chi-Chi's? Strawberry margaritas were sounding really good all of a sudden.

Priscilla put her hand on his arm. "Marni's wrong," she said. "You *can* be objective."

Rosemont shrugged her hand away and brushed his arm where she had touched him. "What's the plan here? Is there one? Are you three just making it up as you go?" His voice was strained and it cracked as he said, "I can't believe you just left me at the café."

Priscilla's widow's peak stood black against her paling skin. "I know. It couldn't be helped. The festival on the Aventine was about to begin so the *templum* had to be closed." Her voice was soothing, an alarming contrast to her vampire-esque look. She held up her hands and patted the air before Rosemont. "Please believe me. You were taking so long and we were in danger."

"I was in danger, too," he hissed, "and the shit I just saw in this festival? What made you think I was equipped to deal with it? I walked in here—la dee da—and Transom grabbed Miles's binder like he was picking cherries. How did—?"

Rosemont shut his mouth.

Priscilla dropped her hands. "What?"

His anger guttered and went out. "I was—"

Marni crossed her arms and grinned. "I thought he had it."

Priscilla's head snapped toward Marni, but she said nothing, looking at the old woman gloat. Then her head turned slowly back to Rosemont, seething. The track lighting directly above her cast horror-show shadows down her face. "You lied to Miles?" Priscilla said.

Rosemont slumped, as if his heart was dragging his shoulders down. He wondered where Miles was now, if he was hurt. Would it have changed anything if he'd given Miles the binder at the café? "I know. I'm sorry."

"You kept it from him when you knew how badly he wanted it?" She stepped forward and the light softened, but her voice didn't.

"No one was telling me anything," Rosemont said weakly.

"Yes"—she nodded broadly as if explaining something to a child—"we were telling you everything—far more than a potential authenticator should be told." Her voice dropped to an angry whisper and she leaned toward Rosemont on the balls of her toes. "They dismiss us. They dismiss what we're about to look at. They've seen it with their own eyes and they dismiss it. Do you have any idea what will happen if they claim the deck for—"

"Ssst," Marni said, shushing Priscilla. "Stop it." She pushed out a chair next to her. "Sit down, Priscilla."

Rosemont clenched his jaw and then said, "See? You don't tell me what matters. Never enough to understand what's happening or even what's at stake." He turned to the old woman and whispered in a rush, "What? What will happen, Marni? If Visconti gets this item you want me to look at, what terrible thing will happen?"

"No one can tell," Marni said.

"Why?" Rosemont shouted. "Why can't you just tell me?"

Marni's face was set in anger, but she leaned her chin on one hand, as though this conversation both wearied and infuriated her. "You think that 'being told' is the same as 'knowing,' " she said, almost snarling. "For us, and for Visconti, Transom, Blackleafers, Babylonians, and tyros of traditions across the planet, *finding out* is knowing." Her voice hit a sing-song cadence implying that her own words tired her. "We live by that. We die by that. We fail and succeed by uncovering, discovering. Not by being spoonfed."

"Well, I'm *not* a tyro," Rosemont said, aiming a thumb at his chest. "I need the goddamn spoon. I keep getting thrown into the dark. I need a handrail or a guide wire or *something.*"

Rosemont's words seemed to wake something in Priscilla. She laughed quietly and said, "You came to Rome when the Monk called you."

Marni nodded at Priscilla, folded her hands in her lap as if the conversation were over. "Exactly."

" 'Exactly'?" Rosemont snapped at Marni. "What, 'exactly'?"

Priscilla said in exasperation, "You *are* a tyro."

"I'll be the judge of that," Marni said in a croaking, sarcastic voice.

"No, Marni. *Rosemont* will," Priscilla said. She looked back at him out of the corner of her eye, as if spying at him through a keyhole. "Well, you'll find your own way or you won't. I've said your whole life that it has to be this way. Now I must stand by that."

Priscilla's words whirled through him. *My whole life?*

He was about to ask what that meant, but her face was a cold, shut door and she raised a finger to quiet him.

"Here he comes."

A moment later, a man in a flowing, shapeless black caftan entered the hall. The robe took away all the sharp angles on him so that from the top of his rounded head and soft cap of black hair, sloping down to his rounded shoulders, barrel body, and Buddha belly, the man was almost a perfect circle.

"Who's that?" Rosemont muttered.

"It's di Trafana, the Mad Monk who showed Miles the deck," Priscilla said, stepping close to Rosemont. "Don't be worried, but he's a little crazy from a possession, Miles says. That's how Miles learned so much about Remus, by talking to di Trafana. The man is half-possessed by a ghost from Remoria."

Di Trafana wasn't what Rosemont had imagined from the condotierre's description in his journal. He had pictured a gaunt, haggard court astrologer, but this man looked downright jolly. Di Trafana smiled a faint smile that barely put a dent in one baby cheek, and crossed to join them. In a pleasant, harmonious voice, he said to Rosemont, "Miles, it's good to see you again."

"No, no," Rosemont said. "I'm Jeremiah Rosemont." He shook hands with di Trafana, and there was something mildly upsetting about him—the all-too-easy slope of his shoulders, the salamander smoothness of his hand.

Di Trafana inclined his head to Rosemont, a little bow that forced him to look at Rosemont from under his eyebrows. "The authenticator. Interesting that you decided to take the ticket that was sent to you."

Rosemont said, "Nothing to lose."

"Hardly makes sense," said di Trafana and closed his eyes, lips moving, speaking soundlessly.

Rosemont looked at Priscilla, who shrugged. Transom appeared at that moment, and while all three waited for di Trafana to open his eyes and stop talking to himself, Rosemont tested the floor with the balls of his toes, as he had on the hill. He could still feel the Aventine's secret platting pulse into him through the soles of his feet.

Di Trafana opened his eyes and they shined at Rosemont. "What are you doing?"

Rosemont said, "Nothing."

"What *are* you doing?" Transom echoed.

"Nothing, I said," said Rosemont.

Di Trafana looked down at Rosemont's feet then back into his eyes.

Priscilla's pallid face gleamed under one of the track lights as she turned and whispered something to Marni, staring at Rosemont.

"How can this be?" di Trafana said to him.

It's not a hallucination, Rosemont thought. *It surprises di Trafana that I can feel this too.*

"Mr. Rosemont has sensitivities that the rest of us do not have," Priscilla whispered to di Trafana. "Many of us have been waiting to see them exhibit themselves."

Rosemont wondered what that meant, *many of us,* or how she knew anything about him. He was about to ask when di Trafana turned and began gliding away toward a small side room. "Mr. Rosemont? Follow me."

In the side room, which was lit with wrought-iron chandeliers and electric candles, a small station had been set up. A microscope. A bright, full-spectrum light on a desk. pH strips and a small magnifying glass. On a long table fifteen paintings were laid out, each in a sealed frame, with one unsealed, ready for examination.

Di Trafana came to stand behind the table and gave Rosemont a disturbing, lingering stare. "Everything you need should be here. But if I've neglected you, pronounce your need and I'll nourish you."

"So you say you created this deck?" said Rosemont.

Di Trafana gave him a dry, canny look. "I never said that."

"You know Visconti. You have held a very low opinion of him in the past." *Testing, testing, one-two-three.* Rosemont couldn't stop feeling the situation out. He examined di Trafana's face carefully as he spoke. "Haven't you, *pontifex*?"

"Priscilla is right about you. Powerful. Resourceful," di Trafana said. "Plus, you are very tan. But what matters now is the future and what you see in these cards."

Rosemont wanted to keep testing to understand what was happening, but he couldn't resist looking, either. The paintings were small, and several were water damaged, but most had survived in remarkably good condition for millennia-old paintings. In fact, if he hadn't seen the Ingebretsen report, Rosemont would have guessed that they were more like four hundred years old.

He walked down the row of paintings. If these were cards that were some missing parent of Renaissance tarots and shared qualities with them, then these had to be fifteen trumps, cards from the trump suit—or the so-called major arcana, as popular culture referred to the twenty-two-card suit of the typical tarot deck. There were no pip cards at all in the fifteen, that Rosemont could ascertain. Did that mean that pips simply hadn't survived from the larger whole? Or were pip cards not part of this ur-tarot, if that's what it was? It was highly unlikely that so many cards of only one suit would survive. More likely, this is what the deck was. Little portraits. Depictions of vanities, archetypes, and human triumphs. That's all. In other words, it obviously wasn't a deck for playing any of the games that tarot was known for in the fifteenth century, namely tarocchi. This "deck" held some other purpose than playing games.

The next thing Rosemont could see that broke with tarot tradition, simply glancing at the cards, was that the Watts deck paintings clearly hadn't been conscripted by royalty. There was no family device, no motto or heraldry as in the earliest tarot decks. The inks were fine, but not of notably high quality—the blues had faded, and all the cards had a red-yellow cast.

Rosemont looked at the lone unsealed card. The image was that of a ram standing in a chariot, and its horns were strangely drawn—flat and rippling outward like a water buffalo's—and Rosemont was reminded of the species of sheep that Kermit the Frog had described. Who would know of this species well enough to draw it in tenth-century Europe? What Italian would know obscure Egyptian gods, ancient even by Egyptian standards? And was Rosemont really seeing this? Or had the image of the ram been planted in his mind, as Kermit claimed he'd done? *No. Don't go down that road,* Rosemont told himself. *You'll drive yourself bat shit questioning yourself like that.* Rosemont inspected the outer lines of the ram figure. It was not a medieval hand that drew this, nor a modern hand, either. It was far older than any era where realism was the norm—perhaps AD 950 as the Guelph report had

said? Even that might have been too young. There was
something, he had to admit, very "barbarian Italy" about
it. The ram's round eyes reminded Rosemont of Etrurian
death masks. Stylized, primitivistic, as they say, like work
from the Haida of the Pacific Northwest, or the bulls
painted on cave walls in the Lucerne. A slashing, solid dy-
namism in the drawing that was not prized in Renaissance
verisimilitude. This artist had more passion for the animal
than for the human. Did Rosemont surmise this because of
what he had been told? Was he seeing what others wanted
him to see in the Watts deck? The ram seemed to reach out
to him in a way that did not seem possible, to lift from the
paper and cast a shadow upon it and to place a wet, stamp-
ing hoof into Rosemont's chest and leave a moist, cloven
print that ...

banner of silver
water lifting

...*but not outrageously beautiful,* Rosemont thought,
like the inks of the earliest tarots. The image on the lone,
unsealed card was that of a shepherd reclining on a hillside
with a sun or a star blazing over his head. Rosemont assumed it was a star since a crescent moon hung low over
the horizon, but it was alone in the sky, not part of a con-
stellation. The shepherd was dressed in an animal skin kilt,
and a staff lay in the grass near him. The same rays that
shot from the sun/star shot from the brow of the shepherd.
The drawing was highly compelling. Emotional. The shepherd with his shaggy kilt seemed to lift off the card stock. It
was not a modern hand, nor a medieval hand, that drew it.
Older, deliciously crude, and a great presence in the card

seemed to swell toward Rosemont as he let his heart rise to
the image of the shepherd, behold it, embrace it. An immense, oceanic personality washed over him. In Latin, the
personality said to him, "I am the half and the other side of
your hope," and he could not bear to resist a word that it
spoke as though forgotten generations were finally...

> lifting water
> in a silver banner

...of native Canadians or the bulls painted on the
Lucerne cave walls.

Though he took this in and marveled at that lone, unsealed card, Rosemont didn't analyze the image itself yet,
but instead examined the cracks in the paint on each card.
The craquelure, as the network of tiny fissures and splits
was called, wasn't fake, per se. It wasn't a paint job itself,
that much Rosemont could see right away, and it cracked
through the subgrade paint in a satisfying randomness like
the web of a drunken spider. Clearly not a bake-and-roll
forgery. Under the microscope, Rosemont examined the
craquelure more closely and saw that the cracks weren't
etched into the dried paint, either. In places, the cracks
went down to the very base, where the paint slightly separated from the card stock like fruit segments ripening away
from the rind.

Rosemont lifted his head from the microscope and
sighed.

It made his mouth water, it was so real. And that's how
he always knew. Whatever the images might have been,
whatever culture or occult tradition might have spawned
them, the paintings spoke to Rosemont's salivary glands,

his stomach, and his body, and that's how he always knew when he was beholding authenticity.

"Are you all right, authenticator?" di Trafana asked.

Rosemont realized he had stopped to rub his eyes. "Fine." He was exhausted from his trip, from the bizarre run across the Aventine. That had to be it. Light-headed and a little buzzed from festival beer. He looked back at the card after blinking his eyes clear. What was happening? He had distinctly different visions of the same card, he suddenly realized. Several visions. A shepherd. A ram. Not just different interpretations or impressions, but he had different... memories of what he had just seen. A ram. A shepherd.

"Are you ready to tell Priscilla and Marni what you think?"

Rosemont nodded vaguely.

Di Trafana's whole body gave a little bob. "After you."

Rosemont entered the banquet hall and saw Miles standing next to Transom and Visconti and three men who looked like hired muscle. Miles seemed fine, unbeaten, but his face looked clammy and damp, even from across the room, so Rosemont assumed he'd at least gotten a good scare thrown into him. Transom and Visconti looked ready to declare victory of someone or something.

Rosemont stretched and made like he was trying to crack his back. "It's a fake."

Rosemont expected that the held breath and tension in the room would release slowly as the players absorbed his words. Or perhaps an outburst of I-told-you-so's or that-cannot-be's. But the room remained tense as they each kept their eyes on Rosemont, poised, as if they yearned to bash him open and snatch the truth out of him with their bare hands.

Miles alone looked deflated, crushed by the news, and when he spoke, he sounded drugged. "How? How do you know, Jeremiah?"

Rosemont slid into a chair next to Priscilla. "The craquelure is phony," he said to Miles, who was about twenty feet away. "It's telltale. Very difficult to forge good craquelure."

"He's right. It's a fake," said Visconti. "I saw it six hundred years ago, you'll all remember. I thought it was phony then too."

Priscilla was still watching Rosemont carefully. "He should have been reduced to a pile of tears and screaming. But he's sane as an egg, look at him. He knows what he's talking about and he sounds convincing."

"Or he survived it," Marni said. "And is now tricking us."

Rosemont said, "I'm just telling you what I saw."

"But what about Ingebretsen?" Miles said, getting his wind back. "What about the Guelph report? They said it was real. They verified it was from AD 950."

Transom apparently thought that was a good point. He crossed his arms and looked at Rosemont.

"Well sure," Rosemont said, "the paint and card stock may be authentic, but I believe someone painted this thing and doctored it to look real. The typical way to fake a painting, make the cracks in it look old, is to throw it in the oven right after finishing it in order to dry it quickly. Then you take it out and roll it over, say, a cylinder or a rolling pin while the paint is drying and becoming brittle to get this web effect of 'aged' cracks. But whoever did this one really knew what they were doing. I'd guess they cracked them from below at several different points.

Pressing upward into the card stock in what we might call the upper middle quadrant. In the upper left. And perhaps at two points in the center," he said, bullshitting freely now. "It's a very similar pattern on each one. That's what tipped me off. That and the crappy paint." Feigning bemusement, Rosemont met every eye in the room, as if he found them to be the dreariest suckers. But his full attention was on the paintings behind him, looping his mind around them, making them his with his every fiber and want. "With better oils, even a century-old painting would look fresh and bright. With these paints, a hundred-year-old work looks ancient."

Rosemont pretended to be fascinated by the proceedings but he was desperately calculating how he could dart away with the paintings. Could he do it now, while they argued? Could he get Miles out of here too? He pretended to rub his ear and stole a look at di Trafana to see if the Monk was equally absorbed in the argument.

But di Trafana was staring at Rosemont, wide-eyed and inquisitive, like a cat poised before rustling grass. And while Rosemont looked at him, the man gave a little nod of encouragement.

Rising on the balls of his toes, he looked back at the paintings again, and feeling the hum of the plats beneath the Aventine, he stared at one, the picture of the stargazing shepherd, until he could feel it begin to lift off the paper. And just as that same curious sensation hit him, of a fish being pulled from a stream and pulling with it a silver banner of water, Rosemont had the sensation of pulling himself from the red Naugahyde banquet room, the Chi-Chi's of the Damned, and Rome.

16

Dead river rushes and the stiff stalks of old weeds and reeds snapped under Boy King's feet as he walked along the Mississippi, headed for the Wiggle Room Saloon and Lara. It was April. The new growth hadn't come in thick yet, and the river had flooded several times recently so the ground sucked at his feet. There was a walkway, a paved riverfront for bikers and joggers up the hill above him, but down here he could walk without frightening people with his bashed face and black eyes. Down here, he could see the symbols and marks left by hunters, and read the messages spray painted by tyros for one another on tree stumps and tumbled concrete pilings.

NO TYRO NO WAY
TAKE BACK WATTS!

Another said:

REFUTE JOHN C. MILES

Boy King stopped and tried to identify the tradition from the handwriting, perhaps even identify the tyro who wrote it, but it had been too many years. Every curve of every letter was a message, he knew, and he could hear the pound of heels on Baghdad streets in the stems and swirls of these letters—but pre-Muslim Baghdad or modern, war-shattered Baghdad, he could not tell.

He stepped back and reread the second message, and realized he knew the name.

JOHN C. MILES

He knew a John C. Miles long ago. Good God, he'd been important to Boy King once upon a time. How could he forget? He stared at the name and wondered what was happening to his mind. First the false vision of an imagined childhood and now he was apparently forgetting crucial people from his past. The seams and fringes of reality were fraying and he assumed the Khnum was on its way, forcing itself through the thin cloth protecting Boy King's world, and important names and people were slipping through.

There would be time for puzzling that out once he was somewhere safe. He pressed on along the river, and when he sensed that the Seven Corners neighborhood was above him, upbank, Boy King lumbered up the hill with his cardboard box. *It was amazing how fast Minneapolis could go from wild to urban,* he thought, as he made his way through mental health facilities, dilapidated student housing, and the outskirts of the University of Minnesota sprawl, making for Cedar and Riverside. Dona Mia's was that way. So was the Wiggle Room Saloon.

The Wiggle Room was an old disco-era club that had been resuscitated as a gay cowboy venue in the nineties and was now slouching into a more comfortable posture as a humble dive bar. Curiously, its multiple identities worked together with stenciled murals of Donna Summer alongside posters of Dolly Parton and Travis Tritt. Rhinestones and pinball machines and a gummy black dance floor that was probably hip once.

Cradling his cardboard box like it held a baby within, Boy King slinked inside and was grateful that Bobby wasn't around. The bouncer always hassled Boy King, had even coldcocked him once, for no reason that Boy King could tell. He was also the only staff person at the Wiggle Room who had a problem with Boy King reading cards. So with the smell of greasy burgers and crispy french fries enticing him from the kitchen, Boy King stashed his box under a table and started hustling for readings, three cards for five bucks. He got two readings right away from a couple that had started drinking around noon, and who needed convincing that they were still in love. Within fifteen minutes, he had enough money for some fries and a cold glass of Pabst.

But word spreads fast in a bar, and as soon as he was finished with his lunch, he had four more readings from a group of young women wearing Twins gear, three more from a trio of older ladies on a shopping junket from Brainerd, and three from a guy who didn't like his first two readings.

But something was wrong. Despite the influx of cash,

the happy parade of whiskeys he'd lined up for himself, and the retreat of the dull ache in his brow and nose, he felt as he had down at the Mississippi, seeing that oddly famil- iar name, that something was slipping through the net. He kept catching visions of strange sights out of the corner of his eye. Bone. Bare bone in the bar's plate glass window. Horn, maybe. But when he looked, it was just a trick of light. Nonetheless, the Wiggle Room didn't feel right, like it was a set for a film about a bar and not the actual Wiggle Room that he knew.

He didn't like this feeling of dread, and worse, he was starting to dither at his clients, really stretching their pa- tience with him. Boy King still hadn't seen Lara, so he took a break from reading, grabbed his box, and skirted to the back of the bar where the games were, just in case she had entered while he was absorbed with cards. That's where Lara would be hanging out if she were here. She wasn't there, but Boy King was relieved to find Garbus, a curly- haired man who always reminded Boy King of a somber Harpo Marx. Garbus was shooting darts with a friend, and Boy King gave him a short wave. Garbus looked away, pretending to be absorbed in the game.

"Garbus," Boy King said, sliding on to the bar stool across from him. He placed his box on his lap.

No response.

"Have you seen Lara?"

Garbus and Boy King had drunk together a few times, or rather, they'd hung out with Lara while she and her friends poured pitchers. Boy King didn't really know any- thing about him, now that he thought about it. The two men were simply part of the wider circle that Lara drew when she wanted to slum, drink hard, shoot pool, throw darts, raise hell. Boy King wouldn't call him a friend, and judging by his expression, the angry set of his jaw, Garbus didn't want anything at all to do with Boy King. He shot his darts and closed out the eighteens, ignoring Boy King through the next two rounds, until finally he said, "You're the crazy fuck that pissed off the Ellings at Dona Mia's."

The man shooting darts with Garbus didn't look at Boy King, but Boy King could tell he had the guy's full attention.

"I didn't mean to," Boy King said. "Pretty high strung, that couple."

"I heard you got your nose broken," he said, finally looking at Boy King, at his nose, his eyes.

Boy King nodded back at him. "And now I'm in trouble," he whispered. "Actually."

Garbus glanced from the cardboard box to Boy King's beaten face, and then shot his buddy a look to say, *I need a minute,* then turned back to Boy King and said, "You bet you're in trouble. You have the cops after you." It wasn't a question.

"I do?"

"Didn't know that?" Garbus said. "The Ellings want you put away."

"Oh, that's rich," Boy King sneered. "Jesus, they had it coming. Besides, I didn't do—"

" 'Had it coming'?" Garbus said, eyebrows arching.

Screaming tires and a sudden burst of piercing, reflected sunlight from outside distracted both of them. A near-accident ended in car honks and swearing, and a burst of engines carried two cars in opposite directions.

" 'Had it coming'?" Garbus repeated, laughing coldly. "How can you say that? I mean, the Ellings are, like, the two most sympathetic people in America. They're icons. Their girl—their daughter's been missing for *years*." He rubbed his curly head and then sipped his beer. "What the hell did you say to them?"

Conversation was hard for some reason. The words in his head were getting logjammed, weren't coming out cleanly. This had been happening in the last few years, but three bottles of booze in the last few days made his thoughts soggy and slower than usual. He wanted to tell Garbus that it was always more complicated, that the people you think of as heroes are really just hopeless, and desperation could make a villain of anyone, anyway. These were the thoughts in his head, but what came out was, "They wanted truth, so I told them a little."

Garbus obviously knew Boy King's reputation through Lara. For the first time, he looked at Boy King like he was something other than a dirty homeless guy. "They wanted some psychic information, eh? What did you tell them?"

Everyone wants a peek, thought Boy King. *Everyone's trapped inside and wants a peek over the wall.* "If I tell you, will you help me?"

Garbus looked angry fleetingly, then a sardonic smile spread over his mouth. "Okay. If I can."

Boy King tucked the cardboard box under his chin and related the entire story, exactly as he saw it. The girl Tanya, her new name, and the parents' helplessness. He wondered if Garbus believed him, but ultimately, he didn't care. Belief was irrelevant. He even related the fight, how Papa Elling broke his nose and the chaos that erupted out of it. "I don't know why that busboy attacked me," Boy King said. "Just looking for an excuse to throw a punch, I guess."

But Garbus was still hanging on to the description of what Boy King had seen when the Ellings first approached him. The girl. Just looking at him, Boy King could tell that everyone in America wanted to know what he knew now. The girl and where she was.

But then Garbus's expression soured and he went back to looking at a dirty homeless guy. "You told them all that? Jesus, you're cold," Garbus said, staring at him with his hands behind his head. "Haven't you been following that story? Don't you know what those people went through? I mean, you're kind of a bastard, you know?"

"But I didn't mean to hurt their feelings," Boy King said. "Garbus, look." He was beginning to feel that even tracking down Lara was going to take too much time. "Can you help me get out of town?"

Garbus appeared aggrieved as he put one hand on his hip. "You want me to help you run from the cops?"

"No. I mean, I didn't even know about *that*. I need— I mean, you can't possibly know what I'm up against," said Boy King. "I mean, if I told you?" He started laughing. What little peek over the wall could he give this man that wouldn't turn him off like a light? "Someone wants me dead. Yeah. Yeah, it might be Papa Elling now that I think of it. But I don't know."

Garbus sighed and finished off his beer with the air of a banker weighing a loan. He took out his cell phone and thumbed through the index, finally nodding and looking at Boy King. "Look, I have a farmer friend who manages a bed-and-breakfast outside of town. He comes in to Minneapolis and drinks on the weekends down at Leaning Tower. I can call him. He might be willing to give you a lift out of town," Garbus said.

Boy King shook his head and shut his eyes in gratitude. "Yes, please. You have no idea how much that would mean to me. Thanks, Garbus. Thank you."

"No worries," he said and punched in the number, stepping away from Boy King.

Boy King felt like his body was going to explode. He was grateful for the ride out of town, but it was a fall-back plan at best. He couldn't wait all night long for the B&B farmer to come and pick him up. On top of everything, the cops were after him. Jesus. He'd have to keep looking for a ride somewhere, anywhere. Maybe he could pry Lara's address out of Garbus or get him to call her. Maybe she'd show up and help him.

Garbus turned back to him and said, "You're in luck."

"Oh yeah?"

"He's been down at the Hard Rock. He says he can swing by and pick you up as soon as he finishes his vegan special." Garbus snapped the cell shut. "How 'bout that?"

Boy King sighed in gratitude. "Garbus, I can't believe it," he said. "How can I thank you?"

He looked down at Boy King's cards, which he held in his hand the way Garbus was holding his cell phone. "How about a reading before you go?"

Boy King passingly thought it odd that just a moment ago Garbus had wanted nothing to do with him and now he was asking for a reading. But he shuffled the cards, glad he was on his way out of town. "Is there anything you want to ask the cards about? Romance? Fortune?"

Garbus stared at him pointedly. "No."

Boy King cut the deck and then started tossing cards. He stopped with just two face up on the table—The Magician and The Fool.

"Looks heavy," Garbus said, watching him.

Boy King stared at them. The Magician and The Fool stared at Boy King. Finally, Boy King said, "It's the whole deck in two cards. Right there, in a basic, binary equation. Fool equals zero. Magician is one. Everything is ones and zeroes, and the whole world is here, in two cards. Quick, how many cards in a standard pack of playing cards?"

"Huh?"

"How many cards in a regular deck?" said Boy King, agitated, not able to speak fast enough.

"Fifty—"

"Wrong! Fifty-three. Everyone forgets the Joker. That is, The Fool. That is, the zero is never counted. See? So it is with Lemuria, or Remuria. Or Remoria. The lost city of Remus. The only thing that could appease Remus and his ghosts, the lemures, was a return to the lost city he created and named for himself. It was called Remuria or Lemuria, you see? Weisman and Versnal most notably have talked about the possibility of this city being located on the Aventine and archaeology backs them up. Now, as John C. Miles once wrote in 'Lemuria: A Roman or American Cult?' there's ample evidence of Remus and his lemures' efforts to get back to their forgotten city. Take the real animals called lemurs, which Linnaeus named back in 1783 for the homeless, wide-eyed, shrieking ghosts of Roman mythology. Right? Linnaeus was a member of the Etruscan Discipline and was the first to purport the theory among tyros that lemurs are not primates. Indeed, they are not even 'real' as we think of 'real.' Lemurs are ghosts, too, agents of Remus, his spies, looking for doorways back into his lost city of Remuria. They now span the globe watching with their wide, shocked eyes the parade of humans and seeking to identify human souls on behalf of Remus, souls brave enough to find the pathway into their master's lost city."

Garbus reached into his shirt pocket, tapped out a cigarette, and offered one to Boy King.

"God, yes," Boy King said and placed it between his lips without lighting it.

"Keep talking," Garbus said, cigarette bobbing as he spoke.

"It's all here," Boy King said, tapping those two cards, again and again as he spoke, the words spilling out of him with impossible, tumbling speed. "The game for which tarot was created was called *trionfi*—that is, 'triumphs.' Remus's death and the ritual it inspired were commemorated with the game. Each hand in trionfi, taken with a 'triumph card,' was a reminder of the triumphator's approach to the *templum*, the Temple, and his petition of the god over the exposed liver of the sacrificial bull. One cannot separate the rite from the myth, the game from the rite, the cards from the occult. Because it's all here like a little city. These two cards might as well be The World card. The brothers. The parade. The evocation of the crime. The question that Romulus needed to know, which was *Am I forgiven for what I did to my brother*?" Boy King covered his mouth. He swallowed a laugh, then realized it was a sob. He looked at Garbus, then dropped his hand and smiled.

"Sounds like you have a lot to say, John," Garbus said.

Boy King put his finger on The Magician's chest. Then he stopped. He looked up at Garbus and said, "What did you call me?"

"John," Garbus said, grinning at him. "John C. Miles."

Who was this? Was Garbus in the real world? How did he know that name?

Boy King didn't want to find out. He grabbed his cardboard box and darted for the front door. He could hear Garbus scrambling after him. Boy King turned over a bar stool behind him to block Garbus's way and saw, at the front of the bar, three police officers and a fourth man in a black suit with a massive white head and dark sunglasses.

That fucker, Boy King thought. *Garbus called the cops on me!*

With the front door blocked, he skidded to a stop and changed directions, Garbus leaping over the bar stool behind him. Boy King barreled through the swinging doors into the kitchen, hoping to find a fire exit back there.

"We got him, we got him!" an officer shouted. "Everyone stand back."

It was a tight fit in the kitchen, so he couldn't help but bash into Elaine and Sarah, the two line cooks on duty, as he shouted for them to get out of the way. Then, having forced them back from the deep fryer, he opened the cardboard box and upended the little paintings into the boiling oil.

"Boy King! No!" Sarah yelled.

Elaine hurled herself back against the refrigerator. "Stop!"

There was a great heave of bubbling oil as the contents of the fryer crested and boiled over onto the griddle. As the oil hit the hot surface, a plume of oily black smoke billowed into the little kitchen.

Elaine and Sarah wormed past him to get out of the kitchen. He stood there, staring. There was no way out. He had imagined a back door, a sprint down an alley, and freedom. Instead, the police easily sealed off his escape and hauled him out of the kitchen, with Sarah and Elaine screaming about the boiling grease everywhere and the bald one-eyed man glaring at Boy King in abject hatred. "Visconti," Boy King said.

"That wasn't the deck!" Visconti screamed into Boy King's face as the police dragged him out of the bar. "Tell me that wasn't the deck!"

Garbus shouted from somewhere in the bar, "Is that John C. Miles? Was I right? Is there a reward?"

"John C. Miles, you're under arrest," one of the police officers was saying as they grabbed him by belt and shirt and hauled him out of the kitchen and the Wiggle Room. "You're being arrested for disturbing the peace. Do you understand me, Mr. Miles?"

Boy King's mind reeled. "Why are you calling me that?" he shouted, twisting to look the officer in the eye. "Why are you calling me by that name?"

"You're John C. Miles. We have a full dossier on you," the officer said.

"You have the wrong man," Boy King shouted. "I'm not! I'm not that man!"

"You destroyed it," Visconti kept shouting, screaming behind Boy King as the officer herded him out into the sunlight. "That's the end? You tossed it into a goddamned deep fryer? That's how it all ends?"

A squad car was parked with two wheels on the curb, perpendicular to the bar's front door. As they emerged from the Wiggle Room, the officer pushed Boy King against the back door and frisked him. A crowd had already formed in a ring around the squad car, and while he was read his rights, Boy King looked across the car's roof and saw a man in a black jacket with wiry hair, herring-bone trousers, and shiny black cop shoes. He wore a sarcastic grin, and he nodded a hello when Boy King saw him.

"You were blowing smoke at me," the man said across the car roof to Boy King, arching his thick eyebrows, "that time in Trudy's."

Trudy's? thought Boy King. That was the name of his favorite bar in Austin, back in the old days when he hung out there with Jer—

Who was this man?

"It's not as amazing as it looks," the wiry-haired fellow said. He wiped his brow. His face was slick with perspiration. "Twelve years for you was just a couple days' work for me, Miles."

Boy King spat at him. "That's not my name!"

"Damn animal." Visconti came to stand by the wiry-haired man with a downward glance at Boy King's spittle on the ground. He lifted his ugly bald head and said to Boy King, "You've destroyed yourself. You're going to pay and pay and pay, Miles."

"That's not me!" Boy King shouted as the officer put a hand on his head, guiding him into the squad car. "That's not who I am!"

17

He was about to finish cutting. The curved blade of
the plow opened the turf, exposed the black soil,
and dust plumed from the muscled bodies and heavy
hooves of his driving team. The long trench trailed behind
the team, circled back around the greatest of these seven
hills, ending dead ahead of him several hundred paces,
where his plow-circle had begun. He pulled back on the
reins, leaning his sweaty, sunscorched body backward, and
the two horses twisted their necks, showing their teeth to
the sky.

The muddy Tiber River ambled through the dry flood-
plain that was amber from drought, and a short way from
the black wound in the turf, a squad of shepherds was gath-
ered with thick staves facing the plowman. One shepherd, as
tall as the plowman, stood forward from the gang, unarmed.

Both were young. Both were big, broad-shouldered and obviously related—brothers. Sunlight shafted down through the spreading orange dust around them.

Watching this scene, Rosemont sat on the northern face of the second highest hill, elbows on his knees. Miles appeared at his side, staring down into the wide river valley. "What the fuck did you do?" He took in the scene but didn't seem surprised by what he was seeing. "How did you make this happen?"

The lone shepherd standing apart from the rest shouted something long and involved, and the plowman stood as if enduring hurtful words, holding gloves in one hand in a fist upon his hip, head bowed, black hair hanging in his eyes.

"What's he saying?" Rosemont asked.

Miles turned his ear to the ringing voice of the shepherd. "So that's Etruscan. Sounds like Greek." The shepherd kept gesturing back to the Aventine and making a sweeping arc with his arm to indicate the valley or the great circle his brother had drawn. Miles quoted, as if translating the shepherd's words, " 'Illium's maidens fled their bowers / Soldiers unmann'd armor'd towers / Fences fell and so did doors / Ulysses walk'd through walls like yours.' "

Rosemont looked at Miles. "That's pretty. Who's that?"

"A contemporary of Jonson's and Shakespeare's," said Miles. "Lionel Crane's *Remo et Romolo*. He knew."

The plowman was now waving his work gloves at the shepherd and shouting back, dismissive and patronizing. He looked past the shepherd at the congregation listening, waved at those shepherds too, shooing them away.

"Romulus is the one inside the circle, right?" said Rosemont.

"Right," Miles said, watching.

"He's going to kill Remus? The shepherd?"

Miles nodded. "That's the story."

"Do you know what they're arguing about?"

"Remus is about to jump across the trench in an attempt to ruin Romulus's magic," Miles said.

"Why?"

"No one's sure about why."

The plowman, his body grimy from the dirt churned up by his team, began walking back along the trench seemingly to inspect his work. The shepherd stalked him.

"It doesn't make sense why," Miles said. "They were both trained in the Etruscan Discipline, which back then was keyed on the art of city building—creating gates, laying down streets, and raising walls. Jumping this circle? After the Trojan Diaspora? It would have been like a Catholic knocking over a Vatican cross on Easter Sunday. This is the climax of a five-hundred-year-old quest for Romulus and Remus's sect of the Etruscans," Miles said, letting his gaze travel across the forests and slopes of this terrain, the Eternal City to be. "They wanted to resurrect Troy here and needed this circle, this wall to do it."

The brother within the circle turned away and began walking back toward his plow team. The brother without kept right after him, the trench dividing them as if a wall already separated them. Rosemont and Miles watched them go back and forth like this several times, with the shepherd shouting and the plowman ignoring him.

Miles said, "This is fucking nuts. How did we get here, Rosemont? What is *happening*?"

Rosemont said, "I wanted us out of that Chi-Chi's. I wanted the deck, and I wanted you. So I got us out."

Miles frowned. "You wanted the deck?"

Rosemont lifted his hand. He was holding fifteen normal-looking cards. Turning them over, they could see the broiling images on each one, and Miles jerked his head away.

"Ach," he said. "Turn them over. Hide them." When Rosemont did, Miles looked back and said, "You took them? You *changed* them?" He looked hard at Rosemont. "What in the name of fuck are you?"

Rosemont said, "I don't know how I did it. I didn't try."

"The idea was to show it to Marni," Miles said. "The idea was to show an unbroken thread between Wilusija, Rome, and us, and claim the deck as part of that. It's not meant for just one person."

The exchange at the bottom of the hill was heating up. Now the shepherd was lying prostrate before his brother, pretending to worship him. Then he flipped up his wolf-skin kilt and bared his ass, crawling in front of the plowman on all fours, barking, braying like a donkey, and making loud farting noises along the trench. The plowman stood stock still, his shoulders back and his chest heaving a little in anger, watching his brother mock him. Finally, Remus stood and seemed to implore his brother to jump across. He was cajoling him, but it seemed sincere too, as if he honestly wanted his brother to break his own spell and join him outside the circle.

"Remus didn't want a city," Rosemont said.

Miles looked at him. "Don't think so? What *did* he want?"

Rosemont shook his head. "Freedom from all that. He wants his bro to want that too."

Romulus unclasped a weapon from his belt that could have been either a spade or a sword, walked briskly to the unplowed section of the circle, held up the tool, spoke to it, and then ran dragging it in the dirt, shouting the same short, rhythmic sentence over and over. When he reached the beginning of his circle, he completed it with a flick of the blade in such a clear gesture of contempt that Rosemont and Miles both chuckled.

But as he swaggered back to face his brother, something appeared behind Romulus inside the circle.

"What is that?" said Miles, standing.

Rosemont stood too. "People."

A moment later, Remus was threatening to jump across the circle and Romulus was sarcastically welcoming him. Neither brother seemed to see the three figures in sand-colored desert robes behind Romulus.

"Maybe they aren't really there," said Rosemont.

"What in the world?" said Miles, voice breaking. "Did Romulus conjure them?"

Remus leapt across the trench and came to stand before his brother. Romulus staggered back as if struck. He dropped the spade and turned away from his brother's consoling hand, staring at the trench with back straight, his head in his hands, like a man watching trains collide. Remus walked up to the trench and, yelling to his mates, gestured for them to come forward, come across, enter the impotent circle. As Remus raised his left arm to them, Romulus spun and snatched up the spade behind Remus's back, then plunged it with one great, two-handed thrust into Remus's ribs, high under his arm. Blood spurted onto Romulus's forearms as he forced his brother down with the tool jammed in his body, down onto one knee, and then to his right side and back.

Romulus stood and flicked the tool toward the earth, like a gardener flipping mud off the blade of his trowel. Then, the three robed figures ran toward the Aventine.

"He's gone," said Rosemont. He meant it literally. Remus was gone, nowhere to be seen in the circle. No body. No blood.

"Shit," Miles said. "What the hell are they?"

Rosemont turned over one of the cards and tried to re-create the same frame of mind he'd used to steal the deck in the first place. He tested the earth with the balls of his toes and was almost knocked backward at the force he felt.

Miles instinctively steadied him. "You got any ideas? Want to try to talk our way out of this?"

Rosemont held his friend's arm and saw that the robed hunters had reached the bottom of this hill. These hills were enormous, but the beings were running in a shifting, dissolving run, like Priscilla had, covering ground at a shocking clip.

I want out. I want the deck. I want Miles. And this time, I want out of Rome altogether.

Stale beer, a smoky mesquite grill smell from Ruby's down the street, stifling cologne in tarrying auras, long-neck bottles on the picnic tables, and the stars at night really are big and bright, high over bent magnolia trees and a growling Texas bar. Rosemont knew this place like he knew how to tie his shoes, a mindless, habitual knowing. He felt that if he turned the corner around this bar that the older tarot reader would have already ordered a pitcher, would be grinning at him over it, like a crazed monkey with a mane of ringlets, lording over his golden idol, pouring Rosemont another glass as the younger reader tried lamely to beg off, both of them secure in the knowledge that neither was going anywhere.

Rosemont turned the corner, where the eclectic jukebox sat in an awkward choke point, and there they were. They were there, like two chess players leaning over an imaginary board. They'd spent the whole day talking between bouts of tarot readings at the Circus of Infinite Wow, and now they'd spend the night unhinged from their own minds, ranting and laughing and quarreling, as if the words couldn't come out fast enough, as if they'd spent the previous eighteen years waiting for the arguments and beer to begin.

Students sporting more tattoos than Rosemont had ever seen as a young man milled through the bar. Day-Glo fingerpolish on nails. Magenta hair. So very Austin. It seemed fresh and so long ago.

An older Miles appeared at his side, staring at themselves across Trudy's. "They look so innocent. Let's kill them now and put them out of our misery."

A moment later, a man in a dark suit jacket with a tight black T-shirt underneath and light herringbone trousers was sidling up to Miles. Rosemont snickered as Miles gave him a complete head-to-toe, from his shiny cop shoes to his wirehair terrier curls.

The man said to Miles, "Who are you?"

Miles glared down at the stocky little man with heavy eyebrows. "I'm Hillary Clinton. Who are you?"

"Hillary, I'm Special Agent Erturk Mehmet," said the man. "And I know you don't belong here, because I don't belong here."

Rosemont started as if to run—but run where? He looked at Miles.

"We're tourists," Miles said.

"Me, I'm flat on my back in a hospital that has no name with an FBI hypnotist whispering sweet nothings in my ear," said Special Agent Mehmet. "I'm looking for someone. A homeless man. He doesn't belong here, either, but I don't know who he is." He turned his head as if catching a far-off tune, and his gaze lifted inexplicably to the ceiling.

"Yeah? We just got here, but I'll keep my eyes peeled," Miles said. "What's he look like?"

The special agent looked back at the two men standing before him. "He looks like you. Either one of you." Mehmet scanned both their faces, back and forth. "You two brothers?"

"We used to get that a lot," Rosemont said.

"Either of you been to Minneapolis?"

Miles shivered. "Hell, no."

"Let me ask you something," Mehmet said. He touched his chest, searching his breast pocket, and swore. "Oh, right. My notebook's back with me in the black ops hospital." His hand went to his forehead, rubbed it dejectedly. "Ibotenic acid and muscimol are coursing nicely now." His thick eyebrows met. He was sweating profusely, Rosemont suddenly realized. "But it makes it hard to remember where and when I am. Listen. Listen up. I need help with two words."

Miles laughed. "What do you mean? Help with words?"

" 'Meschasipi.' " He bit his lip and shook his head. "No? Do you know that word? Meh. *Shah*. Sippy. Something like that?"

Rosemont said he didn't know what it was and turned away. Mehmet made him nervous.

But Miles continued to laugh. Across the bar, their younger counterparts were arguing loudly, slashing the air in front of each other's faces with hands and pointed fingers.

"Might be a city. A whole lot of people I know are headed there, looking for the homeless man I was telling you about. I want to join them but I don't know what it is," Mehmet said, wiping his brow with the flat of his hand.

At that moment, the jukebox went silent and Rosemont shouted into the suddenly quiet bar, "I thought you said the homeless man was here!" "Cherub" by the Butthole Surfers had ended. Rosemont lowered his voice and repeated himself.

"No one knows *where* he is." Mehmet looked about, suspiciously, then said, "What about this? I'm not sure how the vowels land in this name. Khnemu? Khnum? Ring a bell?"

Hank Williams filled the stunned silence with "I'm a Long Gone Daddy." After a pause, Miles decided to laugh some more.

"Is that a city, too?" Rosemont asked coldly, willing himself not to be frightened of this man.

"No." Mehmet stopped wiping his brow and seemed more confident being able to speak about Khnum. "It's the name of a foreign intelligence agency. I've been tracking its movement and lending them support. Here." He flattened his hands, palms down, and looked around the bar. "On this level."

"You're helping them?" Miles stopped laughing but kept his smile nice and friendly. "What are they after?"

"Something pharmacological, I think," Mehmet said. "Must be potent. The full twenty-three expressions allow one to create doppelgängers, which is what Ehirllimbal sent back to the States, of course, but the intervening expressions work up to that." He nodded significantly and cast his skittish gaze about the room again. "You two know all about that."

"The fuck are you talking about?" Rosemont said.

"You tell me. A new way to astral project?" Mehmet mused. "It'd explain a *lot*. Something beyond the twenty-third expression? I can't even imagine what's at stake here, or what everyone is looking for, but I'm sure the Bureau knows." His beady eyes narrowed even further and, amiably, he hit Rosemont with the back of his hand. "Now what is that? I've been seeing that for a while now." He pointed out the window.

Rosemont turned and saw the smooth, lion-colored fabric of a desert robe, just as it disappeared from view. The wall of the bar, there, seemed to ripple as the thing outside walked by, heading toward the door.

Before he could stop himself, Rosemont had the Watts deck cradled in his palm.

Miles and Special Agent Mehmet glanced down to see what Rosemont was holding.

"What's the matter?" hissed Miles, looking up into Rosemont's face.

Mehmet, too, looked up from Rosemont's hand to his eyes, and then he stepped backward, looking back at the deck. He reached beneath his jacket for a gun, perhaps, that was usually there. He swore and looked back at the deck. "That's it, isn't it? An expression. You have it!"

No more. No more! Rosemont recoiled from Mehmet. *Let's go!*

The air in the bar felt cooked, loaded, like too much blood pumping in a single vein as Miles and Rosemont stepped away.

"It's you!"

"Fall apart in the Circus of Infinite Wow." A taped woman's voice wove through the makeshift fairgrounds, cottonwoods nodding overhead. "In the Circus. In the Circus. In the Circus of Infinite Wow." And then reverb, with the cooing feminine voice going. "Wowowowowowowowowowowow."

Acid carnival music in three-quarter time carried sinister whimsy among the stalls of tattooed strongmen and sword swallowers, pony girls in leather skin suits carrying circus-goers by cart to the main stage where Ed Hall was bashing out a set with Fire Goddesses squirting lit jets of lighter fluid on bare breasts, well-muscled giants in skimpy short-shorts and kitty costumes giving piggyback rides, I-Can-Eat-Anything Man ("Because I can eat anything, man"), Jigsaw the Human Contortionist, the Cutter Sisters, Orgasma the Dirty Mentalist—and into this memory came Rosemont and Miles.

"It's more colorful than I remember it," Miles said, reading the main banner.

"I was seventeen," Rosemont was saying. "It was all so new to me after Racine."

They walked over to the tarot tent together, and Rosemont wondered if they were really safe here. He didn't want trouble. He didn't want any more menacing surreality.

Couldn't they just be in this Austin and explore it without worrying about being followed, hunted, chased? "I want to get rid of the Watts deck," he said.

"Now you don't want it," Miles said. "Now you want to throw it in a river."

"No, I just—" Rosemont stopped. He *did* want to throw it in a river. "It's a relief just to be away from Rome."

Miles took the cards and said, "You know what a *templum* is?"

"No."

"It's a safe piece of territory from which to view the other world or work the greater work. In there," he said, pointing to the tarot tent. "That's a *templum*. I know. I drew it before we ever raised the tent."

Rosemont followed. "You drew it back then?"

He shrugged. "I must have known what I was doing," he said. "It's strong. I can feel it now. Maybe why you were able to get a foothold, too, and bring us here. Come with me."

In the Circus of Infinite Wow, the two tarot readers had been bland geraniums among jungle orchids. Even with Miles's trademark wrestling mask, tarot readings simply slowed the pace of the Infinite Wow down to an unsexy halt compared to the raging mayhem of, say, the cross-country jugglers or the Mighty Twelve (boxing midgets), but it turned out that lots of circus-goers appreciated the tarot readers' tent as a brief retreat from the Infinite Wow's symphony of bodily weirdness. It was always full, with young folks lounging and drinking Shiners on folding chairs watching Miles read.

Miles opened the tent flap and winced as he looked at himself. "Yeeg. What a grisly sight."

But Rosemont grinned. When he first met Miles he was seventeen and ripe for exactly the brand of strange that Infinite Wow was cranking out. Rosemont had fallen in love with John C. Miles the moment he watched him read cards for the first time, that love one feels when another's strangeness and oddity feels like a puzzle piece snapping into place. Lucha libre mask over his face, hands folded calmly, a little candle lighting the hot tent, young Miles was leaning across his card table and jabbing his index finger at a farm boy wearing a Longhorns cap.

"Thirteen days!" Miles in Mexican wrestling mask was shouting at him. "That's how long you have to get things right with your sister! After that, things are going to explode like a water balloon right in the kisser. Full of lighter fluid. While you're smoking. So no lit cigarettes and don't come crying to me when your face melts right off your head. Next."

Rosemont recalled the first time he got a reading like this from Miles. He'd been hired by the Circus to be the straight reader because Miles was scaring lots of money away. Young Rosemont thought Miles's reading style was hysterical, which earned him points with Miles, but it was unnerving too. So was seeing Miles's tarot deck. Scrawled over with notes, written in ballpoint. Rosemont simply couldn't get his brain around it. "You *write* on your tarot decks?"

"Sure." The red wrestling mask had faced him. "But only important shit," Miles said, mouth slightly muffled behind the lamprey eel mouth of the mask. "It's not like I'm putting phone numbers on my cards, for chrissakes."

Older Miles and Rosemont stood inside the candlelit tent for a moment, listening to the younger Miles read, and then Miles gestured for Rosemont to follow him, circling around to the back of the big tent.

"The Page of Swords is a trap. He's a vicious little thing and you'll have to chew your leg off to get away so don't play around—hey, you two clowns wanna sit down?" younger Miles said, looking up from his spread. "I'm in the middle of surgery, okay?"

"Shut your cakehole, jackass," said Miles to himself.

The lucha libre mask stayed aimed at them for a second more as they backed into the shadows of the tent, and then younger Miles continued. "So that's The Page. Let's look at The Four of Testicles."

In the back of the tent Miles pulled up piles of S&M gear until he found, on the ground, a blue spray-painted square, like something a utility company might draw on the ground for digging. "There it is. Put the cards right there."

Rosemont looked back at the younger Miles. "Won't someone find it?"

"Nah. Not exactly Remus getting ready for the auspices, but it'll do," Miles said. "Just put it there and I'll draw another *templum* somewhere else and retrieve it."

Rosemont set the cards down in the middle of the blue square and instantly, the deck vanished. He was almost relieved to see the cards disappear.

"What are they?" Rosemont whispered, looking down at the empty square. "What did I steal?"

Miles's eyes narrowed in wonder. "You still don't know."

"How in the world *would* I know, Miles? How in the world would I understand? I get a letter in the middle of the night, and I follow it back to the sender, and, yes, I understand that I was the one who accepted the ticket, I get that. But it doesn't help explain what the Watts deck is or who these people are who are obsessed with it. Or why I just walked from the Aventine to Trudy's with a whacked-out urban mythologist. You see?"

"Hey, asshole," younger Miles shouted from the main room of the tent. "Go have your pathetic mental breakdown somewhere else!"

"Nobody knows, Rosemont. None of them know," Miles said, lifting the tent flap for Rosemont and then ducking out after. "They want it to be something, but they don't know what it *is*."

"Visconti seems to know. He seems to have some control," Rosemont said. He could smell the mutton that On the Lamb caterers always brought in. "You have any money?"

"No," Miles groused, his posture straightening as he smelled the roasting mutton. "See. This is my theory about you and Visconti. But especially you because I know you. What you just said is wrong. Control and knowing aren't the same thing. I think we have a cultural memory of a time when logic did not prevail, when instinct and magic ruled and we routinely bumped up against chaos without it destroying our minds. We rightly call that chaos madness now, but once, madness was an accepted mechanism in human thinking. It was necessary. And I think something like the Watts deck does not exist without it."

"Madness," Rosemont repeated, skeptical and dismissive. "Maybe."

"By our standards, madness, yes. Schizophrenia. Hallucinations. Multiple personalities."

Miles had never liked the way Rosemont contradicted

him—flat out, blunt. Rosemont liked getting Miles's goat. "Bullshit."

"Well, you explain what just happened! Go on. Explain it, you ridiculous motherfucker. Explain how you got here."

Rosemont had been settling into their old rhythm, and he was arguing from his no-bullshit default mode, as if he hadn't just traversed the globe and across time in a heartbeat. "I can't."

"That's right, you can't, because you need control to explain anything," Miles went on. "You're a harnessed horse. You're a good little tool of Romulus and George Bush and the Democrats and the Ford Motor Company. You trust control more than your own eyes."

Rosemont was incredulous. "Are you calling me a control freak?"

Miles laughed raucously, crowlike.

"What's so fucking funny?"

"You. You and your perfect hair and your perfect little work boots," Miles shouted, "and you just *stole,*" he shouted some more, slapping the table, "the Holy Grail. You are the biggest control freak I have ever known in my life. Why? Why did you steal the deck?"

Rosemont couldn't answer him, because he sensed his friend was right. He didn't like to believe it about himself. He liked thinking that he was a libertine, the kind of fellow who could screw a priest and feel okay about it afterward. But he knew Miles was right, and he knew what Miles would say about his motive. His seduction of Aurelio wasn't done out of a love for freedom or a respect for the liberty in the man. He wanted to control the situation, wanted to guide the older fellow down the street, into bed, and say he did it wantonly. Rosemont didn't twirl his mustachios and pounce on the poor man. He did it without thinking, like grabbing a smoke or following his stomach to a restaurant, except that want inside him, that need to fulfill, commit, control, was frightening.

Rosemont recalled long ago, how, after Miles had watched Rosemont read cards for a big-haired Dallas lady at the Infinite Wow, Miles had said, "You're too smooth for your own good." Hearing it was like a concussion for Rosemont—it was one of the truest things anyone had ever said about him. And it remained true. Readings, explanations, artifact analyses, lectures, historical reports, articles, truths, lies, all could spill out of him faster than thought—so fast, sometimes, that he would later wonder where all the right words had come from. Standing in the Chi-Chi's of the Damned, when he realized that the Watts deck was as real as the Guelph analysis said it was, Rosemont had coveted it—so when he'd turned and faced the room, ready to tell them what he thought about the deck, the words were already flowing. He had taken control of that room without knowing it, without planning it. He just did it and he didn't know why.

There had been a day when Rosemont proved to himself that he was this way, a controller—though he'd thought of it as something playful, challenging, and freeing of his hungers. That day with the funhouse mirrors when he'd shown Miles who he was. That day that a duel of bodies, hearts, and selves began, which had never ended, which still clashed and parried, clashed and parried.

"We could be brothers," Miles had said, pulling Rosemont close and looking at themselves in a mirror, side by side.

A blue balloon had levitated to the peaked roof of the funhouse tent, and young Rosemont watched its reflection slither up the funhouse mirror.

Rosemont's shoe-polish black hair and clean-shaven face had been oddly matched by the harder, scruffier version of himself in Miles. *We* could *be brothers.* But the way Miles said it, it was like a hint, a proposal. Was Miles really coming on to him? Three swallows darted in the air around the blue balloon, and Rosemont pushed Miles away playfully, but didn't know why, except it just felt like too much all of a sudden, after days and days of drinking, throwing cards, drinking, and locked up in conversation with Miles over drinks, and some more drinking. But before the break of contact, there was a tangy recognition of skin and muscle finding its own and wanting more, and Rosemont looked back at Miles, the moment stretching out and out and all the days of schoolboy kidding around, the strategies of getting close to each other in roughhouse intimacy, of smear-the-queer and swimming pool chicken fights, which Rosemont played with a smirking self-knowing, even at a very young age, now filled him with stage fright, looking at Miles and the shape of his delicate chin. Because behind all of John C. Miles's veils—brash Texan, fast-talking bullshitter, leaping, unrestrained intellect, mad fortune-teller—was a disorienting heaviness. Rosemont hadn't felt it in his friend before, but Rosemont understood it, that weight like a massive planet in the heart, warping gravity around it, and caving reality in on itself, because to look at Miles and see it, feel it, was to feel it in his own self. Being pulled from Valhalla like a fish pulled from its own silver waters. Guns and flak jackets. Thrown into his grandparents' home. A new name for a new school. Forced to make it all normal. And no mother to explain it, protect him. All executed as if he didn't matter. And he didn't matter, never had. Not like now.

"We *could* be," Rosemont hinted back, feeling raw and exposed, seeing Miles this way.

And then it was Miles's turn to shy and shirk, turning his shoulder to Rosemont and mugging in the mirror. "Hey. I'm Elastic Man."

Most men were boys, really, even older ones, Rosemont had learned in high school. They felt most at ease turning innocently intimate moments into games, and most did not care for hearts. Rosemont had expected something more from Miles, that the young man would be a guide, not a boy. But that weight, that dense planet turning in him—it was a wonder Miles could stand upright, breathe, let alone offer guidance.

Standing slightly behind him, Rosemont leaned against Miles. "I've never been pinned."

Miles grinned at him in the distorted mirror. "Bull."

"Never. And you can't do it, either."

"I could pin you blindfolded."

Rosemont shook his head, looking at their reflections over Miles's shoulder. "Sorry."

It was an off-day. There were no guests, no customers. Most of the Infinite Wow's performers had road tripped to Mustang Island on the Gulf Coast to eat mushrooms. Like that, Rosemont found his wrist in Miles's fist, pulled forward, his neck under Miles's armpit in a headlock, and a moment later, he found himself driving Miles forward, onto his hip, knocking his yellow tinted glasses across the grass, breaking the hold, straddling him, winning.

"Come on!" Miles said from beneath Rosemont,

laughing and trying to catch his breath. "Come on, buddy."

"I'm not letting you up."

Miles put his hands on Rosemont's thighs. "I didn't ask you to."

Good thing. Rosemont couldn't have stood if he wanted. Their bodies were magnets snapping together, too powerful to pull apart, so Rosemont kept Miles pinned and kissed his delicate chin, his throat. Then Rosemont raised his head and looked at Miles, stunned to realize that the soap opera details of whatever had hurt his friend didn't matter—Rosemont might as well have been looking at a shell-shocked version of himself, looking down at Miles. "Don't worry, I'd never hurt you," Rosemont told him.

"What?" Miles said, and then he laughed raucously under Rosemont. But he fell quiet. It was no use, his shining eyes seemed to say. Rosemont had seen.

"I'd do anything," Rosemont whispered, not sure what his words meant but knowing they were true.

Miles's head nodded, a little boy's earnestness. "I know. Me, too," he said. "Wherever I go, you come too. Okay?"

Rosemont nodded, unbuttoning Miles's shirt down to his stomach. "Okay."

Skin pressed against new skin, and their bodies crushed together and held. One mouth fed, another gasped, a hand slipped over it to silence the cries, and a quiet grinding yearned for itself over and over. Might this moment stay? Would the pain stay away? Would the world make this much sense when it was over? A quake shot through all that muscle and bone. A wild, looping release, and the pleasure that came was a sad, shredding split. It wouldn't stay together. It was over, and this was all.

"You wanted to be in control, didn't you?" Miles was saying in the Circus of Infinite Wow, a few years older but just as excitable. "You wanted Visconti and Transom and me to know that there was another force to reckon with at that bargaining table."

That might have been true but Rosemont said, "It's not always a competition, Miles."

Miles smiled slyly as if sharing a delicious joke. "It is with you."

Rosemont shook his head, toying with the notion that he had once loved Miles but knowing that the truth of that was far away. Miles never told, never told about the vicious hole that had been torn in him. So all they had was the game. If that was love, then what was Casa Evangelista, finding the old priest's delicious fear of being caught and leaning on it, commanding it? Was that love? And when the young Professor Rosemont had drawn a cadre of students and fellow teachers, most older than himself, but all devoted, frighteningly devoted—was that love? And when one of his young students received a birthday card written in his dead father's hand and another was possessed by a spirit that burned alchemical symbols into his skin with match heads, when irrationally straight lines were drawn back to Rosemont, and the shovel handles came down one night—was that love? Professor Rosemont's strangeness, his witchy charisma and otherliness was something Rosemont had vowed to relinquish lying on that hospital gurney. He'd fallen down through Mexican and Central American highways and rows of coffee plants, only to wind up here, back in the Circus of Infinite Wow, a stolen talisman in his pocket, John C. Miles before him, and the old duel about what they were still clashing with every word he chose or didn't choose. "No. Not always, John."

Miles gave him a goofy grin, obviously didn't know how to respond, could not see Rosemont, now, as anything but a gamesman who got what he wanted, and he admired him for it.

Over Lake Travis, a storm was swooping into town with wind and rain coming across the water. All around them canvas flapped in the sudden storm, and it was strange not to be joining the team in breaking the circus down. Whipping tents unstaked themselves and banners lashed, so that Rosemont did not hear the swish of robes or see the shift and dissolve of sand-colored fabrics. Lightning cleaved the blackening sky in the northwest and froze there, didn't wisp away, but remained a glowing, brazen streak, brandished in the dark. Hands upon wrists. A wrist across the windpipe. Someone was being muscled to the ground, and Rosemont was pretty sure it was him. What followed was very, very dark. So black that Rosemont could barely breathe. How had this happened? How had he wound up here? With duct tape over his eyes, and a pillowcase upon his head? Duct tape on his hands too, and he was lying somewhere cramped, in something like windshield-wiper fluid.

There was a sound like bungee cords scraping on a bumper, and as they snapped and lashed, the noise was deafening.

Because I'm in a trunk, thought Rosemont. *How did this happen? Am I Miles suddenly? Back in Rome? Who is opening the trunk of this Volvo? Is that me coming to save myself?*

A moment later he was being hauled, carried, like a sack of flour over someone's shoulder. All he could smell was oil. Machinery. A garage? He tried to ask what was happening but his brain was foggy and he didn't care right now what was happening to him enough to speak or to complain about the hard chair in which he was placed. A deep, echoing cavern of time hollowed him out as he waited and waited and waited.

At last, footsteps scuffed in the room some fifty or sixty feet from him. There was a scratching and scritching too. Nails on concrete. Animals were here in the room with him. A moment later, the fabric covering his head was being removed.

"It's him. We found him," said a woman's voice.

"Priscilla?" Rosemont said.

"Yes," she said, close to his ear. "Are you hurt?"

His wrists were bound in place, he realized, fixed to the arms of this uncomfortable chair. "No, I don't think so. But I can't move."

"Rosemont," she said, "you don't have the deck with you, do you?"

"No," he said, and for a flash, he doubted if this were really Priscilla. "It's safe," he said.

"Good, good," she said. "Because you aren't safe. We can't let them yoke you—your mind won't survive it. Now listen. I'm not really here. I'm hunting for you along with Marni, and Miles is searching too. He's closer than I am but I don't think he's going to get to you in time."

Rosemont's head turned toward Priscilla's voice. "In time? For what? Where am I?"

"Visconti is going to get the location of the deck out of

you," she whispered. Every syllable was like a tender secret in the vast, empty room. "He has to hurt you in order to do it."

Rosemont's head turned left and right as he thrashed against the bindings. "God, Priscilla, get me out of here!"

"Quiet, quiet," Priscilla whispered urgently. "Stop saying my name!"

He stopped wrestling against his ties and forced himself to calm down. "Where's Miles? Is he coming? Is he near?"

"Yes," said Priscilla. "But he—he's being an idiot. So I need to tell you something."

Rosemont felt a resigned sob well up inside of him. He swallowed it, assuming he was going to get the ridiculous apology now for having sent for him, for having thrown him into a situation for which he wasn't prepared. "What? What do you have to say?"

Her voice was so close he was sure her lips were inches from his ear, his hair. "I've been watching you your whole life," she said, and it was almost a coo, "since you were a little boy in Madison. I was your mother's teacher, and Thyme Goldblatt was mine."

Thyme Goldblatt. He turned the name over in his head like a locket. Thyme? He hadn't thought of her in years, hadn't thought of Valhalla Commune, really, since the winter he was taken from it. Her name was like something from a fairy tale—it *was* a fairy tale, because those days didn't exist in anything like reality, rubbed out as they were by the FBI agents who came to transplant him in Racine. As he grew up there, his grandparents had simply iced over everything from Madison as if it had never happened, as if their own daughter hadn't been involved. His new name, Jeremiah Rosemont, was given to protect him from the figures of the Madison underground movement who, federal agents advised, might come for him. Figures like Thyme Goldblatt.

"What happened to Anita?" Rosemont said. "Where's my mother?"

Priscilla whispered, "Safe. In Prague."

"Well, good for fuckin' *her*," Rosemont said. "I take it she's not floating into this final scene like Glenda in a bubble to send me back to Kansas."

"No, Jeremiah," Priscilla said.

"Heh. One last betrayal," he said. He turned toward the voice. "Why the fuck are you telling me this now? Just to mock me? Why didn't you tell me this years ago, if you've been watching me?"

"Because we couldn't find you. You don't think we would have come and spirited you away? We had to wait for you," Priscilla said. "We all were waiting. Your mother too. We've been waiting to see if you would shuck off that blind normalcy that your grandparents put on you. That gets put on just about everyone." She paused. "It's time for you to realize that you don't need cards. You don't need the Aventine. You don't need anything, not even the Watts deck. What you are—"

"Yeah, I'm special," Rosemont said in a sneering mockery of Mr. Rogers, "just because I'm *me*. Get the fuck out of here, Priscilla. Stop it! Go! If you can't lift a goddamn finger—"

There was a loud whump, like a body hitting the floor. A body *had* hit the floor, right in front of him, Rosemont realized, and he jerked back in his chair from it. A woman's voice groaned and then started sucking for air. "Oh no," she said.

It was Priscilla.

"Got her," said a voice, and it was Kermit the Frog's distinctive tenor. "Was she talking to him? Was she freaking communicating? Christ, the nerve of—"

Kermit let out a shriek of laughter, and a second later, there was a gun blast. The report echoed sharply, made it sound like the walls were made of metal. In the smothering quiet, the pain of the gunshot kept stabbing Rosemont's ears.

"Transom," a rumbling voice said.

"Don't," said Transom, sharp and tense. "Just don't."

"That wasn't necessary," said the resonant, rolling voice. "I'm going to need a greater degree of discretion from you in the next half hour. Take the pillowcase off Mr. Rosemont's head."

"You heard him. Take the pillowcase off Rosemont's head," Transom snapped.

The hood came off, the duct tape was stripped from his eyes, and Rosemont found himself face to face with Kermit the Frog again. But now the balding fellow with the tender green eyes was wearing a beige linen suit and his general air of ridiculousness had been burned away. He was standing before Transom, who was dressed in that tight-fitting black Cardin jacket with his thinning hair slicked back. Transom had a hand on Kermit's back and Rosemont didn't like the look in Kermit's green eyes. Hard. Vicious.

Now he seemed desperate.

A mechanic's garage or a machine shop. Against one wall, a tangle of old transmissions was stacked. On another, tools hung on pegboard. Thirteen car doors were stacked nearby against a press or forge of some kind.

Priscilla's body lay several yards away on the concrete floor of this wide, open space.

Like the Japanese woman he'd seen in the Roman apartment, his forearms were lashed to long rectangular pieces of wood, like placards. The placards' wood was very fine—excellent hardwood. Rosemont tried to lift his forearms, to examine the boards, but duct tape was wound around chair arm, wood, and his arms.

Kermit and Transom were staring down at him, and Rosemont took in his new surroundings.

"I think you've changed," said the rumbling voice, and Visconti stepped into Rosemont's view, eclipsing Transom and Kermit. Tall, imposing. He was far uglier too than Rosemont had originally thought, with his pale fish eyes and large, unfinished sculpture of a head that looked like a skull hacked hastily from white chalk. He leaned down, and on a little chain, a pendant swung forward. The Khnum symbol. "I said, I think you've changed," Visconti said. "Everyone says so."

"Everyone says so, huh?" Rosemont said, eyes darting from Kermit to Transom to Visconti.

"How *have* you changed? Can you say?" said Visconti.

Rosemont couldn't pretend that he didn't know what Visconti was talking about, but he was busy trying to control his panic, to keep himself from looking at Priscilla. After Rome and Austin, he felt like his synapses had been rerouted with exploding stars, and he would have been shocked if a tyro like Visconti hadn't been able to smell it on him.

"Why don't you tell me about it?" Visconti said.

"I'm a quarter Italian." Rosemont looked down at his arms. "Hard to talk without using my hands."

Transom, after a little smile to show how unimpressed he was, reached out of Rosemont's view and a moment later had a hammer in his hand.

Rosemont's cockiness fell and broke when he saw the hammer, knowing what was about to happen.

All the while, Visconti's absurdly round eyes were lifeless in his great rock of a skull, staring down at Rosemont.

"Tell me about the Watts deck and what happened last year in Rome," the Duke said. "Quickly now. Before the others figure out where we are."

Last year? Is he bullshitting me? A year has gone by? Before he knew what he was doing, Rosemont's imagination had reached out for Visconti, a friendly arm and hand curving around the ugly man's shoulder, and he convinced himself that he believed what he was saying as he said, "I haven't changed. I'm me. I'm just me."

Visconti's face slackened in sympathy, disappointment. "Oh."

Rosemont said, "I'm a victim of circumstances that I don't understand. Only a few minutes went by for me."

"I see. Well, that can happen to a tyro like you or me," Visconti said. "Time, time. Who can tell with time?"

Transom glanced sidelong at Kermit, who glanced sidelong at Transom. Then Transom looked at Visconti in an angry squint.

Priscilla had said that Miles was near, but called him an idiot, so Rosemont wondered if he was having trouble finding where Rosemont was. He needed to stall, buy Miles more time to track him down.

"I didn't take the Watts deck. I was sent away," Rosemont said. "It was that di Trafana person."

"I see," Visconti said. "Di Trafana, then, has the deck?"

Rosemont shrugged. "I don't know who has it."

"Di Trafana told us *you* took it," Transom said.

With the swagger of a tomcat lording over prey, Visconti said, "Di Trafana was the Mad Monk, as we called him back then. A lemure—our term for priests of the lost city of Remoria. We think he created the deck, but that doesn't mean that there isn't something of Our Lord Khnum in his work. Khnum was the first. As the god-potter, his fingerprints are on everything."

"What are you talking about?" Transom asked Visconti. "Why are you nattering on about—?"

Rosemont pulled Visconti close, imagining his arm nice and snug around the ugly old bastard.

"A creature of extraordinary powers and length of life. That's what I'm talking about," Visconti said to Transom, as if rebuking him. "Like you, Jeremiah, I attracted the attention of ancient powers in my youth, 568 years ago. Di Trafana and a magician from Khemet, a disciple of Khnum, Our Lord the Spinning Wheel. They vied for my allegiance in my Citadel of Milan. I listened, because I wanted to unite Italy under my duchy."

Kermit was rapt. He'd obviously never heard this before, and his soft eyes seemed to fill with thoughts of Renaissance Italy. Transom was listening now too, though his eyes kept sliding over to Rosemont in his chair.

Rosemont didn't know if any of this was true, didn't care; he just wanted Visconti to keep talking. "So you were given the ancient cards and asked to look into them," Rosemont said. "By di Trafana?"

Visconti nodded and frowned as if this were a judicious concern on Rosemont's part. "What di Trafana did not see was that the answer to his riddle was not Remus. The twin Italy needed to remember was the triumphator, the heir of Troy, the conqueror. Romulus. And Khnum and Romulus were one, I saw. They were shapers. Builders of empires. Di Trafana saw power in hiding and camouflaging, and I saw power in—"

"Stop this!" shouted Transom. "You deformed, stupid mongoloid! He's playing you from the torture chair. Stop it!"

Visconti lunged at Transom, and the two tussled for a moment, until the duke grabbed the hammer from Transom. He swung it at Kermit, and then at Transom. "Will you stop interrupting me?"

"What is wrong with you, you drooling, moronic—"

"Go out in the office and wait there!" He took another swing at Kermit. "And take this shithead with you!"

Kermit backpedaled and then placed a hand upon his chest, as though wounded. "I'll have you know that I escaped Rosemont while I was at gunpoint! There's no need to insult—"

"Get him out of my sight, Transom!"

"And leave you alone with—"

"Go!" bellowed Visconti, raising the hammer.

Rosemont could tell he'd lost Visconti. He had lashed at Transom like that because he was furious that his underlings had seen him spun on his head. Rosemont felt all of this as if they were his own feelings, furiously boiling in his own heart—and he was terrified of the released, unleashed Visconti, for he had never felt anything so threatening, sadistic as the man when he raised that hammer. Visconti would have killed Transom had the smaller man not cowered and retreated.

"Bloated retard!" Transom stamped away, stung and petulant. He grabbed Kermit by the shoulder and shoved him through the doorway, into the outer room. "Imbecile!" Transom shouted at Visconti. He drew his gun and stepped outside, frowning childishly at Visconti through the crack in the door as he shut it between them.

Visconti turned back to Rosemont and his face showed his humiliation and bitterness. "What did the Khnum give you, Jeremiah Rosemont?"

Rosemont dangled from the image of the painting, not understanding its significance, not knowing how to tell Visconti what he wanted to know. It wasn't Khnum. Khnum was there, he supposed, but only insofar as Rosemont had been poisoned ahead of time by Kermit. It wasn't Khnum, no matter how the old man repeated the claim. There was some other presence within the cards and it wasn't Egyptian, wasn't what Visconti wanted it to be. The image had reshaped Rosemont, the thought of it reshaping him even now as he recalled it in his mind's eye. All he could say was, "Paintings. Paintings from the Watts deck is what I was given."

"That's what you took." Visconti hefted his hammer. "But that's not what he *gave* you."

Eyes on hammer. Eyes on hammer. Eyes on blessed, goddamn hammer. "I don't know what he gave me."

"Think. It was just a few moments ago for you. Think. He gave you something. What was it?"

There was no thing. There was no item. Had di Trafana given him something? There was the nod of encouragement and that strange moment of double-memories while viewing the deck, a light-headed disorientation and the image of fish leaving water that hardly seemed worth remembering at all. Was that it? Did Visconti want to hear about that? "I can't say. It was—"

Like a carpenter finding a knot in the wood he was cutting, Visconti said, "You really don't know, do you?"

"No," Rosemont said and sighed.

"It's too difficult for you to remember."

Rosemont nodded, relieved. "That's right."

Visconti removed a long, heavy nail from his suit coat pocket. He nodded the nail's head at Rosemont. "Torture is a failure, I've always said, because it's a recognition of equal power."

He may have cried out when he saw the nail, but he couldn't be sure. All over his body, Rosemont's skin broke sweat.

"You have something I want, that I cannot simply take," Visconti said.

Rosemont's face, the backs of his legs, even his feet seemed to be pouring sweat. "It was a painting. Some shitty little paintings. We don't need the nail. We don't need to do that."

"But it's a long-held Roman tradition for putting down magicians—or putting them up," Visconti said, crossing himself with a laugh, "as the case may be."

Rosemont clamped his eyes shut and, gloriously, there in the dark of his closed eyes, he could see Miles, who was looking this way and that, as if waiting for someone. He was standing next to a cash register and a tire display. A door behind him read Employees Only. If he screamed, Miles would hear him. But what if he didn't respond in time? Visconti could kill Rosemont with a quick hammer blow if he didn't handle this correctly. *Oh Jesus Christ, Miles, why can't you hear us talking? We're so close. Open the door and walk through it!*

To Visconti he said loudly, "I took them because I wanted them. I'm sorry. But I don't need them. I don't need them that badly."

Visconti made a little noise in the back of his throat as if he found this fascinating. "What were they of?"

Rosemont had just enough presence of mind to realize that even though Visconti had seen the deck with his own eyes at Chi-Chi's, seen it other times in his long life, he may have never *seen* the deck. He may have only seen what he hoped it would be. Why else would he want to know such a thing? He wanted to know what the authenticator saw. He wanted to see what Rosemont saw. Rosemont shut his eyes again to see where Miles was. In his mind's eye, Rosemont could see that Miles didn't even seem to notice the door into the machine shop. He was being cautious, unsure of himself. He was casting out with his mind, searching for Rosemont, but unable to latch on to his location. It filled Rosemont with contempt to see him so close to the Employees Only door. *God, you idiot, turn around and walk through it! Walk through the fucking door!*

But he wouldn't. He remained positioned outside, as if guarding it.

A moment later, Transom and Kermit stepped into the office where Miles was, carrying Styrofoam cups of coffee, and the three of them began talking, chatting, like old acquaintances trying to place one another.

Miles!

"Now, now," Visconti said. "Don't squirm like a fish on the line. No scheming and plotting, because it takes a character like you nowhere good." He took the nail, leaned forward, and placed the point on the back of Rosemont's right hand, digging it in painfully between the tendons. "Childlike? Savage? Frightening in its simplicity?"

The duct tape was too tight. No matter how he thrashed and shook he couldn't squirm himself out from under the point of that nail. "What do you want? What are you asking me?"

"The images on the Watts deck," the duke said patiently, firmly. "Describe them."

"Yes." Rosemont nodded frantically, eager to be able to say something that he knew. "That's right. Primitive. No way could it have been a modern hand."

"I see. So you lied about all of it to us. Do you have it, Jeremiah?" Visconti's great chalk-white face loomed close. "Is it in this very room with us, somehow?"

"No. No, it's not."

"You're lying. As evident to me as a stoplight."

"I'm not lying!" Rosemont shouted at the top of his lungs. "It's not here! It's not here in this machine shop! It's not anywhere near us, I swear!" Rosemont shut his eyes.

Miles was lunging toward the Employees Only door. *Jeremiah!* Kermit got between him, and then Transom grabbed Miles around the upper body.

Oh, God, that little geek has never been in a fight in his life, Rosemont realized in hopelessness as he watched the two small men easily subdue his friend. Miles didn't see the letter opener on the counter. The box cutter. The pipe at his feet. Rosemont thrashed harder in the chair. "Goddamnit! Get me out of here!"

"Jeremiah!" Rosemont could hear Miles from the office. "Jeremiah, what's happening?"

"Ah. I see. I do see now. It's hidden. *You* hid it. In a *templum*. Very wise of you. But it could be anywhere then." Visconti looked down at the nail between his fingers. "Now just relax."

And to his horror, Rosemont relaxed. He was actually unclenching his fist and laying his hand flat, as if readying himself for the nail. Visconti had control of his body. Total control. But Rosemont could still think, could still lie, could still fear, and overhead was a stone structure, the smooth underbelly of a spanning arch with cruel characters carved into it.

The yoke, a voice told him. *The arch is a yoke. Look up, slave, and see the arch that Romulus built. Look up, slave, and see the sight the captured enemies of Rome saw in their lament.*

"Miles!" Rosemont shouted.

But the voice was Miles. The voice in his head was Miles's voice. The hand he felt upon his shoulder, guiding him forward, beneath that arch, was Miles's controlling hand.

"Stop! No!" Rosemont cried.

A multitude of jeering and mocking people milling about the base of the arch were screaming at the two of them, and Rosemont felt certain they were castigating Miles for his betrayal.

"Why are you doing this?" Rosemont screamed over his shoulder. "Miles, no!"

But the deed was done, and Rosemont felt his whole being, his very self, kneeling in subjugation to Miles. Then he could feel himself retreating into that loneliest deep, that oceanic presence he'd felt in the deck, sinking to the bottom of an unmapped sea where whole worlds go to be forgotten—and landing in Miles's body.

"Because I'd do anything to save you," Miles was saying. *"Even this."*

Rosemont felt Transom's hands on his shoulders. He felt Kermit bear-hugging his hips. A sign that read Employees Only was right in front of Rosemont suddenly. So was the box cutter. Then who was strapped to the chair? Arms and bodies and legs were trying to drag Rosemont down to the floor, and a rage boiled inside him, shaking loose of his attackers and lunging for the box cutter.

"Kill them, Rosemont! Save me! Get rid of them and come get me, goddamnit."

Rosemont was yanking Kermit's head back by the thick locks at the base of his skull, making a fat bulge of his neck, and the box cutter was opening the man's throat like an envelope with one bright red slit.

A loud series of pounding metal notes clanged from behind the door, followed by a scream like an animal being slaughtered.

Kermit crumpled, thrashing and gurgling, beneath Rosemont. Transom released him and backed away in horror from Rosemont as he landed on top of Kermit and, with two more savage slashes of the cutter, stilled Kermit's throes.

Transom turned and fled through the shop's front door.

Blood dripped from fingers and box cutter. He was breathing heavily. Madison, Racine, Austin, and Nicaragua were all far, far away for the person who had once been Jeremiah Rosemont. His body was not his own body.

His self was subjugated, submerged. He was an absent person now.

"I'm in trouble, Jeremiah! I'm in trouble. I'm in trouble. I'm in trouble. That was. That didn't. I can't. The worst is coming. Oh, God, Jeremiah Rosemont, I need you, I need you, I'm in so much trouble."

Through the crimson nova of pain that this absent person felt coming from the screaming, he understood that he had to help. Attend. It walked through that red cloud, feeling doorways literal and supernatural open as it beelined for Visconti and the bound Rosemont-Miles in the chair.

Visconti was crouched over Rosemont-Miles, who sat slumped beneath him, one hand on his shoulder and the other spinning the hammer. "It's here. It's in this city of Austin," Visconti was saying. "In a *templum*."

"I don't know, I don't know, I don't know," Rosemont-Miles cried.

The unperson saw only Visconti, the bow of his back and his obliviousness. His only concern was to get close enough, to leap upon that huge back and slit the throat as he'd done to Kermit.

But Visconti straightened as if he'd heard the thought and looked right at him. "Transom?"

The unperson paused. Why would Visconti call him that? Even Rosemont-Miles in the chair looked confused under sweaty, matted bangs.

"Now!" a woman shouted.

The unperson leapt. The tunnel of red mist focused on Visconti like a frame, and the unperson felt as though its body were tumbling inevitably toward the duke. Visconti raised his hammer to defend himself, baffled, it seemed, why his own henchman would attack him. But the hand that held the box cutter was too quick, and it slashed across the duke's left eye. As he fell backward, blinded, Visconti's hammer landed hard, uppercutting and hitting the unperson's chin. They landed together, the unperson atop Visconti, slashing madly at his arms and face. He could feel the blade entering and leaving, opening and splitting.

But then, there was nothing. Nothing beneath him but red mist and the machine shop's concrete floor. No duke. No hammer.

"Stop, stop," an old woman was saying behind him. "He's gone." A kind hand held the unperson's arm while he caught his breath. "You scared him off. Thank you." She stepped toward him and peered into his eyes, holding his shoulders and forcing him to look down at her. The Armenian/Turkish/Arabic woman. So old. What was her name again? "Come. Here. Down here. Look," she said.

From deep down in that unnamed sea, beneath cool strata of water and darkness, Rosemont sat on its ocean floor and began to weep. The unperson, too, sat, and then collapsed to the floor.

Rosemont-Miles sat sprawled in the torture chair, weak from blood loss, and all he could say was, "I'm sorry! I'm sorry! I'm sorry!"

The unperson lay on the machine shop floor, crushed and dropped there by Marni's penetrating gaze and complete lack of volition.

"He's gone. Jeremiah's gone. You took him," Marni said to Rosemont-Miles in his chair. She wore the same blue peacoat she'd worn a year ago in Rome.

"I'm sorry, sorry for taking away your beautiful self. I thought I was sparing you the torture. But then I was in

trouble. *Oh, please forgive me, Jeremiah!"* said Rosemont-Miles.

That's what Jeremiah heard, anyway, down there beneath the deep blue sea, broken as he was by Miles's yoke.

Blood dripped from the chair. A clock ticked loudly by the office door, the ocean ebbed away from Rosemont-Miles, and the tide took away Miles's name, his face. It inhaled his two-year-old cousin, his aunt and uncle. It took the tragedy, the sorrow, the blame, the fuming acrimony, his epic instinct to flee, and the harrowing encounter in Sarajevo when he saw her again. The ocean drew back like a great muscle, lifting all that he had been as John C. Miles and swallowed it whole into its leviathan self, and swam away.

Marni stepped back from the inert unperson as if what she saw in its eyes horrified her. Then she swiped the bloody box cutter from the unperson's hand as easily as if she were taking something dangerous from a baby, then slit the duct tape, releasing Rosemont-Miles. A second later, the nail in his right hand was gone, though the hand continued to bleed. Rosemont-Miles lifted his left hand for her to help him up. She looked down at the spray and puddles of blood on the right side of the chair and stepped backward. "I'm not helping you anymore," she said to him. "You're on your own from now on."

"I know," said Miles who was Rosemont, now.

"I have to choose one of you to help, and I choose this one," she spat. "The Egyptian will get him for sure otherwise. And, don't kid yourself, they're coming for you, too. Now get up." She reached into the pocket of her peacoat and took out a set of keys on a chain. "I stole this van but you can have it. I masked it. It might keep you hidden for a little while, but not forever. Good luck, Miles."

He watched her leave and blinked at her by way of waving or saying good-bye. Already, he felt like the name "Miles" was wrong for him. He was this. This was him. He wanted nothing to do with that bastard John C. Miles, and by the time Marni had left the room with the old, unperson's body, he knew that this new Jeremiah, his new stitched-together self, was the being he needed to preserve. He stood and pain shot up his arm in volts.

They're coming, came a voice from the bottom of the ocean. *You have to escape! It doesn't matter where you run,* Jeremiah said to his new self, sweetly whispering the childhood name that he called himself in the scariest of moments to encourage and strengthen himself. Distantly aware that other tyros' minds were turning to his own, to this place in Texas, Rosemont who was now a new Rosemont staggered from the torture chair, right hand still dripping.

Boy King, you have to run and don't look back!

18

Boy King sat with his elbows on his knees, hunched over and facing the blank white wall. He was alone in an empty room that was big enough, the ceilings high enough, but it didn't matter how big the room was. He felt strangled, trapped, in this room with no doorknob.

He had nothing, no toehold from which to spring himself out of this place. A week ago, he might have slid through the crack in the door like a shadow. But everything had been stripped from him in the last week. He had no van. No maze of spells to deter trespassers in Bryce & Waterston. No Bryce & Waterston. No hidden neighborhood. No Aventine Hill beneath his feet. No circle of friends to give him a lift, no Lara, no Marni to come riding in and save him in the end, or no childhood that he could blame or long for or try to comprehend. Even the laces of his shoes and his belt were gone.

"Boy King."

Now he was trapped and consequences were coming, swift and sudden as those desert hunters had come for him in Austin. So fast he didn't even know from which direction, or who might be a betrayer, or who would deliver the blow. He'd seen FBI on his way into this room. Tobacco and Firearms. TSA and HSA jackets with Khnum pins on the lapels. Minneapolis Police and National Guard. He'd even seen one-eyed Visconti and a new protégé talking to young men and women with the classic, dark throat-veining of Blackleaf addiction. The duke had taken enough time to pause as Boy King was ushered past to say, "The left hand is next, whoever you are."

Because now it wasn't about information. Or submission. Or even subjugation. It was about justice, or at least, the powerful's sense of justice, and Boy King knew he had a lot to answer for in their eyes. Stealing and hiding and arrogating ancient powers to himself that the powerful had wanted rubbed out. Insulting the Ellings. Ruining that batch of fries.

The deck.

Romulus had slain his twin for doing something similar—destroying their Holy Grail—and empire and power in this world were built on such blunt sentiments. Romulus's wasn't a world that prized mercy. There was no power in pity or forgiveness from Khnum.

"Boy King? Boy King!"

He faced the wall more fully, refusing to look at the source of that voice.

He kept wondering where the ram-headed god was.

Was it all pins and pendants and no mud-slicked delegate from ancient Khemet? When would *that* hammer fall? When he learned that the most powerful was coming for him, he'd felt a certain thrill, he could now admit. He felt flattered, worthy of the challenge. Was it still coming for him? Would he yet face it in a Room 101 like Winston Smith, or would he be disappeared into some archipelago of supernatural gulags? Now he wished there really *were* a primordial half-beast coming to confound this too, too normal status quo.

Even the spell he'd cast upon himself was gone, that effort to save, protect, and spirit himself and his friend away. He was no longer Boy King, couldn't think of himself so. Beneath that, he was a cracked and reglued Jeremiah Rosemont, a self barely thriving on life support. There was no other name he cared for, no other self he wanted. Without even a glove upon his right hand, he was completely laid bare in this horrid little cell, and his guilt and shame were hatching things, unable to shed the shell and come into the sun, nor crawl back in the eggs they'd shattered.

The thing he'd done. The thing he'd done to his Jeremiah. He looked down at his left hand. He'd let Visconti have this one too if he knew that Rosemont might remain safe and whole.

"Boy King!"

He clapped his hands over his ears for a while, and then he tugged off one shoe, spun on his rump, and hurled it at the huge two-way, wall-sized mirror that reflected this room back at him.

"Look at me."

He looked. And he looked away in panic. The same

feeling he'd had in Rome, seeing the reptilian thing morphing into flower and fractiled images of himself filled him with dread and revulsion.

"That didn't happen to me!" he shouted to remind himself. John C. Miles had never seen his "tyro self" as Kermit had called it. "I'm not Rosemont. I'm not Boy King."

He looked again and saw his reflection standing, arms crossed, while he sat trying not to look too long at the reflection.

"Do you know what it is?" said his reflection, once he caught his eye. "Mirrors are intimate, but they aren't *that* intimate. No heat. No wet. No touch."

The man who had been Boy King said, "There's no magic left! This shouldn't be happening!"

His reflection said, "Come here."

He looked at the reflection, really scrutinized it for the first time in a decade, examined what it was wearing, how it stood. So like him, as he'd come to think of himself. But not him. The right hand was whole. The face was unbroken. It was Rosemont as he should have been. No. It was really John C. Miles's face.

"Do you see who I am?" said the reflection.

The man who had been Boy King nodded.

"Come here. I figured it out. Come on, buddy," the reflection said.

The man crawled to the mirror, and his reflection hunkered down to look at him, whispering, "You know what a mirror is, Boy King?"

He shook his head. "Don't call me that."

"Do you know what a mirror is?"

"I hate mirrors."

"Me too. But, look, it has four corners. It has four sides. It allows you a safe vision into another world," it said, leading him. "Get it?"

He smiled a little in admiration. He didn't know why the thought struck him so, but he breathed, "Ahh."

"You do see," the reflection said.

"A *templum*."

"A lifting of the plow," said his reflection. "A doorway. Right? A breach in the wall of Romulus. Go on. Touch the mirror where my hand is."

It was the reflection's left. He would have to raise his ungloved and shattered right, look at it. "I can't do that."

"Do it."

"I can't. I can't do what you ask. I can't even hear your voice without dying inside—and it used to be my voice."

His reflection lowered his hand and looked at him with pity. "Because of what you did?"

The man's mouth turned down and he willed himself not to cry.

"You saved me, Miles," the reflection said. "You saved me from all that horror and took it on yourself."

He turned his profile to the mirror, but his reflection did not look away. "Don't say that."

"Then touch me."

The man turned back and raised his hand. He held it against the mirror, as flat as he could manage, the ugly, brutal wound right in front of his eyes.

Hot. The reflection felt warm, hot skin, not glass.

He jerked his wounded hand away.

"Don't stop now," said the reflection. "Come on, buddy. Up, up, and away."

The reflection put its hand to the mirror again, and the

man touched it, pressed his palm against the other palm. He gave a little shout as his hand dissolved into the mirror, into the warm, moist skin of the reflection.

Then he raised his other hand, the reflection did the same, and they pressed their other hands together through the glass.

"Head," said the reflection.

The man pressed his head to the glass, just as the reflection did so too. And as they touched, felt, pulled back, and pressed again, there was no turning back as the man who'd once been Boy King, his head, his thoughts, his mind, his memory, his fears, and his body began to press through the mirror into the head, thoughts, mind, memory, childhood, and body of the mirror him. It felt cool and warm as the membrane, the barrier of the mirror slid over the crown of his head, over his eyes, and along the bridge of his nose like a loving finger. Lips. Chin. Throat. And he kept pushing and pushing.

"He's leaving!" someone shouted, thin and far away, on the other side of the two-way mirror.

Shoulders and chest—laughter into laughter—and a glorious joy burst through him as his heart and the heart of his reflection pushed into each other.

"Don't let him go! Grab him."

Stomach. Penis. Butt. Thighs. Knees and foot and other foot.

And then Miles and Rosemont were so very far away.

About the Author

Barth Anderson is an award-winning author who has been reading tarot cards for over thirty years. His first novel, *The Patron Saint of Plagues,* received wide critical acclaim. Barth lives in Minneapolis with his wife and two children.